UNREPENTANT

Eilidh Maclaine

This novel is entirely a work of fiction.
The names, characters and incidents portrayed in it are the work of the author's imagination. Any resemblance to events or actual persons, living or dead, is entirely coincidental. All localities and businesses are used in a fictitious manner.

For Dad
never forgotten, miss you

CONTENTS

CHAPTER 1

For the second time since arriving home, Michael listened to the voicemail Louise had left him.

'Sorry darling have to work late tonight, last minute order to get out, you know how it is.'

He stared at the flat device in his hand and sniffed in disgust, his fingers curling around the piece of equipment that was such an integral part of everyday life. Walk down any street, board any bus or train and there it was; the mobile phone. Firmly clamped to the ears of the masses, dangling on headphones or connecting with fingertips; making it possible to have a conversation without uttering a single word. How much it had contributed to the art of deception, how easy to lie when you did not have to look someone in the eye or answer awkward questions. Just type a little untruth and press the send button. Or if you prefer the more personal touch; call at a time when you know the recipient will be unable to answer and leave a well-rehearsed fabrication on their voicemail service.

Until recently his wife had always refused any overtime offered, however, in the last two months she had worked late at least once a week, usually twice and on occasions three times. When he'd remarked on the amount of overtime she'd worked lately, the colour had drained from her face. However, he had to give her credit for recovering quickly. Looking at him defiantly she'd answered.

'Old Gerry, the Office Manager is retiring next year, and I've got my eye on his job. Got to show willing, darling, the competition will be stiff.'

He hadn't believed her. She seemed so detached nowadays and went out more often on her own.

Pouring a large whisky Michael sank into the nearest armchair. He was convinced his wife was having an affair and he could not, would not ignore the issue any longer. The thought of losing her filled him with dread, she was his whole world. He had been merely existing with no real purpose in his life until he'd met her. Louise had given him hope, a future and finally he'd started living. Gulping down the whisky in one mouthful, he poured himself another and reflected on how much Louise had changed. His wife was no longer the easy going, moderate living person he'd married. Nowadays she was an over confident demanding cow. Of course it was all down to the influence of that bitch Shona she'd once worked beside. Picturing the snooty expression she always wore, the upturned nose, which gave the impression there was a bad smell about and her irritating nasally voice, he slammed his fist down on the arm of the chair. Although Shona had long since left work, divorced her husband and moved to Berkshire, she had certainly left her mark on his wife. Under her guiding hand Louise had moved them from a modestly furnished, comfortable flat into this three-bedroom detached property. She'd also insisted they decorate the house from top to bottom. When he'd suggested leaving a couple of the bedrooms as they were, she'd given him a withering look and said they needed to make their own stamp on the property.

The price of some of the furniture she'd suggested buying had shocked him. Disagreeing with her had resulted in him being cut out of the loop, and her buying what she wanted without consulting him.

He glanced around the room. The Mocha coloured Italian leather suite nestled comfortably among the solid oak furniture. Cream silk curtains hung in perfect folds, skimming the top of the polished hardwood flooring. Cushions in the same material as the curtains all plumped and standing to attention graced the sofa and two chairs. Two large abstract canvases, both painted in neutral colours, by someone Louise assured him was an up and coming artist and therefore justified the exorbitant price she had paid for them, hung on opposite walls completing the décor. Even the television sat at just the right angle, appearing inconspicuous, and, blending in nicely.

Sloshing more of the amber liquid into his glass, he grudgingly acknowledged she had done a good job, the house was lovely, but then so it bloody should be; it cost enough.

A car door slamming shut outside roused him

from a drunken slumber. What was the time? He squinted at the clock, rubbing his eyes. Half past ten or was it half past eleven. He couldn't focus long enough to see. The almost empty whisky bottle loomed into view. Christ, had he drunk that much, he could only remember pouring a couple and the bottle had been three quarters full when he'd started. Feeling the urge to empty his bladder he dragged himself from the chair and began staggering up the stairs. The front door opened and he heard the sound of Louise's heels on the wooden floor. He ignored her and continued negotiating the stairs. The effort of standing in the toilet practically made him blackout. He lurched from the bathroom into the bedroom, banging off first the door then a wall. Finally he reached the bed, pulled back the plum damask covered quilt and collapsed on to it. With no intention of undressing, he kicked off his shoes and leaned backwards against the pillows. Downstairs he could hear Louise moving around. She would be furious when she found him in bed fully clothed. He had done this once before after an office Christmas party and she'd made it clear she disapproved, pointing out how unhygienic it was.

'Well fuck her,' he slurred, feeling a childish satisfaction at her impending displeasure. He rolled on to his side and pulled the quilt cover over his head.

CHAPTER 2

The flight home had not been delayed and Sarah's case had been the first one out on the baggage reclaim conveyor belt. She nearly missed it, staring into space not expecting to see it quite so soon. She moved quickly and pushed her way through the throng of people gathered around the conveyor belt to grab her case. A few minutes later she was sitting comfortably in the back seat of a taxi. It had only travelled about a hundred yards when she heard the inevitable question from the driver.

'Been somewhere nice?'

'Yes Benidorm.'

'Never been there myself, me and the wife have gone to Greece for the last three years, we love it there, it's much better than Spain.'

No way could she be bothered listening to this guy all the way home. There was one sure way of stopping that little scenario from happening. She opened her mouth as wide as she could and faked a loud yawn.

The grey haired driver looked at her in his mirror and laughed. 'Tired eh?

'Yes very, wake me up when we get there.' She

smiled at him before closing her eyes. That trick always worked. However, she did not find anything to smile about fifteen minutes later when he pulled up outside her tenement building and demanded sixteen pounds more for the fare than it had been on the outgoing journey. Even allowing for airport taxis being dearer the final price still shocked her and resentfully she handed it over. Noticing there was no tip; the driver dumped her suitcase on the pavement at her feet, jumped back in his cab and sped off without saying a word.

Bastard. He probably added a few pounds on because she stopped him babbling on about his bloody Greek holidays. She dragged her suitcase up the stairs and stared at her front door. She was dreading entering the flat, knowing how empty it was going to feel without Gordon. Fighting back tears she straightened her back, lifted her head high, stuck her key in the lock and turned it. The door swung open and she walked in, kicking aside the inevitable pile of junk mail and bills that had poured through the letter box while she had been away.

The first thing she noticed as she walked down the hall was how bare the coat stand looked. Only one jacket hung on it; hers. Her heart gave a jolt; Gordon had been back whilst she'd been away. With a feeling of dread she walked into the bedroom and looked in the wardrobe. All his clothes were gone.

He'd only packed a couple of holdalls when he'd left three weeks ago. That fateful day when he'd ripped out her heart with three words. *Sarah I'm leaving.* No real explanation why. Only a bunch of clichés about needing space, time on his own. He'd said he would make arrangements to collect the rest of his belongings later. There were also financial practicalities to be settled, which he assured her they would sit down and discuss. As he had not been in touch with her before she had left for Spain, Sarah had sent him a text message to let him know she was going on holiday, a cheap, last minute break she had desperately needed to recover from the shock of him leaving, and the date she was due back.

Brilliant; he's sneaked in while I've been away, taken the rest of his belongings and left me to deal with the rent and bills. 'Bastard; selfish bastard,' she yelled, slamming the wardrobe door shut and collapsing on to the floor in floods of tears.

CHAPTER 3

A mischievous little monkey was playing a drum inside his head; at least that's what it felt like.

'Michael get up you're going to be late.' His wife's voice drifted up the stairs. It was the third time she had shouted to him. Raising his head slowly from the pillow, he threw back the quilt, dragged himself from the bed and headed off towards the shower. When he entered the kitchen twenty minutes later Louise was placing a plate and mug in the dishwater. She looked up at him and immediately pursed her lips and shook her head before turning away again. He made a coffee hoping it would make him feel better but only managed three mouthfuls before heaving them back up and into the sink.

'That's disgusting. You'd better scrub that sink with bleach.' Louise lifted her handbag from the worktop and marched from the room. Minutes later she left the house without a word, banging the door behind her.

One glance at the kitchen clock told him he had missed the train; he would never get to the station in time. The bus was out of the question; the journey took forever. No way could he drive; apart from probably still being over the limit from last night's binge, he knew there was a chance he would not be able to keep his eyes open long enough to negotiate his way through rush hour traffic. He phoned a taxi and dozed on the sofa until it arrived. Inside the taxi he slept the journey away and by the time it arrived outside the insurance company where he worked, he felt slightly better. The Ibuprofen had finally started to kick in. Once inside the building he headed straight for the water cooler.

'Oh God I'm so jealous of your tan,' Linda said, patting Sarah's arm.

Oh no, not again. All Sarah had done yesterday was drone on and on about her holiday. How nice the hotel had been, how good the food had been, how brilliant the weather had been, and a blow by blow account of everywhere she had visited. By five o'clock last night he'd felt as if he'd been on a day trip to Benidorm. In addition, the other two women had raved about her tan. It was beginning to look like a repeat performance today. He was in no position to chastise anyone for not working, as he had arrived twenty minutes late himself, however, he felt sufficiently lousy not to care.

Drawing level with the three chattering females he announced with a note of sarcasm to his voice. 'Well ladies, reality check this isn't Benidorm, it's Glasgow; time to work.'

Sarah, Anne and Linda all turned and looked at him. A slow smile spread across his face. It was like a scene from Macbeth; three witches cackling round a cauldron. The smile quickly disappeared as Sarah lifted her head, eyed him defiantly and asked.

'Are you sure it's safe for you to be out before sundown Michael?' She raised her eyebrows for effect and Linda and Anne dissolved into laughter. Smirking at him she slowly walked towards her desk.

What a bitch, one day I'll wipe that smug smile off her face and take great delight in doing so, he thought, pouring himself some cold water and sipping it before slowly making his way towards his own desk.

CHAPTER 4

Louise was driving home from an afternoon of successful retail therapy, a pair of dark grey trousers and a little black dress, nestling in John Lewis bags on the back seat of her car. The dress would look great with the black and grey shoes she had bought the previous week. She imagined how good she would look wearing the dress and shoes with her hair piled high and the arousing effect it would have on Simon. Realising it would have the same effect on Michael she felt a slight pang of guilt. What the hell am I going to do she asked herself. Leave Michael? She was not sure if she really wanted to leave the life they had built for themselves. After all she had been content enough until Simon had come along. Ok, so she wanted a bigger house, flashier cars, more exotic holidays, whereas Michael seemed quite content with the house they lived in, the cars they drove, a spring break in Britain and a two week holiday abroad in late summer. Louise, however, knew she could always talk Michael round to her way of thinking and slowly but steadily she was changing their lifestyle together into the lifestyle she wanted. Did she really want to walk away and leave it all behind? She couldn't answer that question.

Simon had suggested she move in with him. The thought of waking up every morning next to Simon sent shivers of anticipation through her body. She found him incredibly sexy, with his good looks, toned body and great sense of humour. It was intoxicating just being in his presence. She wasn't stupid and realised a lot of the excitement was because the affair was illicit, and their stolen moments together were precious. Moving in with Simon would change that. Although Louise was not ready to give up Simon she had to make a decision soon. She was beginning to worry Michael might suspect her of having an affair. Several times lately she'd caught him staring at her and when she'd looked up, he'd turned away. He seemed quieter somehow and was drinking more. A couple of times she'd asked him if anything was wrong, but he always said no and walked away from her. He'd remarked on the amount of time she spent working late and last week when she'd told him she was going to the cinema with Julie from work, he'd complained she was hardly ever home. Something in the tone of his voice had triggered warning bells.

Of course, she had not been at the cinema with Julie. Instead she had gone to Simon's flat as arranged. That night had been the best ever. Louise could feel her body tingle with excitement at the memory.

Simon opened the door wearing only a bathrobe,

hair glistening wet from the shower. She shoved some junk mail that she had extricated from the letterbox towards him and said mischievously. 'This is for you; I hope you have something for me.'

'Oh I do,' he replied, untying the belt of his bath-robe.

She kicked the door shut, reached inside his bath-robe and dragged her nails lightly along the in-side of his thighs. Shoving his hands under her tee shirt, Simon undid her bra in record time. When he started caressing her nipples Louise could not get her clothes off quickly enough. Still in the hall Simon pushed her gently against the wall and lifted her from the ground. She gasped as he placed her on his hips. Her arms snaked round his neck, between her legs already moist and aching as her body eagerly welcomed his erection. The sex was fervent; over in minutes, culminating with Louise screaming his name before they both slid to the floor in heap of entangled limbs. When her breath-ing returned to normal, she got up and walked naked apart from her skirt, which was still clinging haphazardly to her waist, into the kitchen. Simon followed her. She downed most of a can of coke she found in the fridge before offering him some. Tak-ing the can with one hand he encircled her waist with the other and drew her to him. Seconds later they were writhing around on the kitchen floor. This time when the sex was over Simon took her hand and led her towards the bedroom. They climbed into Simon's bed, and made love, long and leisurely, before Louise showered and made her way home.

So caught up in the memory of that night Louise did not see the red light. What did register in her brain was the car in front was no longer moving. Slamming her foot hard on the brake she realised there was no way she was going to be able to stop her car before it ploughed into the one in front.

'Oh shit,' she screamed, turning the steering wheel left as fast as she could. Mercifully there were no vehicles in the inside lane and her car screeched to a halt just over the white line. 'Jesus! That was lucky,' she said aloud, her face beginning to sting with embarrassment as she realised the occupants of the car on her right, the one she had almost written off, and several pedestrians were staring at her, some of them shaking their heads.

Putting all thoughts of Simon out of her head, when the traffic lights turned to green, Louise put her car into gear and drove home more cautiously than she usually did.

CHAPTER 5

Michael was on a mission. He'd decided the best way to find out if Louise was having an affair was to follow her the next time she went out on her own. He'd also stopped moaning about her working late or going out alone so often. Two days later, Louise announced she was going out with the girls for dinner on Friday. 'Going anywhere nice?' he asked her.

'Yes my favourite, Mitchells,' she replied, the pleasure obvious in her voice.

By the time Friday night came Michael could hardly contain himself. While Louise was in the shower he paced up and down the hallway. When she finally entered the bedroom to get dressed, he forced himself to stop moving around, switched on the television and sat down in his favourite chair. At last Louise came down the stairs. She looked radiant in figure hugging black trousers and white blouse and Michael felt bile rising to his throat at the thought she might be looking this good for someone else.

'I won't be late, darling, I'm taking the car.' She pecked him on the cheek.

'Have fun,' he replied, keeping his voice even, trying to blot out the image of the black trousers and white blouse lying in a heap beside a stranger's bed.

The front door closed, and he waited a full minute before he leapt from his chair, grabbed his jacket and stuffed his feet into a pair of shoes he had earlier placed in the hall closet.

Opening the door cautiously he was just in time to see Louise's car pull away from the kerb. The black Golf GTi had been the cause of a massive disagreement between Louise and himself the year before. Until then they had both shared the one car and when Louise said she intended to buy her own car Michael told her he thought it was a waste of money. She'd retaliated by pointing out it was her money to waste. Michael had also assumed she meant a cheap economical run around and had been stunned when Louise informed him of the car she intended to buy, adding she was paying five hundred pounds extra for leather seats. He'd hit the roof.

'For God's sake Louise, you don't need to spend that much on a car just to get to work. It's ridiculous, an unnecessary expense.'

'You bought the Focus because it was a good deal and you knew I wanted something a bit sportier.'

'But...'

'No buts Michael you bought the car you wanted and now I intend to do the same.' True to her word Louise had gone to the car showroom the next day and signed the paperwork, by the following weekend the black Golf GTi had been parked outside the house.

Shaking his head at the recollection he quickly slipped out of the house, locked the door and got into his own car. He could see the Golf further along the road and knew he would have to keep well behind it until she reached the main road to avoid being seen by her.

He followed her from a distance for a couple of miles and began to relax. From the route Louise was taking it appeared as if she was indeed headed for Mitchells. Minutes later he saw her indicate and turn into the restaurant car park. Thankfully no one was behind him and he was able to slow his car down almost to a standstill when he saw Louise indicate; to avoid being noticed by her. He drove past the restaurant and parked further along the road. He wished it was winter instead of summer. The car park was tiny but in the dark he could have risked parking at the back and climbing into the backseat. He would then be able to observe who she left the restaurant with. That was not an option in the summer; she would spot his car immediately. Instead he sat in his car staring out the window for the next twenty minutes.

When Louise had said she was going out with the girls Michael knew she was referring to Grace Black and Liz Walker, two friends she had known from school and with whom she met up regularly for a meal and a chat. Well let's see if you really are with the girls. He removed his phone from his jacket pocket.

The telephone number of the restaurant was

saved in Michael's contact list as they often went there for a meal and always booked in advance to make sure they got a table. Leaning forward, he reached into the glove compartment, grabbed a pen and an old petrol receipt. He scrolled through his contacts and scribbled the telephone number of the restaurant onto the receipt then keyed the numbers one four one first, to withhold the number, before keying in the number of the restaurant. The telephone started to ring and Michael could feel his heart pounding in his chest. On the third ring someone answered.

'I'm sorry to bother you but I'm trying to contact Grace Black and I understand she is dining in the restaurant with some friends.'

'One moment please.' There was a brief pause and Michael could hear pages being turned. 'I'm sorry sir we do not have a table reservation under that name. The restaurant is very busy tonight; do you have any idea what other name the reservation may have been made under?'

If she really was with the girls and the reservation had not been made by Grace then it had to have been made by either Liz or Louise herself.

'I think she is dining with two friends Barton or Walker maybe?'

'Ah yes table eight, one moment sir.'

The seconds ticked by; each one felt like a minute. Suddenly a loud voice bellowed. 'Hello,' in his ear.

There was no mistaking Grace Black's voice. In

fact that was the very reason he had asked for Grace rather than Liz. Grace sounded as if she was shouting rather than talking when she was using a telephone. Even more identifying was the way she said hello. She made it sound like two words, hal low. He'd noticed it the first time he'd met her.

Michael ended the call, he wasn't sure if he felt relieved or disappointed. He had been so certain Louise was having an affair and had convinced himself tonight was the night he would catch her out. Had he been wrong? No, this does not prove she is not having an affair he reasoned, turning the car around and heading for home.

When he arrived back at the house the first thing he did was reach for the whisky bottle and a glass. Without even taking off his jacket he sat down on the sofa and began drinking until he fell asleep.

CHAPTER 6

Everyone apart from Sarah, appeared to be in good spirits and enjoying themselves. To her left three girls with impossibly high heels and dresses barely covering their backsides were chatting excitedly, their gazes unashamedly roving over the room, seeking out the unattached males. Beside them stood a young couple, the boy had tousled blonde hair and as he spoke the girl reached up and touched it gently. The open adoration in her eyes was almost painful to witness. The look of passion that flashed across the boy's face as her fingers connected with the pale strands made Sarah turn away embarrassed at witnessing such intimacy. She was ensconced in a booth with Penny in an overcrowded bar on West George Street. She hadn't wanted to go out at all, but Penny had insisted.

Her friend was a good listener and Sarah was taking advantage of that. They were three quarters of the way through their second bottle of wine. Ever since Penny had come back from the bar with the first, Sarah had moaned constantly. How devastated she was, how lonely she was, how short of money she was.

Although Sarah loved her friend to bits, she was not sure Penny really understood how she felt.

Penny had never lived with anyone full time and was currently single. In fact, sometimes Sarah thought her friend preferred being single.

'You just don't know what it's like to have your heart broken; you've always been the one to break hearts.' The minute the words were out of her mouth she regretted saying them. 'I'm sorry, I really am I should never have said that. I didn't mean it.' She bit her lip, nervously.

'It's ok, I know you didn't.'

The reply was barely out of Penny's mouth when Sarah suddenly cried out. 'Oh my God he's here. There's Gordon. He's coming over.'

Although he was indeed heading directly towards them it became obvious he hadn't seen them when seconds later he stopped short in front of their table, a look of sheer panic crossing his face, reminding Sarah of a rabbit caught in a speeding car's headlights.

'Hello Sarah, Penny,' he said, not quite meeting their eyes.

'Hello Gordon.' Sarah replied, a note of coldness in her voice, noticing he was holding two drinks and looking anxiously around him.

As if on cue a small blonde female sidled up to them. 'Oh there you are Gordon; sorry I took so long, you know what I am like once I get started chatting. This must be for me,' she said, while at the same time extracting one of the drinks from Gordon's hand. Finally she looked up and appeared to sense the tension, which hung like a curtain, around the other three. She looked at Gordon enquiringly. Gordon, however, was looking at his feet.

'Aren't you going to introduce us?' Sarah asked, her voice loaded with sarcasm.

Gordon mumbled in response. 'Err, Sarah, Penny this is Prue.'

At the name Sarah a flicker of recognition passed across Prue's face. An uncomfortable silence ensued as Penny and Sarah eyed Prue.

Finally Gordon blurted out much too quickly. 'We were just leaving.'

'Really!' Penny replied, looking pointedly at their obviously recently poured drinks.

Sarah felt dizzy everything around her appeared to be happening in slow motion, voices were distorted. Gordon was staring at her and she got the impression he had asked her a question.

Pulling herself together she took a deep breath and heard Penny say in clipped tones.

'No thanks we are just having a wee roadie anyway.' Gordon must have offered to buy them a drink she realised.

'A wee roadie?' Prue asked, looking puzzled.

Penny turned to Prue and stared at her. Then patiently as if explaining something to a small child she spoke slowly with exaggerated timing between each word.

'A wee roadie: as in one for the road.'

For the first time that night Sarah finally found

something funny and started to giggle. Gordon and Prue both glared at her.

Stifling the giggles Sarah found her voice and said. 'Well don't let us keep you.' Lifting her handbag she stood up, turned her back on the others and walked towards the ladies room with as much dignity as she could muster.

By the time she returned to the table where Penny was seated, she was furious and glad to note Gordon and Prue were now nowhere to be seen.

'Bastard. I'd put money on it he was seeing her when he was still with me. They just looked too comfortable together as if they'd known each other for a while. And she seemed to know who I was. Did you see the expression on her face when he said my name?' Before Penny had a chance to answer she continued. 'How insulting to be dumped for some dumb blonde called Prue. For God's sake; who the fuck is called Prue nowadays?' Pouring the last of the wine into their glasses she held up hers and said. 'Well good riddance to Gordon, the bastard, and his bimbo Prue.

Penny raised her eyebrows in surprise. 'That's my girl.'

One look at Penny's expression on top of all the wine she'd drunk and Sarah started to laugh, really laugh, for the first time in weeks.

Shards of light escaping through a gap in the curtains fell across Sarah as she awoke on Sunday morning. The first thing she remembered was seeing Gordon the night before, with that awful blonde called Prue. The day, dull and grey, visible through the same gap in the curtains reflected her mood. She had secretly hoped once Gordon had some time on his own, he would miss her and want her back. She had never voiced these thoughts to anyone, not even Penny. However, seeing him, last night, with Prue, Sarah now knew for certain that was not going to happen.

Witnessing Gordon with someone else had really hurt and knowing he had left her for someone else was insulting. Hurt slowly turned to anger at the thought of him having an affair, with what Sarah could only describe as the original dumb blonde, while they had still been together. It was not only offensive it was humiliating. She had loved Gordon with all her heart and had believed he felt the same. Now she had to face up to the fact; obviously he hadn't. Not only was he a cheat he was a coward too, she realised. He hadn't even had the guts to tell her the real reason he had left her. She fumed at the thought of all the times he must have lied to her, saying he was going out with his mates, when all along he had been sneaking off to meet that awful woman.

Getting out of bed Sarah headed for the kitchen intending to make herself a cup of coffee. However, by the time she got there she decided she wanted a bacon sandwich as well. While the kettle was boiling and a couple of rashers sizzled on the grill, she routed about in one of the cupboards, looking for some tomato sauce which she intended to spread thickly on the bread instead of butter. A habit which Gordon had always told her was disgusting. Not quite as disgusting as cheating on your girl-friend mate.

Seeing Gordon with someone else had made her realise their relationship really was over. She no longer wanted him back. She could never trust him again and she had too much pride to even try. It was time to move on.

CHAPTER 7

Michael decided to have another attempt at following Louise. Last night she'd told him she intended to work late tonight. Instead of travelling to work by train this morning he'd driven to the city centre and left his car in the multi storey car park in Oswald Street.

He'd left work early, claiming he had a doctor's appointment, retrieved his car and was now driving towards the logistics company in Hillington where Louise worked. He was slightly agitated; an accident not far from the car park had played havoc with the traffic and he began to panic knowing there was a chance he might not arrive at Louise's workplace before five o'clock.

Finally, her office building was in sight. He glanced at the clock on the dashboard. The time was five minutes to five. Louise's office was located to the right of the building and didn't overlook the car park so there was no chance she would spot him driving in. He saw her car immediately and was pleased to note it was directly opposite the entrance to the building. He parked his own car at the back in a bay that afforded him a good view of the entrance and a partial view of the Golf. He turned off the ignition and settled down to wait never taking his eyes off the entrance. If she came out he would follow her. If she had not come out by twenty past five he would assume she had been telling the truth and was indeed working late, and he would drive home.

Michael waited and watched. Some workers had already started to leave and every time the door opened, he felt his heart beat faster. At five minutes past five Louise strode out and walked quickly to her car. He need not have worried about being seen. Louise did not even glance around her.

Gotcha! Now comes the difficult part. Slowly he drove out of the parking bay. Another car was emerging from a bay further down and Michael waved it out; the driver waved back in gratitude. Of course Michael's reason for letting him out was purely selfish. It meant a car between him and Louise. He watched as Louise turned right and exited the car park. He was thankful it was a quiet side road and not a main road otherwise in rush hour traffic he may have lost sight of her at this point. As luck would have it the car in front was going the same way which meant a car still between himself and Louise. He had been following her for about ten minutes when she indicated and changed lanes. He had to do the same, if she turned right at the traffic lights up ahead, he would lose her, and he was not about to let that happen. He indicated and tried to force his way into the outside lane. The car behind refused to let him in and he was lucky not to hit it. Blasting his horn, the driver drew level and shouted 'arsehole' through his open window. Luckily for Michael, the second car to the rear pulled back enough to let him in. Michael flicked his hazard lights in gratitude. He surmised the driver, a young woman, had probably only let him in front through fear of being hit, rather than kindness. Either way Michael was grateful.

He followed Louise all the way to Shawlands and watched with a feeling of unease as she turned into a quiet street, and parked in front of a block of tenement flats. There was nowhere he could park before he reached her car. Damn, he was going to have to drive past her. Terrified she might see him; he drove along the road and pulled into the first available space. Looking in his mirror he watched as Louise, completely oblivious that her husband had just driven past her, got out of her car and locked it.

Before he had time to make a decision as to his next move, he saw a dark haired man approach her. Then to his utter horror the two of them threw their arms around one another and kissed passionately on the pavement. Eventually they drew apart and Louise laughed at something the dark haired man said. Linking arms, they walked towards the nearest building and disappeared inside.

Michael was stunned. There was no mistaking what he had seen. He stared at the block wondering which flat Louise and the dark haired man were headed for. His gaze travelled slowly over the building where the windows seemingly mocked him as they held onto their secret.

Oh Louise, what have you done? The desolation he felt was almost unbearable. Deep in his heart he had been certain Louise was cheating on him but somewhere fluttering on the periphery of that certainty there had been a spark of hope that maybe, just maybe he was wrong. He had gripped on to that lifeline of hope, his jagged rock on the side of a mountain; hung on because his life depended on it, needing Louise to come along, grab his wrist and pull him back to a safe place. Without Louise by his side and faithful there was no way back up. When the dark haired man had first approached Louise, hope, like his grip on that rock began slipping. When they had kissed; the tiny spark of it left had vanished completely and Michael had been unable to hold on any longer. He hurtled, silently, ever downwards towards a dark place.

Everyone he had loved had betrayed him in some way. His father, whom he'd adored, had disappeared from his life when he was ten years old. His older brother Peter had been twelve. His father had eaten his breakfast one morning and gone to work. He had never returned, a three car pile-up on the Kingston Bridge had seen to that; alive for breakfast and dead for dinner. Although his father had not caused the accident, for years Michael had secretly blamed him for being so careless. If he had really cared for his family, he would have been sufficiently vigilant whilst driving to have avoided the collision that snuffed out his life and stopped him returning home safely that evening.

His mother had betrayed him too; she had been besotted by his father. Michael always felt she had given all her love to her husband and there had never been any left to give to her kids. Once their father had died so had her love. She had looked after them, fed and clothed them but showing them love or spending time with them had never been on the agenda. Fate had dealt a cruel blow when it had taken away the parent who was genuinely interested in Michael and his brother. Peter had been the next person to betray him. When their father had died Peter and Michael had grown closer, clinging to one another for comfort; for none had been forthcoming from their mother. She had worked all day, come home, made the dinner and then either gone to bed and cried herself to sleep or sat up half the night drinking.

Peter had left school as soon as he turned sixteen and secured himself an apprenticeship with a local garage. He had worked hard for the first year and when summer had come he had gone on a two week holiday to Magaluf with two of his friends, Gavin and Brian.

Michael had missed Peter like mad. The house had been so quiet without him and his friends trooping in and out. At last the day had come for Peter's return. His flight was due to arrive at Glasgow Airport at twelve noon. Michael must have looked at the kitchen clock a hundred times that morning. At twelve thirty he sat down beside the window to watch for Peter arriving; anticipating him jumping out a taxi all tanned and smiling. He waited and he waited, but Peter never arrived. At two o'clock Michael's mother had telephoned the airport at Michael's insistence, only to be told the flight had arrived on time. Unable to get a hold of Peter by phone, at three o'clock Michael had gone to Gavin's house. What Gavin had told him had made his blood feel like iced water in his veins. Peter had stayed in Magaluf.

At six o'clock that evening Peter had phoned home to tell Michael and his mother what they already knew. He wasn't coming home. He had a job in some bar in Magaluf and he was going to stay there and see how things went. Probably be back after the summer, he'd told them and laughed. Peter had never come back. He hadn't stayed in Magaluf either; he'd travelled all over Spain. At first Michael and his mother had received postcards from him every other week, then every other month; eventually they had dwindled to one or two a year, and never with a contact number.

When their mother had died Michael had tried to contact Peter at the bar his most recent card had indicated he was working in. Peter, however, had moved on. She had been dead and buried for three weeks before he had managed to track his brother down. Even then Peter had shown no inclination to return. He had told Michael there was no point in coming back; the funeral was over. He'd said

Michael deserved to keep any money or valuables as he had been the one left to look after her. His mother's house had been rented and after funeral expenses there had been less than two hundred pounds left in her account. Most of her jewellery had been costume jewellery, which Michael had given to a charity shop along with her clothes. The only two pieces that had any real value had been her wedding ring and engagement ring. Michael had kept both, more as a reminder of his father, who after all had been the person who had given them to his mother.

His father was already dead. Peter was God knows where, nothing he could do about him. Now his wife had betrayed him. He vowed to make Louise pay for her treachery. He'd get his revenge, he'd certainly got it on his mother.

CHAPTER 8

H-e-l-p meee, h-e-l-p meee, Mic—hael. He awoke with a start, bathed in sweat. Michael had been dreaming about his mother. He hadn't dreamt of her in years. All this business with Louise had dredged it all up again. He glanced at his wife sleeping soundly beside him. Not a care in the world, no guilty conscience keeping her awake.

His mother had been the same; she'd never had any trouble getting to sleep either. Although in her case the drink and or pills had been the reason. How many times in the first couple of years after his father had died had he gone into his mother's room at night? Not late at night; sometimes only nine or ten o'clock. Needing to feel the comfort of her arms around him, only to find her in a deep sleep, snoring gently.

When Peter had left he'd started going to the Library most days after school. It was better than going home to an empty house. At least there had been other people around him and it had made him feel less lonely.

He'd worked hard at school and it had paid off. He'd got both good Standard and Higher Grades and had gone to college. He'd moved out the house exactly three months after he had started working.

Every Sunday evening he had visited his mother out of a sense of duty. He could tell she had genuinely looked forward to his visits. In a strange way so had he. Maybe because they had sat down and talked. Something they had never done when he'd lived at home. On some level he had felt sorry for her. Her health had deteriorated, due to years of drinking and the house had been littered with pills for this, that and the other.

Then out of the blue his mother had been diagnosed with pleurisy. She had collapsed in the street and had been rushed to hospital in an ambulance.

It had taken her a long time to recover and Michael had done everything he could for her. However, throughout her illness she had complained constantly. Even when she'd recovered the complaints hadn't stopped and he had started dreading his weekly visits to her. They were even worse to endure if she had been drinking before he got there. The self-pity had been almost intolerable at times.

The cold February night it all ended was still as clear in his mind as if it had happened only yesterday.

He'd entered his mother's flat as usual around six o'clock with his own key which was the norm. He'd known straight away something was wrong. The house had been too quiet. Usually he'd hear the television when he opened the door and his mother was generally clattering plates about in the kitchen.

However, that night the silence had been almost deafening.

'Hello.' There was no reply. 'Mum.' Still no reply.

He walked down the hallway and looked in the kitchen. It was empty. He continued to the living room and found his mother slumped on the well-worn couch, a trail of vomit on her chin ending in a puddle on her chest. An empty gin bottle lay beside her surrounded by a dark stain where the gin had spilled out. A tumbler was on the floor at her feet. Three empty pill bottles amongst a handful of tablets littered the scratched surface of the coffee table.

A horrible dull ache started deep in the pit of his stomach. He approached his mother slowly and touched her hand; it felt warm. Instinctively he pulled his own hand away quickly. He'd assumed his mother was dead but touching her hand made him think she might still be alive. Reaching towards her again he touched her wrist and felt for a pulse. Yes, it was faint but there was a pulse. Dropping her arm he tugged his phone from his jacket pocket, then swore when he realised the battery was dead. Throwing it down on the couch he strode towards his mother's landline, intending to dial 999 and ask for an ambulance. He had dialled the first 9 when something stopped him from dialling any further. The face of his father stared at him from a framed photograph on the sideboard. He looked so young, so happy in the photograph. He stared at his father's smiling face and then slowly turned and looked at his mother.

An overwhelming feeling of resentment gripped him and he replaced the telephone.

The unbearable sadness he had felt at the loss of his father, the childhood devoid of love from his mother, the loneliness he'd suffered as a teenager aggravated by his brothers' absence all came flooding back.

He knew his mother wasn't to blame for his father's death, but she was to blame for being too wrapped up in her own grief and self-pity to give her kids the love they'd needed. She had driven Peter away and he'd left the house as soon as he could afford to. Now she had done the most selfish act that Michael could think of. She had played cat and mouse with her own mortality. She had not really meant to kill herself of that he was sure. She had known he would find her. He always came to visit her at the same time every Sunday. He was never late.

Michael thought about his father's life, cruelly and prematurely, snatched from him. His mother, in comparison, had treated her life with something almost like contempt. Instead of savouring every precious moment she had been allowed and her husband denied, she had chosen to fritter her life away on drink and self-pity. Now she had done the unforgivable. She had used death casually, as a weapon against him, in a bid for attention. The same woman who had never given her kids the attention they had so desperately craved.

He was incensed. How dare she look for something she had never given?

'Well mother, heads you live, tails you die; and today looks like a tails kind of day to me.' His voice was venomous. His mother had gambled with her life and would pay the ultimate price; death.

Slowly he backed out of the room, grabbing his phone from the couch on the way. Standing in the hallway, he took a few deep breaths before leaving the flat and closing the front door quietly behind him.

He had the dream for the first time that night and many times afterwards. He was in his mother's hallway walking backwards towards the door. His mother was dragging herself along the floor towards him; shouting for help, calling his name. He was trying to get away from her. He was walking more quickly than she was crawling along the ground, but she was catching up on him. Panic set in, he couldn't breathe. She reached him and grabbed his ankles with her hands, only her hands had become claws. They dug into his legs. The pain was excruciating as she tried to drag herself from the floor, screaming his name, calling for help. Mercifully; he awoke at this point.

The morning after he found his mother he telephoned his work and told them he was sick; said he had been vomiting all night. He couldn't stop thinking about the day before. He knew his mother would almost certainly be dead. However, by mid-morning he was having doubts about what he'd seen. Maybe she hadn't taken the pills; the empty bottles could have been lying there for days. She might just have been drunk, really drunk. By lunchtime he could stand the uncertainty no longer and phoned his mother's house. He felt sick listening to the sound of the telephone ringing. Part of him wished she would answer; complaining she was coming down with the flu; her favourite excuse, when she had a really bad hangover, but no, the telephone rang and rang and his mother didn't answer.

If his mother was dead Michael had no intention of leaving her lying in her house until the following Sunday and pretending he had just found her; no that was not even an option, he shuddered at the idea.

He dreamt about his mother again that night and was too afraid to go back to sleep. Eventually morning dawned and at nine o'clock Michael phoned his workplace again and told them he was still sick. He sat about the flat all day in his dressing gown and telephoned his mother's house at midday, five fifteen and again at seven.

At ten past seven he phoned his mother's next-door neighbours; Mr and Mrs Shepherd. Mrs Shepherd had always had a spare key for emergencies. She had let himself and Peter into the house many times over the years when they had forgotten their own keys and their mother had been out.

Mrs Shepherd answered the telephone sounding slightly out of breath.

'Hello Mrs Shepherd. It's Michael Barton here...'

'Oh hello Michael,' she interrupted, sounding slightly puzzled as to why he should be phoning her.

'I'm sorry to bother you but I can't get a hold of mum. I think she might have unplugged the phone again. Could you knock on her door for me?'

'Of course I can. Hang on.'

He heard the phone being placed down and stared at a damp patch on the ceiling as he waited for her to return. Finally she came back on the line, this time she sounded a little worried. 'There's no answer Michael. Do you want me to fetch the key and go in?'

'Would you mind? She wasn't feeling well on Sunday and I just want to check she is okay.'

'Oh Glory! Timothy,' he heard her yell at her husband. 'Fetch Abby's key.' This time she dropped the phone none too gently.

Minutes ticked by. He heard a commotion from the other end of the phone and the voice of Timothy Shepherd filled his right ear. 'Michael you need to come here immediately.'

'Why what's wrong?' Is mum okay?'

'Come quickly boy, just come quickly.' The resigned tone in his voice was all the confirmation Michael needed.

He went directly to the bathroom and stuck two fingers down this throat. When he stopped retching, he looked at his reflection in the mirror and grinned. Unwashed, unshaven and now a white pallor to his skin; yes he definitely looked ill. He threw on an old pair of jeans and t-shirt, left the house and drove the short distance to his mother's home. A policeman stopped him in her hallway and led him gently to the kitchen, sat him down and told him what he already knew; his mother was dead.

There was no point in denying he had been there on Sunday, most of the neighbours knew he always visited that day. He answered all their questions, mentally keeping a tally of the truths and lies. The last time he's seen his mother was Sunday around six o'clock, truth. She hadn't been feeling well, lie. He hadn't stayed long, truth; about half an hour, lie. He had been grateful to leave early, truth, he hadn't been feeling well himself, lie. He had suggested his mother have a bath and get an early night, lie.

He had tried to phone her several times in the last two days, truth. He'd assumed she had unplugged the phone and forgot to reconnect it, half-truth; he had doubts yesterday. Yes she did this often, truth. He had been unwell himself, half-truth; he'd just been sick. By tonight he had begun to worry, lie, and had phoned the Shepherds, truth. Yes his mother drank, truth. Yes she suffered from depression and was on medication, truth. Apart from anti-depressants he didn't know what other medication she had been prescribed, they would have to ask her GP, truth.

Ten truths and five lies; he congratulated himself, sticking to the truth as much as possible was the smart thing to do.

The police had been satisfied; the neighbour's statements had helped. Michael was good to his mother; visited her every Sunday. A reliable son;

not like the other one, Peter, who had disappeared abroad years ago. His mother's death had been recorded as suicide.

He'd got away with it. Everything was fine. Except everything wasn't fine, the nightmares had continued. Then he'd met Louise and the nightmares had stopped. Michael had been at last truly happy; until now.

CHAPTER 9

Sarah and Penny were having their usual treat on a Monday after work, a double gin and tonic.

Sarah hated Mondays and today had been particularly trying. She rubbed the red patch of skin on her toe and winced. She should never have worn these shoes to work. Correction; she should never have worn these shoes at all. They were too tight but they had been a bargain and she had convinced herself they would loosen out; of course they hadn't. Not much of a bargain now, they would probably end up in the bin.

'Boy do I need this,' she said, swirling the ice around in the glass.

Penny grinned. 'Bad day at the office?'

'Just Michael being his usual obnoxious self.'

Penny was used to hearing Sarah complaining about Michael and asked. 'What's he done this time?'

'He had Linda in tears this afternoon; asked her if she was lazy or just plain stupid because she had only left two copies of a form on his desk and he'd wanted three. The cheek of the man. I told him he'd gone too far, and I swear I thought he was going to strike me in some way. I'm sure he wanted to and the look he gave me was the kind only a psycho would give.'

'How would you know what kind of look a psycho gives? How many psychos do you know?'

'Only one, his name is Michael.'

They both laughed.

'You'll never guess who I bumped into the other day?' Penny said.

'Well don't keep me in suspense, who was it?'

'Malcolm.'

Sarah groaned. Malcolm had been a friend of a friend who Penny had tried to set her up with before she had met Gordon. She had introduced him to Sarah at a party. Sarah had to admit he had been a nice enough guy; good looking too, but she had found him a bit dreary. However, Malcolm hadn't found Sarah quite so dreary, in fact he had been quite taken with her and had phoned her a few days later to ask her out. She had been at a loose end and thought, what the hell, it beats sitting in front of the telly. Although after her one and only date with him she had wished she'd done just that.

'I did tell you about the date I had with him.' She mimicked the action of slitting both wrists making Penny laugh again. 'Sitting across the table from him in a restaurant was not an enjoyable experience. It was more like a history lesson as he banged on and on about ethnic African tribes. The man's table manners also left a lot to be desired. Everyone in the restaurant was treated to a rendition of him chomping his way through a salad.' She shook her head. 'And the close up view of little pieces of lettuce flying from his mouth as he spoke was plain disgusting. Don't even think about suggesting I go out with him again. We had absolutely nothing in common. Attractive he might be but boring is almost certainly his middle name.'

Penny looked as if she was about to argue, she opened her mouth to speak but Sarah got in first. 'I mean it Penny; I'm not interested.'

'Glad to hear it because he's now a Roman Catholic priest.'

'You're kidding.' That was the last thing she had expected Penny to say.

'Of course I am, he's Jewish you idiot.'

'Ha bloody ha. I'm glad to hear taking a rise out of me is so amusing,' Sarah replied, trying to sound offended.

'Will another gin and tonic make up for it?'

'Make it a double again and we'll see.'

Penny went off to the bar shaking her head in amusement. When she returned Sarah was checking her phone messages. 'Have you heard from Gordon recently?'

Sarah's head jerked up quickly her gaze flying from the phone to her friend. 'No. Why would I? In fact I don't expect to hear from him again, nor do I want to.'

'Good, you need to forget about that jerk and move on.'

'You're right, of course, and I know you mean well

but please do me a favour;   don't set me up with anyone.'

'Ok,' replied Penny, sounding quite vague.

'Promise me.' There was no mistaking the determination in Sarah's voice.

Penny stared at her before raising her hands in resignation and replying. 'I promise.'

CHAPTER 10

It had been four weeks since Michael had watched Louise meeting her lover. He had said nothing.

He wondered if he had ever really known his wife at all. He had thought he did. He'd been convinced she was as devoted to him as he was to her; obviously not. He was not ready to confront her over the affair. Sometimes when he wakened in the mornings before she did, he had an urge to put his hands around her throat and choke the life from her. It was just a fantasy, he would never do it; no matter how satisfying it might feel. If he did, he knew they would lock him up and throw away the key.

He hated being in the house when she was there and went out most nights wandering from one bar to another to pass the time, anything rather than be in her company. Usually he only stayed home if she was going out for the evening or "working late." Mostly he lay on the sofa drinking when she was out and was in a drunken sleep by the time she returned. Tonight she had gone out again and Michael was glad, it meant he could climb onto the sofa with the whisky bottle. He opened the sideboard and reached in to get it. It was almost empty.

He reached in to get the other one he knew was there and could hardly believe his eyes. It was completely empty. The two bottles had been bought on Saturday and this was only Tuesday. He knew he had been hitting the drink recently, but it was a shock to realise how hard.

My God I'm turning into my mother. The notion horrified him. This was a wakeup call, he could no longer go on like this; his drinking had got out of hand. It had affected his work lately too. Most days he arrived at the office with a hangover and was bad-tempered and irritable. That stuck up bitch, Sarah, had told him off only yesterday because he had shouted at someone in the office.

Time to take stock; the self-pity time was over. He needed to get away, spend some time on his own, evaluate his life and decide on his future.

Louise was in the kitchen when he returned home from work the following evening.

'I've decided to go on a fishing trip next weekend,' he announced.

Louise looked startled. 'A fishing trip; you've never gone on a fishing trip before.'

'And your point is what exactly?'

'Do you even know how to fish?'

'For God's sake Louise we're talking fishing here, not bloody rocket science.'

'Ok, sorry I even spoke,' she replied and turned her back on him.

Michael actually did know how to fish. When his

father was alive they had often packed suitcases, climbed into his father's car and gone to stay with Aunt Belle and Uncle Fred in Dunoon. His father and Uncle Fred liked to go fishing and had taught both boys. The first time he'd caught a fish, he'd had been so excited when he'd felt the tug on the line.

He'd shouted to his father. 'Dad, dad I've got one.'

His father had quickly secured his own rod, before hurrying toward Michael to help him reel it in. He had watched in awe as the shiny silver fish danced on the end of the line. Peter had been so jealous that Michael had caught one before he had.

His thoughts were interrupted by Louise's voice.

'Set the table, darling, dinner is nearly ready.'

Michael stared at her. She was quite the little actress. She looked every inch the devoted wife. Well actress she might be, but he was an Oscar-winner. After all he had played a part before and got away with it.

Time for a bit of role playing--again.

Thursday evening Michael came home from work complaining of a headache. He told Louise he wasn't hungry and said he needed to lie down. Of course, unbeknown to Louise, Michael wasn't hungry because he had gone to McDonalds and wolfed down, two double cheeseburgers, large fries, a chocolate milkshake and a caramel sundae. Taking a packet of paracetamol from the kitchen he called out to her. 'I'm going up to bed maybe an early night will help. Any chance you could bring me up a cup of tea?'

'Yes of course,' she replied, concern obvious in her voice.

Smiling to himself Michael undressed and got into bed. He had planned a lazy evening in bed watching TV while Louise ran after him.

Friday was a replica of Thursday, well almost. He had a big Mac meal instead of two double cheese-burgers. This time Louise looked even more con-cerned, when he announced he had another head-ache and was going to bed. Yes, she's good, he thought, but I'm even better.

The next morning, the sun streaming through the blinds had him awake at eight o'clock. He tossed and turned trying to get back to sleep; at half past he finally gave up. Quietly he slipped out of bed, got dressed, went downstairs and made himself a cup of coffee. Louise never surfaced before ten o' clock on Saturday mornings and then she went to the super-market to stock up with groceries for the coming week. Michael had always gone with her until he had found out about the affair.

He finished his coffee, showered, dressed and quietly left the house.

Louise was about to leave for the supermarket by the time he returned. As he took off his jacket, she walked purposely towards him and asked. 'Where have you been Michael?'

'The library,' he said, not even looking in her dir-ection.

'Do you want to come with me to the supermarket? We could go for lunch afterwards.'

Now there's an offer I can't refuse. 'No actually Louise I thought I'd check out the price of fishing rods.'

Louise pursed her lips and Michael could tell she was not pleased. 'You know Michael I'm getting a bit fed up going to the supermarket myself every Saturday. After all you eat the food too, maybe it something we should start doing together again.'

He wanted to scream at her. If you want some company in the supermarket perhaps you should ask your lover to go with you. Instead he forced a smile and looked directly at her. 'You're quite right Louise and I promise we will start going together again, but today I really need to get a fishing rod.'

'No Michael you don't need a fishing rod, but we need food.'

Cantankerous cow he thought continuing to smile through gritted teeth. 'Let's make a deal here; you go to the supermarket, I'll get a fishing rod and tonight I'll take you out for dinner. You get to choose. Anywhere you like. How does that sound?'

'Ok deal,' Louise replied, sounding somewhat mollified.

CHAPTER 11

In the corner of the room a cable channel on the
television was showing back to back episodes of
Law and Order. Louise leaned back in her chair, a
glass of Pinot Grigio in her hand. She glanced over
at Michael. He was dozing on the sofa, one foot dangling over the edge; a slipper precariously perched
on his toes. As she watched the steady rise and fall
of his chest while he slept, she made her decision.
She would end her affair with Simon. Michael knew
she was having an affair. Of that Louise was certain.
She did not know how he had found out; only that
he had. A few weeks earlier he had started drinking
heavily and instinctively she'd known why. Their
relationship had deteriorated rapidly, and selfishly
she'd let it happen. She had been on the verge of
leaving him; his drinking had got so bad.

Then, suddenly out of the blue everything had
changed.

He had cut down on his drinking and found a
hobby, that's what this fishing trip tomorrow was
about. He had taken her out for dinner on Saturday
night, Wednesday night and again tonight. In addition he had helped out with the chores around the

house as much as possible. He had been so nice to her. He was really trying to get their relationship back on track. She knew she had hurt him deeply, and yet not once had he accused her of being unfaithful, or made any snide comments and for that Louise was grateful. She was not sure she would have acted with the same amount of sensitivity had their roles been reversed. Feeling guilty she admitted to herself she would have hit the bloody roof.

Michael loved her, really loved her. Simon on the other hand wanted her, but she doubted he loved her.

Simon was a salesman for computer consumables. She had met him at work and been instantly attracted to him. The feeling had been mutual, and they had flirted outrageously with one another. He had asked her out for a drink that same evening. Reluctantly she had declined, telling him she was married. Next time she saw him, a few weeks later, he had asked her out for lunch. Initially she had said no, but he had talked her into changing her mind. What harm could lunch do? Lunch had led to a drink after work, the following evening, which in turn had led to dinner the following week, which had led directly into Simon's bed at the end of the evening.

She would miss Simon, he was good fun to be with and the sex was great, but it was lust not love. Simon would be disappointed, probably angry, he would not, however, be heartbroken, she reasoned.

Louise decided she would spend this weekend

with Simon, spend the whole night with him, instead of just a few hours. How ironic that the first time she would be able to spend the whole night with Simon would also be the last. Yes, one final fling then she would tell Simon it was over.

CHAPTER 12

The air conditioning was turned up as high as possible, cooling the interior of the car. The temperature outside was well into the seventies. The radio was belting out the Kaiser Chiefs and Louise was singing along.

She was on her way to Simon's flat, driving as fast as she dared, wanting to get there as soon as possible.

Michael had left on his fishing trip around nine thirty that morning. He had got up at eight o'clock and so had Louise. He'd been surprised she had got up so early on a Saturday. She had told him it was his fault, he was making so much noise it was impossible for her to sleep. The real reason was she hadn't wanted to waste precious time lying in bed

She had asked him where he was going, Loch Lomond she thought he'd said, but wasn't sure, she hadn't paid much attention. Her mind had been on the weekend ahead, with Simon. As he left she had pecked him on the cheek and told him to have a good time.

She had waved him off from the window and the minute his car was out of sight, she had cleaned the house as quickly as she could, showered and dressed then made her way to the supermarket. Once there she had almost run round the shelves grabbing what she needed in record time. Returning from the supermarket she had hurled the groceries into the kitchen cupboards and fridge, applied some make-up, shoved a change of clothes and toothbrush into an overnight bag and climbed into her car.

The silver fiesta in front was driving her mad, the driver more interested in chatting to the person in the passenger seat, than keeping up with the traffic. Louise had already had to toot her horn at the last set of lights, drawing the driver's attention to the fact they had changed to green.

'To hell with this,' she said aloud.

Looking in her mirror, she signalled, pulled out, pushed her foot down hard on the accelerator and overtook the car. It was two elderly women. 'Old Muppets,' she muttered at them as she sped past.

At last she reached Simon's street, parked her car and grabbed her overnight bag from the back seat.

Simon had seen her coming from the window and had already opened the front door for her. She ran up the three flights of stairs into his waiting arms.

'I expected you earlier,' he said, a tinge of re-proach to his voice as he buried his face in her hair

'Sorry darling I got here as quickly as I could.'

'So, he actually went fishing?'

'Yes.'

'I half expected him to call off at the last minute and ruin our weekend.'

'Well he didn't and here I am,' Louise said, breaking away from his embrace and walking into the flat. 'Good God Simon, it's like an oven in here, you need to open all the windows in this weather, not just a couple. I don't know how you stand this heat.'

'The bedroom is cool,' he answered, coming up behind her and nuzzling her neck. Expertly he slid his hands under the skimpy top she was wearing and squeezed her nipples. Louise moaned with pleasure. Still touching one of her nipples, he moved his other hand under the waistband of the short skirt she was wearing and pushed it down inside the scrap of lace she called panties. He had barely touched her when she let out a cry and he felt her whole body shudder with the violence of her orgasm.

Lifting her up like a doll Simon carried her to the bedroom and put her down gently on the bed. There they stayed for the next four hours.

It was ten o'clock at night and still warm outside. Simon and Louise were strolling hand in hand along Kilmarnock Road. They were heading back to Simon's flat after enjoying a meal and some wine. Louise was feeling quite tipsy.

'Happy?' Simon asked.

'Yes very.' She looked at him and smiled.

'You know Louise it could be like this all the time.'

Louise stiffened, she had been dreading telling Simon she was not going to leave Michael. She had not decided when she was going to drop that particular bombshell, but she certainly had not planned on it being tonight. No, she was not going to let anything ruin this weekend. No way was this conversation going any further. She kissed him passionately, pressing herself against him.

When they finally broke apart she whispered in his ear. 'Come on, let's go back to the flat; plenty more where that came from.'

She grabbed his hand and almost skipped along the road. However, by the time they arrived back at Simon's flat Louise was aware he was unusually quiet. She immediately started to pull him towards the bedroom, but Simon had other ideas.

'Louise we need to talk.'

'Please Simon; let's not do this now, not tonight.'

'Yes, Louise, now, tonight; you can't put off leaving Michael any longer. Just go home early tomorrow pack some clothes and tell him when he comes back. You can get the rest of your things later.'

Louise said nothing.

Simon looked at her. Louise avoided meeting his eyes.

'Louise, what is it?'

'I...I'm sorry Simon. I'm not leaving Michael. I can't do that to him.'

'Can't or won't? Jesus are you seriously telling me you are choosing that wimp instead of me?'

'He's not a wimp.'

'Louise open your eyes. You told me you were sure he knows you're having an affair and what does he do? Confront you? Oh no. Get upset, angry even?

Oh no. He takes you out a couple of times and then goes fishing. Fishing that's a laugh; he's probably lying bladdered somewhere. Don't forget it was only a couple of weeks ago you sat in this very room crying your eyes out telling me he was an alcoholic.'

'No, Simon, I didn't say he was an alcoholic. I said he was drinking heavily, and we were to blame. Recently he's changed, he really is trying and I know he loves me.'

'I love you.'

'No Simon, we have a laugh, great sex, but you don't love me. Can you honestly say hand on your heart; you are totally committed to me, you want to marry me, have children with me?'

'Louise we're good together as we are.'

'Good together isn't enough Simon. Michael and I want the same things; things that really matter to me.'

'When exactly were you planning on telling me Louise? Tomorrow? Next week? Next month?'

'I...I don't know.'

Simon glared at her.

'Perhaps I should go.'

'Yes, perhaps you should.'

Shocked that he had told her to leave Louise walked into the bedroom and shoved the clothes she had been wearing earlier into her overnight bag. She walked back into the hall; Simon hadn't moved.

'So, this is it. Goodbye Simon,' he said, his voice loaded with sarcasm.

'Simon I'm sorry. I really am.'

'Save it.' He walked into the lounge and slammed the door closed behind him.

Louise slipped quietly out the front door. When she reached the pavement she turned and looked up at Simon's window. Simon had closed the blinds.

She could not drive home after all the wine she had drunk. Further down the road four inebriated girls were spilling out a taxi giggling. Louise saw the driver had already turned on the yellow for hire sign, before the girls had closed the door. Holding her hand up to catch the driver's attention she ran towards it, throwing herself inside and onto the backseat when she reached it. Thankfully the driver made no effort to talk to her, other than to ask where she was going and then for the fare when the cab arrived outside her house. Once home she sat in the dark and cried; great racking sobs of self-pity, that shook her whole body. Eventually the tears stopped, leaving her feeling exhausted. She wanted to sleep but could not face sleeping alone in her own bed. She should be in Simon's bed cuddled up to him. They should have gone to sleep together and woken up together as she had planned. Instead Louise walked slowly to the linen cupboard, reached in and pulled out a spare duvet and pillow. Returning to the living room, she curled up on the sofa, placed the pillow under her head and pulled the quilt on top of her.

CHAPTER 13

Around the same time Simon had carried Louise off to bed earlier that day, Michael had arrived in Dunoon. Rather than going via Gourock and taking the ferry, he'd driven the entire route, stopping at the bustling picturesque village of Arrochar for coffee and a snack. The long drive through spectacular scenery alongside the banks of Loch Long and Loch Fyne, seemingly more impressive on such a glorious day, had a calming effect on him. The stress brought on by Louise's behaviour slipped further and further behind him with every mile and by the time he reached Dunoon he felt completely relaxed.

He parked his car and pulled a crumpled sheet of paper from his pocket. On it were the details of three B & B's he'd jotted down. The first one was in Alexander Street. He consulted his map and when he was sure he knew where he was going started up the car.

Approaching the B&B he slowed the car down to ten miles per hour and had a good look at it from the outside. It looked charming, the windows gleamed and the front garden was well maintained. In addition, the location was perfect; set on higher ground, away from the town centre. A small sign in the window indicated there were vacancies. He turned his car around, drove by the guesthouse again, turned right and parked his car in John Street. He removed a pair of reading glasses and a baseball cap bought the day before, from the glove compartment and put both on. Funny how much a cap and a pair of specs can change someone's appearance he thought, as he caught a glimpse of himself in the rear view mirror. A wall of heat met him as he stepped from the cool confines of the car. He opened the boot and lifted out the holdall containing a change of clothes before walking back to Alexander Street towards the B&B.

He rang the bell and waited. The door was opened by a pleasant, slightly overweight woman in her late fifties, who informed him she had no one staying at the moment and offered to show him a room. Michael followed her up the stairs. She had incredibly fat ankles and her feet were flapping around in open backed slippers that were at least two sizes too big. He was instantly reminded of old Tom and Jerry cartoons where Tom's owner was on the warpath and the camera shot was usually of her feet as she stomped about shouting "Thom-as." He managed to stifle his laughter as they reached the top of the stairs.

The room was bright and clean and looked freshly decorated. Michael agreed to take it and the landlady, whose name was Mrs Crawford, gave him the room key, a front door key and told him breakfast was at nine the following morning. Mrs Crawford was friendly without being nosey; in fact she seemed eager to return to whatever she had been doing before Michael arrived.

Left alone in the room he lay down on the bed, stared at the ceiling for a few minutes and promptly fell asleep.

Half an hour later he awoke, slightly disorientated. After making himself a coffee he left the guesthouse and slowly made his way back to his car to retrieve his fishing equipment. He headed for the seafront and arrived a few minutes later. He turned right and meandered along the promenade, old childhood memories of happier times spent here when his father was alive filled his head. When he reached the old coal pier, he saw a few people fishing from it and decided to join them.

Michael started to put his fishing rod together, making sure the line guides were aligned. Next he attached the reel, opened the bale arm and threaded the line through all the guides. Once completed, he attached a float and hook to the line and then a small piece of bait to the hook. Feeling pleased at how quickly he had completed this task, he moved towards the front of the pier to cast off.

Twenty minutes later and bored rigid Michael packed up his rod and left the pier. What had been an enjoyable experience as a child had turned out to be one big bore to him as an adult. Strolling back along the promenade he noticed one of the houses on the opposite side of the road was being renovated and had a skip outside. He crossed the road and promptly threw all the fishing paraphernalia including the rod into the skip. He ambled further along the road towards Kirn hoping to get a seat overlooking the water, where he could sit for a while admiring the view, but on a day like today they were all taken. He strolled on, passing Hunter's Quay; his gaze roaming over the blue water peppered with white sail boats and ferries making their way back and forward to Gourock.

Michael had intended to spend the day in Dunoon fishing and visit Tighnabruaich on Sunday. However, now he no longer wanted to fish, there did not seem much point in hanging about Dunoon all day. He turned around and walked back towards John Street to retrieve his car.

Just over forty minutes later, he arrived in Tighnabruaich. It was like going back in time; nothing much had changed. A row of shops, opposite them a hotel and bistro. He drove further along the road. On the left, houses were built into the steep hillside rising high above the shoreline, giving their occupants a panoramic view across the water. His father had told him the word Tighnabruaich was a Gaelic word meaning "house on the hill." He'd never forgotten that. The low building of the old tearoom loomed into view. It even had the same name Susy's. He turned into the car park, stopped and got out.

As he walked back towards the road, the feeling of nostalgia was almost overwhelming. Uncle Fred had often brought him here along with his brother and father for the day. The water shimmered beneath the merciless rays of the sun, dazzling his eyes. He stared at the many boats bobbing up and down and wished, as he had many times as a child, he was on one of them. He yearned to feel the breeze, ruffle his hair and experience the gentle sway of the deck beneath his feet. Reluctantly he tore his glance away from the boats, turned left and made his way along the coastal road. The last time he had walked here, his brother Peter had a ball tucked under his arm. Uncle Fred had bought it for them both to play with. Unluckily for Michael, he had thrown it to Peter when he'd come out of the shop and Peter had decided it was his ball. Michael had wanted to play with it but Peter would not let him. He had snuck up behind Peter and pushed it out from the crook of his elbow. The tide had been in and there was no wall at the side of the road to stop anything falling into the water only a concrete railing. The ball had bounced a couple of times and almost gone over the edge. Peter had yelled at Michael and punched him on the arm. His father had grabbed the ball, laughed and thrown it back to Michael. Peter had been incensed and started shouting he wanted his ball back, at which point their father had calmly pointed out the ball belonged to both of them and told Peter to stop acting like a baby. How different his life was now to what it had been that day.

He walked through the boatyard and continued along the track as it rose upward from the shoreline.

It all looked slightly different to him; the terrain was easier to navigate than he had expected, in fact the whole place looked more cultivated than he remembered. Was it different he wondered, or was it all down to seeing the place as an adult, as opposed to how he had perceived the place as a child? A few yards further along the track and Michael's question was answered. A location board indicated that the route he was walking was part of the Cowal Way; he was sure that had not been the case when he had visited here as a child The information suggested it had been set up with money from the Heritage Lottery Fund; confirming this notion. Michael walked on until he came to a small bridge over a waterfall. There he stopped and drank some water from the small bottle he had brought with him. Strolling along the path a few minutes later, he was glad to note it was now quite level and eventually started to descend.

He encountered several walkers on the path and all either nodded or muttered a greeting, most without really looking at him; it seemed the obligatory action to do and Michael dutifully responded. He walked on enjoying the peaceful nature of the place. The lighthouse on Loch Riddon wasn't far away. He used to chase Peter round and round that lighthouse. He wanted a rest and it would be the ideal place to have a break. However, a minute or so later Michael stopped in his tracks, dismayed. It appeared there was no access to the lighthouse, trees now obscured it from his view and he could just make out a building through the trees which looked like a house. Although there were no signs indicating one should keep out or indeed it was private property, from where Michael stood it certainly gave the appearance that the lighthouse was located on the land of whoever owned the property. In fact it appeared to Michael, the isthmus where the lighthouse stood was someone's back garden. Had that always been the case he wondered. Had his father and Uncle allowed him and his brother to run wild on someone's property? Or had the owners allowed access at that time? Michael couldn't be sure if the house had even been there. Bitterly disappointed he continued along the path as it wound upwards behind another house and back down behind a couple more. Mostly there were bushes and or trees separating the path from the rocks some stretches of the path also had a low wall. He really needed to stop for a break; it was an incredibly hot day. He peered over the wall and was pleased to note that there were only a couple of overhanging branches at this point and he could easily step over the wall and sit on the rocks.

Grateful to sit down, he stared across Loch Riddon. It was not quite the same as sitting beside the lighthouse, but it would do. Michael reflected on how many people he had lost since he'd last been here. His father to a road accident, his brother to life in a foreign country, his mother to drink and self pity and now his wife to another man.

Had he really lost Louise? Was she planning on leaving him? Could he forgive her if she stayed? These questions danced around relentlessly in his head. He'd thought his life with her was perfect. The only thing missing had been children and Louise had always assured him there was still plenty of time. He had believed her because he had wanted to. She was everything he could ever want in a woman. Attractive, intelligent, funny, sexy, and he had loved her with all his heart. Should he forgive her; could he forgive her? He stared around. It really was beautiful out here, so remote and peaceful. Maybe he could resolve the situation with Louise after all. He would bring his beautiful wife to this beautiful place, which held so many dear memories; perhaps that was the solution. Feeling more positive than he had in a long time he drank some more water, before climbing over the wall and retracing his steps back along the path.

By the time he reached his car Michael was feeling quite hungry, it was now late afternoon and he had eaten nothing since mid-morning and that had only been a snack. He flirted with the idea of a bite to eat in the tearoom but in the end decided to go back to Dunoon and get something there. However, by the time he arrived he wanted a drink more than he wanted food.

He didn't take his car back to the guesthouse either. He parked up off Argyll Street, which was regarded as the main street of the town and entered the first public house he came to. He ordered himself a double whisky and secured himself a table opposite the bar. Someone had left a newspaper on one of the seats. Just what he needed; he spent the next twenty minutes sipping the whisky and reading the paper. When his glass was empty he looked up, a few more people had come in. Michael bought himself another drink, this time a single measure before turning his attention to the crossword. He managed to fill in about half the crossword while downing another two whiskies before he got bored. Deciding it was time to eat he stood up and walked towards the door.

Once outside he turned right and walked towards the pier. Just before he got there he found what he was looking for; an Indian restaurant.

Louise hated Indian food and complained about the smell in the house on the rare occasions Michael bought a takeaway. In contrast Michael loved Indian food but seldom got a chance to eat it. The first thing he ordered was a bottle of white wine while he perused the menu. Five minutes later he called the waiter over and ordered his food, determined to make the most of this opportunity to eat what he wanted without listening to Louise complaining.

Slightly over an hour later and sated from the food and wine Michael left the restaurant, crossed the road, walked past the pier hosting its Tudor-Chinese shaped building with striking red roof and headed along the promenade towards the West Bay. It was still hot even for a summer's evening and many people were making the most of the weather and were strolling along the seafront. As Michael approached one of the many benches dotted along Victoria Parade, an elderly couple who had been sitting there vacated it. Michael welcomed the chance to sit down. The walking he had done today combined with the whisky, heavy meal, and wine had taken its toll and he was exhausted. He gazed contentedly at the view around him for a while before his eyelids started to droop.

A dog barking loudly behind him awoke him with a start. Bleary eyed he looked at his watch, it was almost nine o'clock, he had been sleeping for nearly an hour. Reluctantly he got up from the seat and made his way back towards the town. His mouth was dry and he wanted a drink. He saw a pub he hadn't noticed earlier and another couple of whiskies later he made his way back to Alexander Street where a comfy bed in Mrs Crawford's guesthouse awaited him.

CHAPTER 14

The delicious aroma of roast beef and York-shire pudding wafted through the house. Michael smelled it the minute he opened the front door. In the kitchen two pots were simmering gently. Lifting the lids, he saw potatoes in one and carrots in the other. Another larger pot sat cooling on a pot stand beside the hob, it contained homemade lentil soup. Louise appeared at his back.

'Oh, hi I didn't expect you back so soon.'

'I missed you,' said Michael walking towards her.

'I missed you too, dinner will be ready soon.'

He looked at her and winked. 'Let's have dessert first.' She moved towards him and took his hand.

Louise was lying curled up in Michael's arms. They had just made love and Michael had fallen asleep almost immediately. Poor baby, he must be tired after driving home from his trip. Her mind wandered back to the night before and her confrontation with Simon. She knew Simon would not pine for her for long. With his good looks and charm he would easily find someone else and then Louise would become just another ex-girlfriend. She felt sad that she would never be in his company again, but from now on she had to concentrate on Michael she had so much to make up to him. She knew their marriage would survive. They loved one another. She made a silent vow never to betray Michael again and do everything in her power to make him happy.

Today had been a start. This morning after a fitful night's sleep, she had toyed with the idea of lying on the sofa and wallowing in self-pity. Instead she had forced herself to get up and retrieve her car from outside Simon's flat before Michael returned. A small part of her wanted to see Simon again, an even smaller part hoped he would be looking out for her; but that didn't happen. She had stared up at his windows, but the blinds had remained firmly closed. Feeling a mixture of disappointment and relief Louise had got in her car, driven home and spent the rest of the morning making Michael a nice Sunday dinner. He stirred beside her. As she looked at him, he opened his eyes. 'Ready for soup and the main course?' She asked.

The sun had stopped shining leaving the evening air warm and balmy. In one of the gardens nearby children were playing, shrieks of laughter filling the air.

Michael was sprawled on a lounger on the patio. Louise brought out a bottle of wine from the fridge and two glasses. She poured wine into both and handed one to him. She lifted her own glass to her lips. Michael continued to stare at her.

'What?'

'I was thinking you and I should have a weekend away.'

'It's not that long till we go on holiday. September is only a few weeks off.'

'I know but right now I think we would both benefit from a break; somewhere nice and quiet away from the grind. I know just the place; Tighnabruaich. It's completely different from anywhere we've ever been before.'

'Tinna where?'

'Tighnabruaich. It's only about twenty miles from Dunoon. I drove there yesterday.'

Louise looked stunned, she thought Michael had gone to Loch Lomond and had nearly said as much. Luckily, she had caught herself just in time. She shuddered thinking how she hadn't really been listening to what he'd said before he'd left. She hadn't even cared where he was going. Her mind had been on Simon and she'd just wanted him to leave as quickly as possible.

'How about next weekend?' Michael asked. Friday night to Monday. We'll have a night in Dunoon too. What do you say?'

'I don't know about Monday Michael, It might not be possible, remember we are right in the middle of the holiday season.'

'Oh come on Louise your boss can hardly deny you a day's holiday at short notice; it would be really mean after all the overtime you've done recently.'

Louise cringed.

'In fact if he does I'll go see him and point that out.'

Inwardly she shuddered at the thought of Michael approaching her boss; complaining on her behalf and Gerald looking puzzled, telling him Louise never worked late. How awful would that be? How humiliating for both of them. Gerald wasn't stupid. He would realise she'd used him as an unwitting alibi to deceive her husband and Michael would realise just how much she'd lied to him. She made a decision; one way or another she would take the Monday of the following weekend off, even if it meant phoning in sick.

CHAPTER 15

The ringing phone on Michael's desk was grating on Sarah's nerves. Where the hell was he? She had a slight headache caused by too much wine the night before. She had been out with Penny and Jo, a friend of Penny's from work. They'd had a good night; too good a night, when she had work the following day.

She looked around hoping to see Michael hurrying to answer it, but he was nowhere in sight. Reluctantly she got up from her chair, made her way towards his desk and answered it herself.

The voice on the other end sounded surprised. 'Oh, hello I was looking for Michael, Michael Barton.'

'Sorry he's not here; I think he must have gone to lunch. Can I take a message?'

'Could you ask him to call his wife when he gets back? I'm at work,' replied the voice on the other end of the telephone.

'Yes, certainly,' Sarah replied.

'Thanks, bye.'

She had rung off before Sarah had time to reply. Irritably she searched around Michael's desk and found a notepad. She ripped out a page and scribbled.

Your wife phoned - Phone her back at work.

Sticking it on top of the mound of paperwork on his desk, she returned to her own. Ten minutes later Michael came back to his desk, saw the note and lifted the telephone receiver.

At first his voice had been only a murmur to Sarah but now she was aware it was getting louder.

'Yes Louise I know I usually go at one o'clock but I went at twelve today.'

'He won't do that again,' Anne said, winking at Sarah as she walked past her desk.

Sarah nodded at Anne and looked across at Michael. As if sensing she was staring at him the tone of his voice changed completely. Where, before his voice had an air of controlled impatience now it was all sugary. Sarah continued to stare. There was something not quite right. The tone of his voice and his body language were at odds with one another; he was tapping his fingers almost irritably on the edge of his desk.

Ending his call to Louise; Michael glared at her and said. 'Haven't you got work to do, instead of listening to other people's conversations?'

'Don't start Michael, I'm really not in the mood,' she replied, lifting her handbag and storming off towards the staffroom. 'That bloody man,' she moaned to Linda when she got there. 'Who the hell does he think he is? God alone knows how his wife puts up with him. Imagine living with someone like that.'

'Maybe he has got attributes that make it worthwhile,' Linda said and laughed.

'Oh don't, I feel sick enough. Joking aside don't you think there is something odd about him?'

'Like what?'

'I don't know, I just think there's something weird going on with him and I don't trust him.'

'He can be a bit of a prat sometimes, but I've never thought he was weird, it's probably just a personality clash.'

'Maybe.' Sarah replied, sounding dubious as she switched the kettle on.

CHAPTER 16

Louise and Michael were walking through the boat-yard at the end of the shore road in Tighnabruaich. It really was beautiful around here, so quiet and serene. This weekend away had been just what they both needed. Michael had put a lot of thought into this weekend and Louise was really enjoying herself. He was such a lovely man; so kind and thoughtful. She was glad she had ended her affair with Simon. How quickly things change; there was a time when thinking about Simon sent ripples of pleasure through her body, now all she felt were pangs of guilt. As they continued to walk Louise took hold of Michael's hand and squeezed it. He turned to look at her and she planted a kiss on his lips.

***

Michael was feeling really pleased with himself, the weekend had been a huge success. Louise looked so happy, more like the old Louise, the one he had fallen in love with.

He had made reservations for Friday night in a hotel situated on the West Bay in Dunoon. Unlike when he had gone himself, this time he opted to drive to Gourock and take the ferry across. The hotel had been a good choice. The location was excellent, and their room had looked onto the shore. It was well run and boasted entertainment on Friday and Saturday nights. There had been a band playing on the Friday night and they had caught the second half of their set. Michael had to admit they'd been pretty good.

Saturday morning had been spent exploring the various gift and souvenir shops. Louise had been in her element; eventually she'd bought two hand painted mugs and a rather chunky looking bracelet. As she was paying for the bracelet she'd spied a pair of silver cufflinks and insisted on buying them for Michael. Their shopping trip had been topped off with two cappuccinos and a huge slice of apple pie from Perk-Up; an aptly named coffee shop.

The next few hours had been spent on the small beach at Ardentinny before driving to Tighnabruaich.

They'd finally arrived in Tighnabruaich around five o'clock and checked into a lovely hotel, again, overlooking the shore.

Yesterday had been spent relaxing on the seafront reading newspapers before walking along the shore road into Kames. It had been such a beautiful day they'd kept going and wandered round to Ardlamont. They'd arrived back at their hotel completely exhausted. The only downside being his knee had started playing up.

As a child he'd fallen from a tree and damaged it quite badly. He had limped for months afterwards because it had taken such a long time to heal. It had left a weakness and whenever he walked any great distance his leg started to feel heavy and he favoured his left leg more when walking, which meant he tended to walk with a slight loping gait.

As usual, a good night's rest, keeping his leg in an elevated position had done the trick and today his knee was fine.

Yes, all in all reflected Michael, the weekend couldn't have gone any better. When checking out this morning Michael asked at reception if they could leave the car in the hotel car park as they intended to walk round by the old lighthouse, before they headed back home. The receptionist smiled brightly, told them not to worry about their car and to go ahead and enjoy their walk.

They walked on hand in hand in companionable silence along the path as it wound its way round Rubha Ban stopping a couple of times to drink from the bottles of water they had brought with them. Branching off to the left they followed the track up to the small bridge across the waterfall.

'How lovely,' squealed Louise when she saw it.

She took the camera out of her small backpack-come-handbag and snapped a picture of Michael with the waterfall as a back drop. They continued along the pathway admiring the thriving vegetation, winding their way down towards the disused lighthouse. When Louise spied the houses to the back of the lighthouse on slightly higher ground she stopped in her tracks.

'Can you imagine waking up to that stunning view every morning?'

'Bit of a trek to get to work, though,' he replied and they both laughed. 'Give me the camera. I'll take a picture of you and use the houses as a back-drop.'

'Perfect,' she said and handed it to him. He was just about to take the photograph when he froze. The sun was shining down on her and she was smil-ing, looking almost seductively at the camera. He had never seen her look more beautiful. What was she thinking he wondered his eyes filling with tears? Pulling himself together, he quickly pressed the button on the camera and blinked a few times avoiding looking at her as he handed it back.

The track climbed upwards behind the houses and then started to descend quite steeply, bordered, intermittently, by a wall which separated the path-way from the rocks at the water's edge. Michael stopped for a drink and asked Louise for the camera again. He took another photograph of her with her back against the wall. As he walked towards her, he looked over the wall onto the rocks.

'Let's stop for a rest, sit on the rocks for a while,' he suggested.

'Oh I don't know about here Michael,' Louise re-plied, staring dubiously at the rocks. 'Let's go a bit further see if we can find somewhere better to sit.'

'My knee is starting to play up a bit with all the

walking we've done this weekend, I really would appreciate a break.'

'Sorry darling I didn't realise. Do you want to turn back?'

'Yes, I think so, let's sit for a bit give my knee a rest and then head back.'

The wall wasn't very high and they both climbed over easily. The trees were overhanging quite low at this point giving them some shade, as they sat down on the rocks. Michael finished the water in the bottle he had been drinking from and opened another as they both stared over the loch enjoying the view.

Eventually Michael turned towards his wife. Feeling him staring at her she turned her head and looked at him. He said nothing.

'What is it?'

'I was just thinking how beautiful you look. Take off your sunglasses let me look at you. I love looking into your eyes.'

'You old romantic.' Louise laughed as she removed her sunglasses.

Michael took them from her and placed them on the ground beside her bag. He then leaned forward and kissed her. Then patting both his pockets he slowly stood up.

'Ready?' she asked.

'As ready as I'll ever be.' He held out a hand to help her up.

Louise now on her feet was facing him with her back towards the edge of the rocks. As she bent down to lift her bag and sunglasses Michael gently took hold of both her arms above the elbows. She leaned towards him and he realised she thought he was going to kiss her again, instead he stared at her and smiled. Eventually he spoke.

'This is goodbye Louise.'

'Wha...what do you mean, this is goodbye?' Her voice faltered, confused.

He continued to stare at her; an ugly twisted grin replacing the ambient smile on his face.

'Michael stop it, you're scaring me. Let go of my arms.'

He had to be careful not to grip her arms too tightly he didn't want to leave marks on them. 'Don't struggle Louise. One false move and you're in the water.'

That statement had the desired effect on her, and she stiffened immediately. Louise was terrified of deep water; she had never learned to swim. Hence the reason she had been reluctant to climb over the wall onto the rocks in the first place.

'Now I'm going to let go of your arms and you're not going to move, do you hear me?'

Louise said nothing.

'Answer me, Louise.'

'Ok, ok calm down for God's sake,' she replied, her own voice high pitched, almost hysterical.

He released her arms.

'Michael what's this all about?' she asked, trying to sound outraged, but not quite pulling it off because she was so scared.

'Well let's see. Maybe it's all about the fact I've got a dirty little whore for a wife. How long did you think I was going to put up with you screwing another man and then crawling into bed beside me?'

'I'm sorry.' Her voice was almost a whisper.

'Sorry. Is that it? Is that all you can say?'

He watched as she risked a quick glance behind her. 'Michael let's move away from the edge, sit down and discuss this.'

'What's there to discuss. I saw you with him.'

Louise looked startled. 'Please Michael, just listen. It's you I love I ended it with Simon. We can work this out. I love you so much. Give me another chance please Michael,' she begged, starting to cry.

'You can turn off the tears they're not going to work. Not this time. One, if you had really loved me the way I loved you, you would never have fucked another man, two there is no way you're getting another chance, three, we can't work this out, you took me for a mug once and that's once too many in my book. I loved you Louise, really loved you but you betrayed me and now you have to pay the price.'

'Please Michael don't do this please I love you.'

Michael stared at her standing on the edge of the rocks, terrified, crying, begging. Slowly he moved forward and put his arms around her. Yes, today she had paid for what she had done. However, not quite enough he thought as he gently released her from his embrace. As Michael watched her visibly relax, he lifted one of her hands and kissed it then placing her hand gently on her chest he pressed his own hand against hers and pushed hard.

Louise fell backwards over the edge of the rocks and into the water. The look of astonishment mixed with fear on her face sent shivers of excitement down his spine. He had caught her so off guard she hadn't even screamed as she fell, only uttered a slight whimper.

Now you've paid enough. Taking deep breaths to calm himself; he sat back down on the rocks and stared across the water, smiling as his gaze drifted towards the spot where Louise had gone in.

Ten minutes later he stood up took Louise's phone from his pocket switched it on and placed it in her bag. He grinned remembering how she had searched through all the drawers in their hotel room three times this morning looking for it. Of course, it had been in his pocket all the time. He had put it there when she had been in the shower. There was no way he wanted Louise to have access to a phone; hiding it had been a safeguard in case some part of his plan had gone wrong. She had insisted Michael call her number and when that had not helped, because he had switched it off she had said she was going to search the car and unpack the holdalls. Michael had stopped her, by saying if it was in either of the holdalls or the car they would find it when they got home. To appease her he had said he would ask at reception if one had been handed in, while she applied her make-up, of coursed he hadn't bothered. Reluctantly Louise had left the matter there, acknowledging, it was either lost for good or was indeed in one of the holdalls.

Next Michael walked back towards the wall turned left and scrambled over the rocks for a few yards until the spot where Louise had gone over the edge was obscured from his view by the over-hanging tree branches. There he unzipped his trousers and relieved his bladder of all the water he had drunk recently. Returning to the spot where he had pushed Louise from, he lifted her sunglasses and threw them into the water. Next he made his way to the left of where Louise had been standing and where the drop from the rocks was not quite so steep, more of a gradual descent as the rocks reached the water. He scooted down feet first and gingerly entered the water easing himself in until the water reached his neck then he ducked his head under the surface and hastily hauled himself out of the water and back up to the wall.

He took his phone out of his pocket, knowing full well it wouldn't work after it had been in the water, and attempted to call 999. Throwing it down on the ground, he walked to Louise's bag and lifted out her phone and again pressed the nine three times. There was no signal he had known there probably wouldn't be one. He had not been able to get one on his own phone the first time he had come here alone. Climbing over the wall he walked back along the path to where he had gotten the signal on his last visit. Again, he pressed the nine three times. This time he reached the emergency services and asked for the police.

Almost immediately a female voice answered. 'Police, what's your emergency?'

'Please you've got to send police divers and get the coastguard, my wife's fallen in the water.'

'What's your name Sir?'

'It's Michael, Michael Barton.'

'And what's your wife's name.'

'Louise.' The sound of fingers tapping on a keyboard could be heard clearly as he answered.

'You said Louise has fallen in water. Is she still in the water?'

Trying to make his voice sound panicked he replied. 'Yes, I think so I can't find her.'

'Now Michael, exactly where are you?'

'In the middle of bloody nowhere.' He smiled, he knew exactly where he was but he wasn't going to make it easy for her.

'Where did you start your journey from Michael?'

'Tighnabruaich.'

'And what direction did you take from Tighnabruaich Michael, did you go through Kames?'

'No the other way.'

'Towards Loch Riddon?'

'Yes Loch Riddon.' Gasping for effect he continued. 'Loch Riddon that's where we are.'

'You're doing really well Michael, the emergency services are on their way. Are you at the water's edge at the moment?'

'No, I couldn't get a signal on the rocks and had to climb over the wall onto the path.'

'Now Michael I want you to stay on the line until the emergency services arrive.'

'No, No I can't do that. I've got to go back and find Louise.' His finger pressed the button to end the call and he climbed back over the wall, a self-satisfied grin spreading across his face.

So far, he had encountered no one. He'd banked on there being few walkers on the path on a Monday morning and everything was going to plan. Sitting back down on the rocks he began to laugh. He'd certainly resolved things with Louise. Resolved them his way and he was euphoric. No feelings of guilt whatsoever. Eventually in the distance he heard voices. His heart sank as they drew nearer, and he heard laughter. He didn't want anyone else around the scene he had set so diligently. Nor did he want anyone else involved; that would only complicate matters. However, it would look strange if he did not try to get help from anyone who passed by. The voices were getting closer, they were female. Michael chanced a quick look over the wall and was relieved to see two women who looked to be in their sixties walking towards him.

Jumping quickly over the wall he started slowly staggering towards them, weaving from one side of the path to another. The two women immediately stopped in their tracks and eyed him suspiciously. He knew he was frightening them. He saw the look of panic that passed between them. Not wanting to scare them to the point where they ran screaming back the way they had come, he held out his hands in a gesture of helplessness.

'Please, please help me,' he said.

Not moving the taller of the two women shouted at him. 'What's wrong?'

'Please, please my wife, help me please.'

The two women looked at each other and again the tallest one spoke.

'Where is your wife? Is she hurt?'

'My wife, you've got to help me,' was all Michael replied as he made his way backwards along the trail and started to climb over the wall towards the rocks.

The two women now appeared less scared and slowly started walking towards him, both climbing over the low wall.

When they saw him standing on the rocks dripping wet: the shorter of the two finally cottoned on.

'My God, has she fallen in?'

Michael said nothing

'Is she in the water?' This was said more sharply.

'I can't find her. I can't find her,' replied Michael, sniffing for effect.

'Phone the police, Marie,' commanded the taller woman.

Marie dutifully scrabbled about in her backpack and brought out her phone. She tried to make the call.

'Damn, there's no signal,' she said and climbed back over the wall on to the path.

The taller woman's nervous expression, stated clearly she was uneasy at the thought of being left alone with him. He couldn't really blame her after all she was being left with a murderer, even if she didn't know it. However, it was now obvious Marie's only concern was getting a good enough signal on her phone to be able to make a call. She ran along the pathway until she managed to connect with the emergency line. While Marie was away her friend spent the time standing between Michael who was now sitting on the rocks head in hands swaying from side to side, and the wall. Her head going from right to left as she glanced from him to the path nervously awaiting the return of her friend; he heard her breathe a sigh of relief when the woman named Marie reappeared.

Michael sat on the rocks staring at the water in a trancelike state, ignoring all questions the two women asked of him until the emergency services arrived.

CHAPTER 17

It was quarter past nine and no one was doing any work, they were all huddled around one desk in the office. Sarah was late; the first time ever, she had slept in. As she entered the office everyone turned to look at her. She sensed immediately something was wrong and walked towards them. Anne broke away from the others and met her half way.

'Something terrible has happened. It's Michael; his wife's dead.' Sarah stared stupidly at Anne as she continued talking in short stilted sentences, lifting her hands in a gesture of helplessness. 'She drowned. Apparently she slipped. Fell off some rocks.'

Finally Sarah found her voice. 'My God how awful, he must be in some state.'

'He jumped in, tried to save her, but couldn't find her. Police divers eventually recovered her body.'

'I met her once,' said Linda as Anne and Sarah walked towards the others.

'She came to pick him up; she seemed really nice; bright and bubbly.'

The telephone on Bill's desk started to ring and he went off to answer it. One by one everyone drifted back to their desks and slowly started to get on with their work. Sarah found it hard to concentrate; thoughts of Michael and how his wife had died kept flitting into her head. She was glad when it was time to go home and surmised everyone in the office felt the same. She didn't particularly like Michael, but she did feel compassion for him. She remembered how bad she'd felt when Gordon had left her and this was worse, much worse.

Thinking about Gordon made Sarah realise how far she had come in the last few weeks. Penny had been her rock. She'd been there for her whenever she had been down, and slowly Sarah had begun to enjoy life again. She no longer minded being on her own, in fact she realised being single had some advantages. She could come and go as she pleased, eat when she wanted, allow the flat to get in a mess and not feel guilty, and best of all she didn't have to consider anyone except herself.

She'd thrown herself into her painting, a hobby she loved and that had been just the therapy she'd needed.

Several nights out with Penny and Jo, who were both good company, had helped her to move forward. Slowly Sarah had finally started to realise that there was life after Gordon and, as Penny had said, probably a better one.

More than once that evening she thought about Michael and what he must be going through. Sadly she thought also of the woman who had been his wife. A woman she had never met, only spoken to on the telephone. A woman who could not have been much older than herself and whose life had been cruelly taken from her.

CHAPTER 18

The tightly closed vertical blinds swung in the breeze from the open windows. Alexa was playing Green Day tracks so low they were barely audible. Michael was ensconced in his favourite chair, feet resting on a footstool, a crystal glass half full of Glayva in his hand. He had gotten away with murder, how many people could say that. He grinned at the thought.

He was glad Louise was dead. She had treated him like a fool; lying to him, crawling into bed beside him straight from another man's bed. She had also done something else, she had underestimated him, and that mistake had proved fatal.

Revenge is a dish best eaten cold and his revenge had been delicious. He would never forget the look on Louise's face as he pushed her from the rocks. He felt a thrill of excitement pass through his body, a stirring in his groin at the memory.

It had been so simple to get her to sit on the rocks, using his knee as an excuse.

Off course his knee had been fine. Unlike the Sunday the distance they had walked that day had had no impact on it whatsoever.

He could scarcely believe how easy it had been. One hard push was all it had taken, and Louise was gone forever. He knew once in the water she would never be able to get out. Louise couldn't swim. He had found this out the first time they'd gone on holiday together. On their first day in Tenerife Louise had been sitting at the side of the hotel pool dangling her feet in the water. Michael had sneaked up behind her and pushed her in. She had gone berserk, started screaming, it had only been the shallow end, but Michael had had to jump in and help her out the pool. She had told him she had never learned to swim. As a child her father had tried to teach her, but the smell of chlorine had made her feel sick. The visits to the pool were such an ordeal her father had given up. At Secondary School whilst her classmates were off to the local pool as part of the physical education curriculum; Louise had had the misfortune to have been struck down with Glandular Fever.

What had gone through her mind in those final seconds, he wondered.

He hadn't thought it would all be over so quickly, that Louise would disappear under the water and never be seen again. He'd expected her to struggle splash about; he'd wanted to watch her die. He'd wanted her to see him watching her, not doing anything to help. He'd actually felt quite cheated it had all been over so quickly.

He had thought Louise's body might float to the surface; he'd been prepared to pull her body out of the water, make it look as if he had tried to revive her. That was the only part of the plan he'd had any difficulty with. He'd dreaded the thought of touching her dead body. He'd had no qualms about pushing her in. He'd relished that part of the plan.

But Louise hadn't floated to the surface, instead her body had gotten snagged on some rocks and police divers had been called in. All Michael had had to do was immerse himself in the water to make it look as if he had tried to save her. That had freaked him out. When he'd lowered himself gingerly into the water, irrational thoughts of Louise's hands grabbing his ankles, pulling him under the water had raced through his mind. He shuddered at the memory.

When the police arrived, they had found him soaking wet. He'd told them they'd been sitting on the rocks having a break from their walk, enjoying the view. He'd wandered off left Louise alone for a few minutes; call of nature. He'd heard her scream his name, heard a splash. He'd ran back as quickly as he could, shouting her name calling for her over and over. Her bag was lying on the rocks, but she was gone. He'd scrambled down the rocks into the water but still he couldn't find her. He had to find her she couldn't swim. Why couldn't he find her he'd asked the police?

The police told him, after the post mortem had been done Louise had hit her head on the rocks below the surface and had already been unconscious at the time of drowning. He knew this was supposed to make it easier for him knowing she hadn't suffered as much as she might have. However, under the circumstances it had annoyed him intensely.

The funeral had been the next test of Michael's acting skills. He'd been confident he could play the grieving husband to perfection. The only thing that had worried Michael was facing Louise's father, looking him directly in the eye.

Louise's parents, Ruth and George, had been in their forties when Louise had been born. They'd both long since given up hope of having children. Then out of the blue Louise's mother had become pregnant at forty three. Her parents had been devoted to one another and she had been adored by both of them. By the time Louise and Michael had married they'd both retired. Five years ago Ruth had died suddenly from a heart attack. Her father had taken it really badly, in fact he'd never properly recovered. He had a sister, Moira, who lived in North Berwick and she had persuaded him to go and stay with her for a while. He'd never returned to his own home.

As it was Michael needn't have worried about looking Louise's father in the eye. George didn't look anyone in the eye; in fact he never took his eyes off the ground the entire day. Moira guided him in and out of the service, helped him in and out the funeral car and not once did Michael see him lift his head or say a word.

The only time Michael felt any guilt over killing

Louise was when he thought of George. When Ruth had died the light in his eyes had dimmed, now his daughter was dead, the light had been turned off completely.

Michael had thought it likely Louise's lover would attend the funeral. He'd scanned the crowd in the crematorium several times expecting to see him hanging about at the back and was surprised when he hadn't showed. Why wasn't he there? Didn't know? Or didn't care?

***

The truth was Simon had no idea Louise was dead. Louise had been paranoid about Michael finding out she was having an affair and from the very beginning had sworn him to absolute secrecy. Simon had respected her wishes and had told no one. He'd always believed she would leave Michael and then their relationship would no longer be a secret. He'd had the good sense to realise the furtiveness had added to the intensity of their relationship.

Although Louise's death had merited a few lines in a couple of the Scottish dailies, Simon had been in Birmingham all week at a sales conference when Louise had drowned.

***

Everyone had been so nice to Michael. Ken Paterson, his Departmental Manager, had visited him at home and told him to take as much time off work as he needed. Bill from the office had come with him.

Bill had said if he ever needed to talk not to hesitate to call him, night or day.

Swallowing the last of the Glayva in his glass and pouring himself another Michael laughed thinking how he had missed his vocation, working in insurance; he should have been an actor.

CHAPTER 19

Pressing the light switch at the bottom of the stairs he was surprised when nothing happened, and the hall remained in darkness. He started to climb the stairs; halfway up he was sure he heard something and stopped to listen. He stood quite still for a few seconds and when he heard no further noise began to move again. A feeling of impending doom engulfed him and with each step the feeling grew stronger. By the time he reached the top he was certain he was not alone in the house.

He heard the noise again this time more clearly; it sounded like someone sniffing. It had come from behind the closed bathroom door. A slither of light escaped from underneath. The hairs on the back of his neck felt as if they were standing to attention and a pulse was beating fiercely in his left temple. Moving on tiptoe he slowly turned the handle and opened the door. The light in the room was so bright for a second it blinded him and then he saw her. She was stepping out the bath looking at him, eyes blazing with anger. A long, wet, pale green evening gown clung to her body, low cut exposing her cleavage, accentuating every curve. Her long dark hair hung loose, rivulets of water dripping onto the floor. He stood transfixed his heart aching, she looked so beautiful. Slowly she lifted her hand and pointed an accusatory finger at him. She opened her mouth to speak but no words came out, only water. At first slowly trickling from between her lips, dripping down her chin, but as she drew nearer him it poured out more quickly. He tried to step back but his feet wouldn't move. He felt the water hit his face, saw it spewing from her mouth like projectile vomit and he began to scream.

The light went out plunging him into darkness and still he screamed. His eyes snapped open, he was lying in bed, gasping for breath, the quilt around him and pillow beneath his head, both, damp with sweat. He sat up and switched on the bedside lamp. After what seemed like an eternity his breathing returned to normal and he threw himself back down against the pillows.

For the rest of the night Michael remained in bed, staring at the ceiling; the dream still too vivid in his mind to want to sleep.

CHAPTER 20

Where were her bloody keys? Sarah rummaged frantically through her handbag wishing she had got them out of her bag earlier. Knowing the stairs were being washed today and the door to the close would be open at this time, same as it was every week, she hadn't bothered. She could hear the telephone ringing inside the flat. At last she felt the large letter S attached to her key ring. Grabbing on to it she dragged the keys through the rest of the clutter that filled her bag to almost bursting point. As if on cue the minute she fitted the key in the lock the telephone stopped ringing.

She'd been looking forward to a long soak in the bath, followed by a bite to eat and an early night. She was exhausted. Since Michael's wife had died, she'd covered much of his workload in addition to her own. She was starting work half an hour earlier most mornings and she'd worked until seven o'clock for the last two nights. She didn't mind, with the exception of Linda, who was young, free and single and apparently had an extremely busy social life, everyone else in the office either had partners or kids or both to rush home to. Sarah was quite happy to work on after everyone else had gone home, and the money was definitely coming in handy, now she was on her own.

On entering the flat she dumped two bags of shopping, and her handbag on a chair and made her way towards the telephone. She punched in the numbers one, four, seven, one and was dumbfounded to hear Gordon's mobile phone number relayed back to her. Her heart lurched, what could he want. She'd had no contact with him since he had left, apart from the night Penny and herself had bumped into him with that awful woman.

Knowing Gordon had tried to contact her unsettled Sarah. She no longer felt tired. She made herself something to eat had a quick shower and when she noticed a missed call from him showing on her mobile, which was almost out of battery, curiosity got the better of her and she lifted the landline telephone and keyed in Gordon's number. He answered on the fourth ring.

'Hello. It's Sarah, you phoned me.' Her tone was sharp.

He sounded slightly nervous and the words came out in a rush. 'Yes, I did. I...I need to talk to you. Can we meet tonight?'

It was the last thing she had expected to hear him say and she hesitated before replying. 'No Gordon. I've been working late and I'm tired. It's been a long day.'

'Please Sarah it's important.'

'Can't we just talk about whatever it is on the

phone?'

I'd rather speak to you face to face. I could come to the flat.'

Sarah didn't really want him to come to the flat. She wasn't sure how she would react to seeing him there again. She knew she could put him off, suggest meeting him tomorrow instead, but decided if she was going to meet with him at all it was probably better doing it sooner rather than later. She had to admit she was curious to hear what he had to say. 'Ok come to the flat,' she replied.

'Thanks. I'll see you in about an hour.'

He'd sounded anxious; was he in trouble she wondered? She did a quick tidy up, brushed her hair put on some makeup, sat down in front of the television and channel hopped, waiting for him to arrive.

Eventually the buzzer rang. Her heart lurched when she saw him standing on her doorstep, he was so handsome, but she also felt resentment towards him. Both greeted one another rather awkwardly, avoiding eye contact. Gordon followed her towards the living room.

'Would you like coffee or a drink, there's no beer I'm afraid, only wine.'

'Coffee will be fine.'

Sarah headed for the kitchen thinking how strange this felt, they'd once been so intimate and now Gordon felt like a stranger to her, albeit an attractive stranger, but a stranger none the less.

Walking into the living room, two mugs filled with steaming hot coffee, she handed one to Gordon and sat down opposite him.

Gordon sipped his coffee nervously and asked. 'How have you been?'

'Well let's see, I've gone from completely devastated to just tickety boo.' Her voice dripped sarcasm.

'Please Sarah don't be like that.' He placed the mug on the floor at his feet.

'Like wha...' She stopped herself. Looking him directly in the eyes she asked. 'Gordon why are you here?'

'I'm sorry I hurt you Sarah, can we try again? Put everything behind us and start over.'

She stared at him, wondering if she had misheard him. No real apology just the words I'm sorry, no genuine regret.

'And Prue, Gordon; what about Prue?'

'Prue was a mistake.'

Sarah stared at him. In that moment she saw Gordon in a different light, not the gorgeous, sexy, soul mate she'd once thought, but instead an arrogant, conceited, self-centred pig.

'My God, she's dumped you hasn't she?'

'Sarah please, does it matter?'

'Of course it bloody matters. You wouldn't be here otherwise.'

'Yes, I would. I've missed you like crazy. I should never have left. I'm sorry I made a mistake. You and me; we were good together, you know we were.'

'Oh you made a mistake alright, coming here tonight was a mistake and I made one too when I let you in the bloody door.' Sarah retorted, her voice rising in anger.

'We can work this out I know we can, just let me move back in and...'

'Whoa, stop right there. There is no way you are moving back in here.'

'Please Sarah.'

She stood up and banged her mug of coffee down on the mantelpiece. Some of the brown liquid splashed out and dripped onto the carpet. 'Let me get this straight. You cheat on me with another woman, you leave me for her, she dumps you and then you come snivelling back to me. Have I missed out anything?'

Gordon said nothing and had the good grace too look ashamed.

'Get out.' Sarah shouted, by this time furious with him.

'What?'

'You heard. Go on, get out,' she said opening the door of the living room and heading for the front door.

'Sarah calm down,' said Gordon following her out into the hall.

Shaking with rage Sarah turned and looked at him. 'Piss off.' She opened the front door.

Gordon looked at her for a few seconds then shoulders slumped he walked from the flat.

Sarah slammed the door shut so hard she expected to hear the sound of breaking glass from the small panel in the middle of the door.

Walking back into the living room, she collapsed onto the nearest sofa, sobbing, while at the same time half laughing at the look of disbelief on Gordon's face when she'd told him to piss off.

CHAPTER 21

It was time to go back to work. He had stayed off long enough; it had been six weeks now. At first it had been great, staying in bed all morning, lying about the house for the rest of the day, reading books watching movies. In the first two weeks after Louise's death he had not even had to cook much. One of the neighbours, Mrs Liddle, had come to the door most days with food. A pot of soup, a couple of casseroles, a lasagne, a steak pie, a chicken and leek pie; all had been homemade, and all had been delicious.

Now, however, Michael was getting bored. His nightmares were getting more frequent, most nights he either dreamt about his mother or Louise, sometimes Louise even appeared in his mother's dream. As his mother dragged herself along the floor Louise appeared behind her, dripping wet and always pointing the accusatory finger. It was like a double act. He could laugh about it in the cold light of day, but not during the night when he awoke bathed in sweat. He'd asked the doctor for sleeping tablets in the hope they would knock him into such a deep sleep he wouldn't dream. When that had not worked, he had taken slightly more than the prescribed dose, he had not had either of the dreams that night but the next day he was so zonked he had decided that was not an option. Maybe getting out the house and going back to work would break the pattern a bit and they would lessen.

He lifted his phone and contacted his work. He told Ken Paterson he planned to return on Monday. Next he showered quickly and threw on a pair of jeans and a t-shirt. Checking his driving licence was in his wallet, expecting he would require identification; he grabbed his car and house keys and left the house. He was off to join a health club. He had decided it was exactly what he needed. It would get him out the house, keep him in shape and give him a chance to meet new people.

Although he was glad Louise was dead, he had to admit he was beginning to feel lonely. He had built his life around her, planned his future with her and he had loved her in a way he had never loved anyone else. Obviously Louise had not felt the same, she had thrown everything back in his face and now she was out of his life for good. It was time to move on.

After registering at the club, which was only a couple of miles from home and had a decent sized gym, Michael drove to Glasgow and left his car in the car park at the Buchanan Galleries shopping centre. Meandering around the many shops, he treated himself to a new pair of trainers, two pairs of shorts, two t-shirts, two pairs of jogging pants and a sweat shirt. That should be enough to start him off at the club. Then he had a bite to eat, re-trieved his car from the car park and drove home. When he reached the local shops, he stopped out-side the florist. He would send Mrs Liddle a small bouquet of flowers in gratitude for her kindness. After all I might be a murderer, but I am not ill man-nered. He sniggered at this thought as he entered the shop.

CHAPTER 22

'Speed dating; that's what you need my girl.' Penny said, hiccupping because she had drunk so much wine.

Sarah stared at Penny in disbelief. Jo, Penny's friend from work, started to giggle. 'You should see your face it's an absolute picture.'

The three of them were lying on massive cushions on Penny's floor, empty wine bottles and pizza boxes littering the coffee table.

'No really, we should all go. It'll be a laugh.'

'A laugh,' Sarah said, looking horrified. 'What's funny about moving from chair to chair, listening to a bunch of weirdoes droning on and on about themselves?'

'It's not like that,' Penny said, sounding slightly defensive.

'Somebody's been before,' piped in Jo.

'No I haven't, but I know someone who has.'

'Who?' Sarah asked, her curiosity now aroused.

'Remember Mary, who used to live next door?' Sarah nodded. 'Well that's where she met her boyfriend.'

'No!' Sarah said, sounding incredulous.

'Yes, and he wasn't a weirdo,' replied Penny.

Sarah had to agree. She'd met him a couple of times and he had always struck her as a decent sort of guy and rather good looking too.

'Well I'm game,' said Jo.

'I don't know,' said Sarah doubtfully.

'Oh come on, where's your sense of adventure?'

'I'll think about it.'

'That's settled we're going,' said Penny topping up their glasses with more wine.

***

Sarah looked around the room staring at the men suspiciously.

'Lighten up.' Penny whispered in her ear.

What the hell was she doing here? She had said no to Penny and Jo so many times in the last week she had lost count and still here she was at a speed dating event. The venue was the function room of some trendy bar in the merchant city.

'How did you find out about this place?' Sarah asked.

Penny ignored her. 'Don't thank me now, wait till you meet the man of your dreams, then you can thank me and reimburse me for the nineteen ninety five it cost to register.

'My God, paying to meet men, what next?'

'Pole dancing,' answered Jo with a loud raucous laugh.

The sound of a small brass bell ringing brought their attention to the host, who asked everyone to take their seats.

Despite all the misgivings Sarah had about speed dating, once it was over she had to admit she'd actually enjoyed the experience, and the biggest surprise of all had been discovering there were two men in the room she'd been attracted to.

Jo and Penny hadn't fared so well, but they'd talked Sarah into leaving her contact details with the host.

Afterwards they'd gone to The Guitar, a pub recommended by Jo and one neither Sarah nor Penny had ever visited. Once there, they'd dissected the night and had a laugh comparing notes on the various men who'd been at the speed dating event.

CHAPTER 23

Michael had been back at work four weeks. The first day back had been another test of his acting skills. Everyone had been so nice to him, even Sarah. They had all shown genuine concern. At first, he had felt slightly guilty, with the exception of Sarah, he liked everyone in the office. However, by mid-week he was beginning to find it all slightly wearying.

'That poor man; what must life be like for him now,' he had overheard someone say in the staff-room.

Thankfully when everyone had realised he wasn't going to burst into tears every now and then, they had stopped treating him with kid gloves and now life in the office was the same as it had been before Louise's demise.

He had settled into a routine at the health club; he worked out at the gym on Tuesday and Thursday nights and Saturday mornings. The nightmares hadn't stopped but they were less frequent since he had gone back to work.

There was one thing Michael wanted to do. He wanted to go back to where he had pushed Louise off the rocks. He wanted to relive the moment again; but he was scared someone might recognise him. He had never been under any suspicion at the time of Louise's death but going back to where she had drowned so soon; would that be wise? Or was he being irrational?

Michael finally decided to take the risk. On Saturday he would visit the spot where Louise had died. If he avoided the ferries and drove the entire journey there and back, he wouldn't come into contact with anyone other than those he passed on the trail from Tighnabruaich. Surely the chances of anyone being on the same route on Saturday, and at the same time on the day Louise had died must be pretty remote.

The decision made he poured himself a large whisky and drank it in two gulps.

**

He was standing on the rocks, smiling, remembering the fear in Louise's face. The water began to gently ripple. Michael expected to see a fish darting about and was surprised when he didn't. Meanwhile he heard voices behind him, he half turned to see two policemen. The water started to ripple again, only this time the gentle ripples quickly turned into small waves. They gathered in momentum each one coming higher up the rocks than the last.

The voices behind him grew louder. He stepped back and someone laughed. He turned around; the two policemen had been joined by several others. Michael began to panic, the next wave washed over his feet and ankles and he slipped. Two of the policemen grabbed him, tried to pull him back but the waves were becoming more violent. He lost his balance and fell into the salty water. He was aware the policemen on the rocks were shouting but he couldn't make out what they were saying. A couple of them were taking off their jackets and he tried to swim towards them. The strong waves held him back. The policemen were getting smaller with every second and he was drifting further and further away from them.

He was exhausted, his arms and legs felt like lead; he no longer had the energy to stay afloat. His head slipped under the surface, and his feet came up, water poured into his mouth and nose; he couldn't breathe. His right hand hit against something hard as his arms flailed about. He threw his head upwards, disorientated and gasping for breath. He had fallen asleep in the bath. His knuckles were red and sore where they had hit against the tiles at the side of the bath. How long had he been asleep? The water was freezing, and he began shivering from both the cold and the all too vivid dream, still fresh in his memory.

Leaning forward to pull out the plug he screamed. Louise's face stared up at him from below the surface of the water. He scrambled out of the bath, moving backwards, not stopping until his shoulder smashed against the wall on the opposite side of the room. He began to retch and only just made the toilet bowl before throwing up. Once the vomiting had stopped, he grabbed the towel from the rail and wrapped it round himself then gingerly walked towards the bath and forced himself to look down into the water. Seeing it was completely clear, he breathed a sigh of relief and quickly yanked on the chain of the plug and wrapped it round one of the taps. He almost ran to the bedroom and threw himself on the bed. Tears of self-pity stung his eyes and the whisky he had drunk earlier and just thrown up stung the back of his throat as he lay in the dark.

He would never visit the scene of Louise's death now. The vivid detail of the dream, together with the trick his imagination had played on him with Louise's face in the bath water had made sure of that.

CHAPTER 24

Sarah was on her way to meet Robert; one of the men from the speed dating event. They had been dating now for just over a month. The first time they had met up Sarah had been really nervous, in fact she had almost called off at the last minute; but she had forced herself to go and much to her surprise she had really enjoyed herself. Robert seemed to be a pretty nice guy, although you can never really tell she had pointed out to Penny after their first date.

Tonight they were going to the theatre. Sarah loved the theatre and so it appeared did Robert. Another box ticked. She hadn't been to the theatre in ages, Gordon had never really enjoyed going.

She crossed the road directly in front of the entrance to the King's Theatre and was pleased to note Robert was already there waiting for her. He waved to her as she walked towards him.

Penny had been right; there was a better life awaiting her after Gordon. Last Saturday night when she'd been out with Robert, a taxi had stopped a few yards ahead of them. Robert had run towards it and Sarah had followed, as she was pulling the door shut she'd spotted Gordon walking towards them. He'd been on his own and she knew he'd seen her and Robert getting into the taxi.

The following evening he'd phoned and asked who she'd been with. She'd told him Robert was her new boyfriend. Although it was really none of Gordon's business who Robert was and Sarah hadn't really started to think of Robert as her boyfriend; she had wanted to make it clear to Gordon she had moved on with her life. That had been on the Sunday night; on Tuesday night Gordon had phoned Sarah again and this time he had asked to meet her. He had suggested they go for a meal. When Sarah had said no Gordon had sounded really disappointed. He had tried to persuade her; telling her they should remain friends. Sarah had stood by her decision not to go and told him she thought it best to leave things as they were. She knew he wasn't pleased, but by now she couldn't care less what Gordon thought.

When Sarah awoke the next morning, Robert was lying beside her. He was still sleeping, and Sarah slid quietly out of bed. Tying her dressing gown around her she padded barefoot to the kitchen and made herself a cup of coffee. She had asked Robert back to the flat last night and now she had mixed feelings about doing so. They'd had such a good night; the play, a comedy, had been hilarious and they had both really enjoyed it. When the play was over, not wanting the evening to end Sarah had suggested they go back to her flat for coffee. Coffee finished; one thing had led to another and now Robert was lying asleep in her bed.

She liked Robert and she knew he liked her. In fact, after last night she liked him a whole lot more. That was the problem. When she had first met Robert at speed dating, she had been attracted to him and when he had contacted her, she had been flattered. The first couple of dates had been light hearted good nights out; but last night had changed that. Sarah realised she had deeper feelings for Robert than she wanted to have at this point. After she had gotten over the shock of her break up with Gordon, she had vowed to have some time to herself, keep any dating she did on a casual basis. She was falling for Robert and she wasn't sure if she was ready to go headlong into another serious relationship. The other question that was niggling at her was; how did Robert feel. Was he falling for her, the same way she was falling for him. Or was it all just a bit of fun to him with the added bonus of sex now thrown in.

A sound behind her brought Sarah out of her reverie. She felt Robert kiss her neck and she turned round. As she felt his hands slip under the top of her dressing gown Sarah put all the questions she had been asking herself for the last few minutes to the back of her mind.

CHAPTER 25

Joining the health club had been a good move. He had a date with a petite brunette called Tina he'd met there. In a buoyant mood Michael whistled as he dressed. He hadn't felt this way in years; full of excitement at the thought of a first date, wondering if he would be able to charm her into bed at the end of the night. He glanced at the clock, he wanted to be early. Waiting for her, feeling nervous, would ultimately add to the excitement of the whole experience. Smiling, Michael lifted his jacket and left the house. He was not smiling a few hours later when he returned.

The date with Tina had been a disaster. The night had gone badly from the outset. Arriving at the restaurant fifteen minutes early he was peeved to find Tina already there. Bang goes the anticipation of waiting for her to arrive he thought, smiling through gritted teeth as he walked towards her. No thrill of the chase either. Tina made it clear throughout the meal she expected the evening to end with sex. She was wearing an extremely tight, low cut top and leaned over the table at every opportunity, affording Michael several eyefuls of her more than ample breasts. She kept brushing her leg against his, touching his hand, licking her lips and on her way back from the ladies' room she snuck up behind him and whispered something in his ear. Michael could not recall what she had said, what he did recall was feeling her boobs pressing into his neck and shoulders.

They both ordered a starter and main course. Michael had barely finished eating when she brazenly suggested they go back to his house for coffee and winked at him.

No way had that ever been a remote possibility. Louise had only been dead a couple of months; he couldn't afford to be seen taking women back to the house so soon.

When he suggested they go to her house instead she agreed immediately and signalled for the waiter to bring Michael the bill.

'You don't really want coffee?' she asked, her voice husky, as she stood in her hall and kicked off her shoes.

'Well actually I do.' Michael by this point was desperately trying to regain some measure of control and watched as Tina flounced off to the kitchen to make it.

When they reached the bedroom, things got worse. He was given the distinct impression Tina was less than impressed with his performance. The final straw came when she egged him on to go faster and he ignored her. She yelled impatiently. 'I said faster you bastard.'

Michael was incensed and lost the plot completely. He slapped her hard across the face. She stiffened momentarily, her eyes snapping open; a look of shock crossing her face. Seconds later the look of shock was replaced by a look of ecstasy as she moaned with pleasure. The slap across the face had done the trick which was just as well for Tina because it had certainly done the trick for Michael. Almost immediately she reached out and grabbed her cigarettes. Michael watched as she lit one and thought probably the only reason she went to the health club was to meet men. To him she was a most unhealthy person. This was the third cigarette she had smoked since they'd arrived at her home. Taking a deep draw, she winced and tentatively touched her jaw where Michael had slapped her.

'Whew, Michael that was just a touch too hard.'

'Sorry,' he mumbled, rising from the bed and starting to dress.

'You're not leaving already?' she asked, sounding incredulous.

'Yeah; can't stay, not tonight.'

Tina turned away, a look of disgust crossing her face. Michael hadn't been able to get out of the house fast enough. He had really lost it when he had hit Tina. He had been lucky Tina had taken it well; put it down to the throes of passion. Only Michael knew different; she had annoyed him, and he had been incensed with rage, he had really wanted to hurt her. He would have to be careful. After all, he acknowledged, slapping women because they annoyed him would only land him in trouble, no matter how satisfying it may feel.

It would probably be best if he avoided going to the health club on Thursdays, he concluded. This was the only day when he visited the club, he had ever seen Tina there. However, by the time Michael arrived home he had decided to give the club a miss completely for the next two weeks, just in case Tina should go there at other times to try and seek him out.

CHAPTER 26

A blast of wind and rain hit Sarah on the face. Her umbrella had blown outside in for a third time since coming up the stairs from the underground. As she struggled to right it, she almost decapitated a tall thin man walking past her. Luckily, he ducked out of the way at the last minute.

It was Saturday morning and Sarah was on her way to meet Penny. Penny's cousin was getting married in three weeks and she needed an outfit. She also needed a partner and, in the absence of a steady boyfriend, had asked Sarah; which meant Sarah needed an outfit too.

By the time Sarah arrived at Starbucks to meet Penny; she was cold, wet and grumpy.

Her friend was already there and waived to her as she stood in the doorway, fighting with her umbrella; this time trying to put it down, only the umbrella had decided it wanted to stay up. Sarah finally won the battle; breaking a nail in the process.

Two lattes and a blueberry muffin later Sarah felt less grumpy and ready to face the shops.

Three and a half hours later they had both finally managed to choose an outfit, shoes and a matching handbag each. Their next stop was Penny's favourite tapas restaurant in Renfield Street.

'Seen Jo recently?' Sarah asked as they ate their food.

Jo no longer worked beside Penny. She had only been on a temporary contract which had now ended.

'Err, no; not for a while.'

Sarah noticed the strange look that passed over her friends face. 'What's wrong?'

'She stole some money from me,' Penny blurted out.

Sarah dropped her fork and sent a prawn flying onto the table as it clattered off the side of her plate. She was completely shocked by her friend's answer. 'Are you sure?'

Penny shook her head slowly. 'She took the money from my purse.'

'Are you sure?' Sarah knew she sounded stupid repeating herself, but she was having great difficulty believing Jo was a thief. Surely Penny must have got this wrong.

'Let's put this another way,' said Penny, who by this time sounded slightly riled by Sarah's reaction. 'You leave a room. A few minutes later you return to the room in time to see someone remove a twenty pound note from your purse. Is that person a) trying to steal from you, b) not trying to steal from you, or c) you are not sure whether or not that person is trying to steal from you.'

'Sorry, if I'm being a bit insensitive about this, but

I'm finding it hard to get my head round it.'

'You're finding it hard to get your head round it. I suppose I probably wouldn't have believed it either, if I hadn't seen her with my own eyes.'

'What did she say when you caught her?'

'Nothing really, she didn't even look embarrassed, just laughed it off and muttered something about being caught red handed. I asked her what she wanted the money for, thinking she must have been really desperate to do such a thing. When she didn't answer I told her I would have given her the money if only she'd asked. She just stared at me for what seemed like an age, shrugged her shoulders, replaced the note in my purse and left. Her reaction really freaked me out. I think she took the money because she wanted to, not because she actually needed it and I don't think it was the first time either.' Sarah opened her mouth to say something but thought better of it as Penny continued. 'A few weeks earlier the two of us had been out and I thought I should have had more money in my purse than I had at the end of the night. At the time I thought I must had been careless and dropped it, now I am not so sure. I think she may have stolen money from me that night too.'

'She always seemed so generous with money; always first to buy a round of drinks, that sort of thing.'

'Maybe because it was other people's money she was being generous with,' Penny replied, bitterness obvious in her voice.

'When did this happen?'

'About three weeks ago.'

'Why didn't you say anything before?' Almost immediately she added. 'Oh God it's me isn't it. I've been so wrapped up with Robert lately to notice anything else.'

'No; it's not that. To be honest although I did want to tell you, I didn't feel able to talk about it before now. I'm actually glad you asked me about Jo today.'

'Oh Penny.' Sarah covered her friends hand comfortingly with her own.

As she looked across at Penny, she thought how well her friend appeared to have handled the situation at the time. She wasn't sure how she would have reacted if it had been her instead of Penny.

The rain was battering off the windows by the time they had finished their meal and Sarah and Penny decided to get another drink in the hope it would subside before they left. Another drink turned into another three. Drinking during the day didn't agree with Sarah or Penny for that matter. By the time they left the restaurant they were both more than a little tipsy, and Penny had decided she needed a hat to complete her outfit. They spent the rest of the afternoon trying on hats and giggling before both purchasing hats they could ill afford.

The only thing they hadn't bought was a wedding present; which turned out to be a blessing in disguise.

A week later Penny telephoned to say her cousin

had called off the wedding. With a bit of luck we can return the hats and get a refund, thought Sarah, wishing she had never bought hers in the first place.

CHAPTER 27

The tall, athletic looking, blonde woman walked towards him and Michael smiled as she approached. He needn't have bothered; she didn't even look at him. Michael was on a treadmill and watched as the blonde stepped onto the one beside him. It was Friday night and Michael was in the health club. After his experience with Tina he had stayed away for a few weeks and when he had ventured back, he had gone on Friday nights instead of Thursdays. He had noticed the blonde woman immediately and had been instantly attracted to her.

Engaging her in conversation was proving to be a challenge. She neither acknowledged nor talked to anyone and constantly had music blasting in her ears from her iPhone while working out. He watched her from the corner of his eye. The last two weeks she had finished her workout around eight forty-five and had entered the changing rooms. He looked up at the clock on the wall, ten minutes to go.

At eight forty-seven the blonde woman walked towards the ladies' changing rooms. Michael immediately started making his way towards the men's changing areas. He quickly showered and dressed and made his way to the reception area. His plan was to hang around and strike up a conversation with her as she left the club. He expected to be waiting for a while; remembering how long Louise had always taken to get ready to go anywhere even the supermarket. He was, therefore, amazed, when sauntering out of the changing room, he saw the blonde walking towards the exit. Michael hurried after her as she strode confidently outside.

'Damn,' he muttered under his breath as he followed her through the door. Something caught his eye. A membership card lay on the ground slightly to his right. Michael bent down and picked it up, then running to catch up with the blonde he shouted. 'Excuse me.'

The blonde did not turn around in fact her stride never faltered.

Michael tried again. Slightly louder this time. 'Excuse me.'

There was still no response. By this time Michael was right behind her. Transferring the card to his left hand he reached out with his right and touched her arm. The woman shook her arm, while at the same time turning with such force that Michael, involuntarily stepped backwards.

Taking a deep breath and trying to look slightly apologetic; he held out the membership card towards her. 'I'm sorry if I startled you but I think you dropped this.'

The woman, eyes glittering with anger, glanced

down at the photo card and then glared at Michael. 'Does that really look like me?' she asked, her voice loaded with sarcasm.

The outside of the club was particularly well lit making the photograph on the card clearly visible. For the first time Michael looked down at the card; the face of a fair-haired young man was smiling up at him. Of course, Michael hadn't cared who it belonged to when he had picked it up, he had only wanted to use it as an excuse to stop the woman. A feeling of overwhelming rage took hold at the way the woman had spoken to him. His hand shot upwards, toward her face and flailed in mid-air, the woman had already turned dismissively and marched off toward parked cars completely unaware that he had tried to strike her. A voice beside Michael brought him to his senses.

'Oh good, you've found it.'

'Wha-at.' He stammered, confused.

'My membership; I realised I didn't have it when I got in my car and came back to look for it. Thanks.'

Michael looked into the face of the man whose picture was on the card he was holding. 'No problem,' he replied distractedly, handing it over.

The blonde was now nowhere in sight and Michael walked towards his car. Climbing inside he thought back to his encounter with her; he had lost it again. If she hadn't been so quick off the mark, she would be nursing a sore face and he would probably be handcuffed and on his way to a cell by now. What a bitch she had turned out to be, her sarcastic reaction had been completely over the top. How had she managed to get ready so quickly? Probably hadn't bothered to shower; mangy cow.

He was going to have to make a real effort to keep his anger in check. He decided not to go back to the club on Friday nights either. He didn't want to risk being in the blonde's company again in case she said or did something to trigger off another rage. That was Thursday and Friday nights now off limits. Christ at this rate there would soon be no nights left in the week he could visit the club. He started the car and pulled out of the car park.

CHAPTER 28

It was Wednesday night and Michael was driving home from the cinema. He loved the cinema, so had Louise and they had gone often on Wednesday nights. Since returning to work, Michael had resumed this practice. Usually he returned from work, showered, changed and had a bite to eat first; preferring to go to the later showing. Tonight he had been a bit later than usual leaving work and had decided to go to the earlier showing of the film and pick up something to eat on the way home. As he drove, he pondered over what to get to eat; a takeaway didn't much appeal to him. Approaching the next roundabout Michael came to a decision, he would treat himself to a meal in Mitchells; it wasn't that far from here. Hopefully midweek he would be lucky enough to get a table without a booking. It was worth a try he reasoned. Indicating right he moved into the outside lane and turned right at the roundabout.

Would you like to join me for a meal Louise? Oh sorry, I forgot you can't; you're dead. He laughed as he drove.

Not only would Louise have been over the moon

to be going unexpectedly to her favourite restaurant she would probably have enjoyed the film too, he surmised. He, on the other hand had been disappointed and thought it had fallen short of the reviews he'd read. To make matters worse, one of the characters; a blonde with a bad attitude, had reminded him of the blonde at the health club. Every time he thought about his encounter with her, he bristled with anger.

His stomach rumbled and he silently prayed a table would be available in the restaurant; he really was feeling peckish now. Thank God he was almost there. A lone figure was walking further ahead and as he drew nearer a look of surprise crossed his face. As if by magic, thinking about the female from the health club had conjured her up. She was unmistakable; tall, thin and wearing that same distinctive jacket Michael had seen her wear at the health club. The jacket was a bit garish for Michael's taste, black with large zigzags of fuchsia pink on the back front and sleeves. He watched as she stepped out onto the road without looking. Typical of the haughty bitch; don't bother to look, just expect the cars to get out your way.

Glancing at the speedometer, Michael realised he was speeding slightly and moved his right foot to brake a little. As he did so he started to fantasize the outcome, if instead of pushing his foot down on the brake he pushed it hard down on the accelerator. That would sure teach the bitch a lesson.

The car shook violently, bringing Michael out of

his fantasy.

'What the hell was that?' he said aloud, looking in the mirror.

'Oh no; oh dear God no.' He hadn't just fantasized about running the woman down he had actually done it. Instinctively he braked hard, he knew he should stop, try to help. He could say it was an accident. There were no other cars about but there were houses on either side of the road, if anyone had been looking out of their window at the time, it would have been obvious Michael hadn't tried to slow down. There would be tyre marks or lack of them as he had not braked until after he had hit her. A voice inside his head was telling him to keep driving, it was too late to go back and Michael listened to that voice.

He had only driven a few yards when he spotted headlights in the distance. A car was coming towards him. Real panic gripped Michael, the car coming towards him would find her. He had to get off this road; he turned left and the restaurant he had been headed to loomed into view on his right. All thoughts of eating now banished from his mind Michael kept going.

He had to stop the car and think what to do. He couldn't risk stopping on this road it was too close to the accident. The car must be damaged, and Michael wanted to see how noticeable it was. Thankfully he had not encountered any more vehicles. He had to find somewhere safe to stop. Another roundabout loomed into view and without indicating he turned right. On one side, the road was bordered by woodland on the other, however, a row of houses stood and the road itself was well lit. He couldn't risk stopping here either. As he reached the top of the hill it got suddenly darker and Michael calmed down slightly. Some of the street lighting was out and although there were flats to his left the right hand side was still bordered by woodland and there were cars parked on both sides of the road. Michael felt sure stopping here for a while would be safe.

He felt sick at what he had done, the fact he had deliberately run the blonde down because of the way she had spoken to him was bad, but worst of all; it hadn't even been her. He forced himself to remember that horrifying moment he had looked in the mirror and saw the woman lying on the road. Her hood had fallen from her head and Michael had seen her hair; it had been dark. Was she dead or just injured? Had he killed someone else; this time without meaning to?

First things first, get of out the car. He didn't want to look, but knew he must. Stepping out of the car he walked around it, surveying the damage. It was bad, even in the darkness he could see it was bad. There was a large dent on the bodywork at the front on the passenger side. Slowly he climbed back into the car. He would never be able to repair the damage himself and he couldn't risk taking it to a garage. He had to get rid of the car, burn it out, that should get rid of any evidence or would it? Nowadays the police had all sorts of clever ways of retrieving DNA.

The faint sound of shouting broke into his thoughts and Michael looked in his rear view mirror. A teenage boy jumped out from the dark mass of bushes, quickly followed by another two. Sounds of laughter pierced the air before all three disappeared back into the darkness.

A plan was starting to formulate in his mind. What if he could get them to take the car? In all probability they would drive it around for a bit then set it on fire. If they got caught driving, they would get blamed for the accident and even if they didn't get caught driving or didn't burn the car out; their fingerprints would be all over the inside of the car. All he had to do was report it stolen; first, however, he had to make the car appear attractive enough to steal. He couldn't risk leaving it where it was, they might not come up this way. He would have to take the car to them. He didn't want to turn the car round either; he didn't want them to see the damage to the front of the car before getting in.

Gently easing the car out of the space and without switching on his headlights, he started to reverse slowly back to a few yards in front of where he was sure the youths were in the bushes. The flats on his left didn't go as far back as he had thought, beside them was a low building. Whatever it had once been it was now uninhabited, the windows were boarded up, half the roof was missing and bushes from the adjacent property were encroaching into the grounds.

Michael could hear the sound of voices and laughter coming from the bushes. Leaving the key in the ignition; and touching the switch that opened the boot from the inside, he quietly climbed out of the car. He didn't shut the door completely, which meant the inside light stayed on. Going to the back of the car; he eased up the lid of the boot and lifted out the hooded waterproof jacket he kept there. As he slipped it on and pulled up the hood he debated with himself whether to leave a twenty pound note lying on the front seat; but decided against it; afraid they might just take the money and scarper. Instead; he leaned back into the car and turned the radio on, raising the volume slightly. As he stood outside the car, he could hear the radio and knew whoever was larking about in the bushes would too. Quickly he walked away, back towards the spot where he had originally stopped. He heard their voices getting louder and knew they had ventured out from the bushes onto the pavement. He was desperate to turn around and see what they were doing, but didn't in case it scared them off. A few yards further on, he could no longer hear their voices and dared a quick glance behind him. Two of them were inside the car; one was still standing on the pavement. Michael kept walking, he had done the best he could. He quickened his step and crossed the road. He had to get away from here as quickly as possible. He had just reached a small road that branched off to the left at the end of the block of flats when a car sped past him; his car.

Michael reckoned he was in Castlemilk somewhere but didn't have a clue what the name of the street was or where it led to. He kept walking and when he reached a mini roundabout he stopped. He had two choices, straight on or turn left. A bus was coming towards him along the road to his left. Michael squinted to read the destination board and as it drew near he saw the word Castlemilk. Not much good to him, it must be near the end of its route, it might, however, come back this way. He decided to take the chance and turned left.

He had walked on for what seemed like an age before he heard the faint drone of what sounded like the engine of a bus. Michael turned round, he had been right a bus was indeed coming down the road towards him. He was only a few yards away from a bus stop and he hurried towards it, sticking out his hand; while at the same time fishing around in his pocket for some change. He had no idea how much the fares cost. Amongst several ten and five pence pieces nestled three pound coins, surely that should be enough. The destination on the bus said Govan and not wanting to draw attention to himself by asking what route the bus took, Michael dropped the money in the coin box and muttered. 'Govan please.' The driver didn't even look at him as he punched a couple of buttons and from the machine out popped a ticket.

Michael sat down; he had to report the car stolen, that was a worry. Where was he going to say it had been stolen from? He couldn't say from outside his house, someone might have seen him drive away earlier and if the neighbours were questioned, he would be caught out. He didn't think it was a good idea to say it had been stolen from outside the cinema either; he had been parked in the car park and it was a certainty there would be CCTV there. Same with the cinema so he daren't pretend he had gone to a later showing or even different film.

As these thoughts were swirling around inside his head he looked out of the window. Nothing looked familiar in the darkness, there were houses on either side of the road the bus was now travelling along and Michael did not have a clue where he was. Panic started rising from somewhere deep within again and he had to force himself to take deep breaths; he had to stay calm. He also had to go somewhere where other people were around and establish an alibi, but where he thought, staring at his feet. Furtively he looked around the bus, there was only one other person on it; a young woman who was chatting to someone on her phone. He wished he knew the route the bus was taking, nothing looked familiar. The bus stopped and a couple of men got on and Michael turned to stare out of the window again. It stopped at a set of lights the first set to be at red, all the others had been green and the bus had sped through making it even more difficult for Michael to try and work out the direction the bus was going in. When the lights changed back to green the bus turned left and he relaxed slightly. The bus was slowly making its way along

King's Park Road and Michael knew exactly where he was. He breathed a sigh of relief when it turned into Battlefield Road; there were pubs and restaurants in this area.

Having a meal would prove to be a better alibi than drinking in a pub, but Michael knew there was no way he could force himself to eat anything at present, in fact, even thinking about food now was making him feel a bit queasy. He made his way to the front of the bus and alighted at the next stop. He removed the jacket he had put on earlier when he had left the car, rolled it up as tightly as he could and was about to shove it in a roadside rubbish bin when he spied a white transit van parked a few yards down a street to his left. The rear doors were open, and a young man had just jumped out carrying some slats of wood. The man disappeared inside the nearest close mouth. Michael sprinted quickly towards the back of the van and peered in. As well as the timber, which had been carefully stacked to one side, there was an array of building materials. Glancing furtively towards the close the driver of the van had disappeared into, Michael jumped into the back of the van and stuffed his rolled up jacket as far down as possible behind a bucket which had been quite clearly used for mixing plaster. He had only just managed to get back out of the van before he saw the driver coming out of the close. He held his breath, had the driver seen him? Obviously not; as completely oblivious to Michael the driver reached back into the van and removed more of the wood. Unknown to Michael the driver's only concern was removing his ill-gotten gains from the van as quickly as possible.

Hastily he walked away from the vehicle, entered the first pub he came to, made his way to the bar, ordered himself a double whisky and carried it carefully to a table. He wanted to gulp the whisky down, drain the glass completely; but instead he forced himself to sip it. He had to think things through and he needed a clear head. He was desperate to know what had happened to his car. Had the youths who took it smashed it up, crashed it, burnt it out or been stopped by the police? One thing was certain he could not afford to report the car stolen tonight not now he was attempting to build himself an alibi in a pub. As Michael continued to sip his whisky a plan started to take shape.

He would report the car stolen in the morning. He would get up early, phone a taxi to take him to Battlefield to collect his car and when it wasn't there he would phone the police and report it stolen. Even if the police caught the youths driving it and came to him before he reported it stolen he could still use the same story. He would tell them today had been the anniversary of the day he had first met his wife. They had always celebrated it by going for a meal and this year Michael had decided months ago to take Louise to Battlefield Rest He was so lonely since her death he had planned on going to the restaurant himself. He thought it might make him feel closer to her. As the day grew nearer, he wasn't sure if he could face going on his own. He hadn't made a reservation he had decided to wait and see how he felt on the day, then if he did decide to go, he would leave it up to fate whether there was a table or not.

He had driven there but couldn't face going in. He had got so upset he'd had to stop driving and park the car. Once composed he had got out of the car and walked aimlessly about. He'd dreaded the thought of going home yet again to an empty house and had decided to leave the car where it was, go to the pub and collect the car in the morning. Michael ran through, one more time in his head, the scenario he intended playing out to the police tomorrow when he reported his car stolen, or sooner if they came to him first. Then drinking the remainder of the whisky in the glass; he made his way towards the bar and ordered another, this time a single. Now to get the barmaid on side.

As she pushed the whisky towards him he smiled sadly, looked around him and said.

'Quiet tonight.'

The barmaid, with the name badge Debbie, nodded and almost immediately Michael sensed her interest in the heartbroken stranger he found so easy to portray. By the time Michael had called a taxi to take him home Debbie was putty in his hands. The exact phrase that had gone through his mind was, like a bitch in heat and he would have liked nothing better than to have gone home with Debbie. Of course, he hadn't, he wasn't stupid and sense had prevailed. Instead, he glanced at the clock above the gantry and said. 'I really should get home, I've been here since nine o'clock,' planting the notion in Debbie's head that was the time he'd arrived.

CHAPTER 29

By the time the paramedics had arrived Jill Mason was already dead. Her head too full of thoughts of her new boyfriend, she had stepped onto the road without looking. She hadn't stood a chance at the speed Michael had hit her.

D.I. James Stanford, Stan as he was known to friends and colleagues, had promised her parents he would find whoever was responsible for their daughter's death. Small consolation, he knew, what they really wanted was their daughter back, but that was something Stan couldn't deliver. He understood what the Masons were going through. He knew only too well the pain of losing a child.

Dean, his son, had been the centre of his wife, Carol, and his world. At three and a half years old Dean had been struck down with meningitis and died. Cruelly, Stan had not only lost his son but his wife too. Carol had not been able to cope with Dean's death and had suffered a breakdown. Her recovery had been slow and painful for both of them. Finally, she had told Stan she was leaving. She could not go on living the same life without Dean. She had to move away, start afresh; it was the only way she would be able to survive. Stan had known in his heart things were headed that way, but had hoped he was wrong. He had loved Carol dearly, and looking after her had kept him going through the months after Dean's death. After Carol's speech he had been forced to face the facts; their marriage was over. They had not lived as man and wife for a long time; their relationship had become one of carer and patient.

Carol had left the next day. She had gone to stay with her sister in Surrey and never returned. That had been ten years ago, and Stan had been on his own ever since. There had been a handful of girl-friends over the years, but Stan's inability to make any sort of commitment after Carol and Dean, had in the end pushed them all away.

For Jill Mason's parents, life had changed forever and bringing their daughter's killer to justice was the only hope Stan could offer them.

Jill had been on her way to her friend Susan's house, Jill's mother had told him, tears streaming down her face.

There had been no witnesses to what had happened. The driver of the car Michael had seen coming towards him had found her and called an ambulance. She'd remembered seeing a car coming in the opposite direction which had turned on to the road to her right, just before she had come across Jill Mason's body lying on the road. She'd thought the car was silver but had no idea of the make or model.

***

Michael couldn't sleep a wink; he kept expecting the police to appear at his door. He knew the girl was dead; he had been listening to the news on the local radio station most of the night and checking on-line news reports. Morning couldn't come quickly enough, he wanted to report the car stolen before it was found. By the time morning did come the last thing Michael felt like doing was going to work; all he wanted to do was report the car stolen and crawl onto the couch with the whisky bottle. He knew that was not an option, he had to make today appear to be as much like any other day as possible. Forcing himself into the bathroom, Michael showered, shaved and dressed. Next he went downstairs and made himself a cup of coffee, which ended up in the sink after a few sips. Anxious to get the encounter with the police over with; he lifted the telephone and called a taxi.

***

Sarah watched Michael as he walked towards his desk, she had never seen him so agitated, and, like everyone else in the office was full of sympathy for him. He was over an hour and a half late. He had telephoned earlier and said his car had been stolen and he would be there as soon as he could. Sarah didn't own a car, but she imagined having one stolen would be a real hassle for someone, and coming so soon after his wife's death, must be nothing short of devastating for Michael.

When returning from lunch; Sarah walked into the office to find Michael sitting at his desk head in his hands; her heart went out to him. She approached his desk and gently touched his shoulder.

'Michael, if you want to go home I don't mind finishing anything that's urgent for you.'

'Thanks Sarah, I might ask Ken if I can leave a bit earlier than usual. It would be great if you could look over a couple of files and tie up the loose ends for me'

'Sure, no problem.'

'I'll pass them over to you before I go,' he said sounding genuinely grateful.

***

He was more grateful than Sarah could ever have imagined. He was in no fit state to do any work; apart from being fatigued, through lack of sleep, he couldn't stop wondering about his car. What had happened to it? How long before the police would find it? Had it been burned out? These questions floated round and round in his head. He desperately wanted a drink and couldn't wait to get home. He forced himself to stay in the office until mid-afternoon, before calling a taxi to take him home.

***

D.S. Sharon Thomas walked quickly towards Stan's desk. 'Sir, I think we might have something here.

Silver Focus reported stolen. Owner; one Michael Barton; parked it on Battlefield Road last night around eight o'clock; went back to get it this morning and it wasn't there.'

Stan reached out, took the report from her and swiftly read it. 'Right; let's go pay Mr Barton a visit.'

***

Michael was peeved to find the police turning up as he arrived home from work. He'd jumped out of the taxi and hurried towards the front door, desperate for a couple of whiskies to steady his nerves and a good sleep. Instead as he turned the key in the lock, he heard footsteps behind him. He turned round and was confronted by a man in his forties and a much younger woman.

'Michael Barton?' The man enquired. When he nodded, the man shoved a warrant card towards him and continued. 'D.I. Stanford and this is D.S. Thomas, it's about your car.'

Michael had been caught so off guard when they approached him, he could feel the colour start to drain from his face.

'My, my car,' he managed to reply stuttering slightly. 'Have you found it?'

'Not as yet.'

'I don't understand; why are you here?'

'Perhaps we could go inside.'

Michael felt light headed as he entered the house followed by the two detectives. He walked directly to the lounge and took a deep breath.

'Please sit down; can I get you anything, tea or coffee?'

'No thanks,' Stan replied, he looked around the room before continuing. 'Mr Barton, why did you leave your car in Battlefield last night?'

'I explained this all to your colleagues this morning.'

'Please Mr Barton, if you could just tell us.'

'I recently lost my wife and yesterday was a particularly difficult day. It was the anniversary of the day we met. I had intended to go for a meal to the restaurant I'd planned to take Louise to. We'd always celebrated this day and I stupidly thought it might make me feel closer to her, but in the end I couldn't face going alone.'

'Had you booked a table?'

'No; I wasn't sure if I really wanted to go or not. I thought I'd leave it up to fate whether they had a table or not. In the end it didn't matter. I never went in. I'm afraid I got pretty upset while driving and had to pull into the side of the road. I thought a walk would clear my head.'

'But you went to a pub.'

'I walked about for a while and on the spur of the moment I decided to go to into a pub and collect the car the next day.'

'What time did you park the car?'

'I am not sure, probably about eight.'

'What time did you enter the pub?'

'Just before nine.'

'Was the car still there when you went into the

pub?'

'I don't know.'

'Mr Barton, surely you checked your car was securely locked after all you intended to leave it overnight.'

Michael stared at the detective, his heart beating so loudly in his chest he was sure the detective must be able to hear it. 'I am afraid I didn't. I was feeling so low I just went to the pub, had a couple of drinks, phoned a taxi and went home.'

Stan stared at Michael for a few seconds, and then abruptly stood up. 'Ok thanks Mr Barton, we'll be in touch.'

He was shaking as he closed the door behind the detectives. What the hell was all that about? Christ they hadn't even found the car and they were questioning his word. He almost ran towards the whisky bottle and with quivering hands poured a large measure into a glass. Seconds later he was refilling it.

***

Stan surveyed Michael's house from the outside before getting into the car. 'What do you make of Mr Barton?'

Sharon shrugged her shoulders. 'Seems pretty shook up. If he's telling the truth, wife dying, car stolen can't be easy for him. On the other hand, he could be shitting bricks because he was the one driving. What do you think Sir?'

'To be perfectly honest I don't know. He has a certain vulnerability about him which makes what he is saying plausible; but there's something about him I don't trust.

CHAPTER 30

Where was his lighter? Danny was sure he had left it beside his fags on the kitchen table. The fags were still there, or were they? He opened the packet again and counted them. A quick calculation and it was obvious he hadn't smoked that many since he had bought them. Wee bastard, he simmered realising his younger brother, Joey, had nicked a few fags plus his lighter. The fags he wasn't bothered about, but the lighter was a different story.

The zippo, had belonged to his father and now it was Danny's and he intended to keep it that way. Not for sentimental reasons; he hated his father. He'd beaten both Danny and Joey black and blue when they were younger, their mother too, on occasions. It had been after one of those beatings Danny had taken the lighter. He'd waited until the snoring had started, a sure indication his father had fallen into his usual drunken stupor, tiptoed into his mother and father's bedroom, grabbed the lighter and hidden it in the room he shared with Joey. He'd pulled back the carpet in the corner and hewn out part of the floor board with a penknife. He had put the lighter there and replaced the carpet. He knew his father would never find it.

Taking the lighter from his father and hiding it had made him feel in control and that night Danny had vowed every time his father beat him, he would take something from him. It hadn't come to that, a few weeks later his father had buggered off; much to Danny, Joey and his mother's relief. They hadn't seen or heard from him in years and Danny secretly hoped he was dead. However, according to his cousin Phil who claimed to have seen him recently, he wasn't dead but very much alive and living with some woman in Easterhouse. Must be an evil bitch to want to live with him, Danny had said when Phil told him this piece of news, well good riddance, at least it keeps the bastard away from us.

Joey had taken the lighter before and Danny had given him a clip round the ear. This time Danny vowed to give him a good kick up the arse, make sure he didn't take it again. He waited all evening for Joey to come home and finally gave up at a quarter to twelve and went to bed. He had just dropped off to sleep when Joey sneaked in and silently tumbled into his own bed.

When Danny awoke the next morning Joey had already left the house.

'Gone to school.' His mother informed him, when Danny asked where he was.

CHAPTER 31

The telephone on his desk was ringing as Stan walked into the office.

'Hello, D.I. Stanford,' he said picking it up.

Sharon watched as a smile slowly spread across his face. When the conversation ended, he turned to Sharon and rubbed his hands together.

'Michael Barton's car just turned up in Rutherglen. Traffic cops spotted it being driven erratically and gave chase. The driver hit a lamp post. Seems there were three youths in the car. Idiots lost them; they all scarpered in different directions. Looks like it might be our car. Signs of damage not sustained from hitting the lamp post and traces of what looks like blood on the bumper. Forensics are checking it out.'

'Right Sir, I'll phone Mr Barton and let him know.'

'No let's visit him, tell him in person. I want to see his reaction.'

***

Michael was standing at the window, swaying slightly, a tumbler of whisky in his hand. He was half cut; he had started drinking the minute he had returned from work. He knew he should have eaten something first. He couldn't afford to get drunk; he needed to keep his wits about him in case the police turned up again. Since the accident, he hadn't been able to eat a thing, all he had wanted to do was drink. On one hand he wanted his car to be found as quickly as possible to get the inevitable encounter with the police over with; on the other hand, he was dreading facing them again. Emptying his glass, he poured himself another generous measure of whisky and returned to the window. It was pitch black in the room. He hadn't bothered to put a light on when darkness had fallen outside. He'd gone directly for the whisky bottle the minute he had returned from work and had done nothing in the house other than drink.

Fuck them he thought, lifting the glass to his lips. If the police come tonight; fuck them. I won't answer the door, the house is in darkness, they'll just assume I'm not at home and go away.

A movement outside caught his eye. Squinting and staggering slightly, he leaned nearer the glass and felt the colour drain from his face. The two detectives who had visited him yesterday were outside the window and the man was signalling for him to come to the door.

Michael backed away from the window. He had to let them in, he had no choice they had seen him. Don't say anything unless you have to, he told himself over and over before opening the door.

'Power cut, Mr Barton?' Stan asked him, raising

an eyebrow.

'No, I was about to go to bed.'

'At eight o'clock?'

'I don't feel well,' replied Michael.

From the corner of his eye, he caught the wry smile the detectives shared behind his back as he weaved his way drunkenly towards the lounge.

'You'll be glad to know we've found your car,' continued Stan once Michael had switched on the light and all three of them had sat down.

'Where?' Michael asked, not quite meeting Stan's gaze.

'Rutherglen.'

'Rutherglen,' repeated Michael. 'Did you get the people who took it?'

'People?' Stan asked, looking puzzled.

Michael could have bitten off his tongue. Think before you say anything, he silently warned himself.

'I just assumed it would be joy riders, kids who'd taken it. There's usually more than one, isn't there?' Michael slurred.

Stan stared at him.

Michael stared back waiting for a reply which never came. Eventually Michael spoke again. 'What happens now, do I go to Rutherglen and collect it?'

'I don't think you're in any fit state to collect a car, Mr Barton, do you?' Stan said raising his eyebrow again.

'No, no, of course not; I didn't mean tonight.'

'Actually, at the moment your car is being examined by our forensic investigators.'

Michael's heart began to beat faster. 'Oh for fin-gerprints,' he said hopefully.

'Something like that.'

Even though Michael was drunk the man's tone of voice made him uneasy.

'What I don't understand, Mr Barton, is how, who-ever stole your car managed to get hold of your key. I presume it is your key that was in the ignition.'

Michael had been expecting this question and had rehearsed his answer over and over in his head. Putting his hand to his forehead, in what he hoped appeared to be a gesture of enlightenment, he re-plied. I must have dropped the key when I dropped my wallet. I couldn't find the key on Thursday morning; I had to take the spare key with me when I tried to collect my car.'

Stan and Sharon continued to stare at Michael, both saying nothing.

Michael was feeling more and more uncomfort-able with every second that ticked by. 'When I got out of the car I dropped my wallet, I must have dropped the key as well, only I didn't notice at the time.'

He waited for one of them to reply; neither did. Fear gripped Michael, like a snake slowly coiling its way around him. He was finding it difficult to breath. He was too drunk; he couldn't risk saying anything else tonight. He had to get them out of the house as quickly as possible.

'I'm really sorry, but I don't feel at all well. I need to lie down,' he said trying not to slur and making his eyebrows droop as if falling asleep.

Stan stood up first followed by Sharon.

'Ok Mr Barton, we'll be in touch. Don't bother getting up we'll see ourselves out.'

A photograph caught Stan's eye and he lifted it to get a better look, the man was obviously Michael Barton. 'Is this your late wife?' He asked, pointing at the woman in the photograph.

'Wife; humph.' Warning bells rang fuzzily somewhere in his brain the minute the words were out his mouth. Although he was drunk, he knew he'd made a grave mistake. Shit, he'd need to be careful. Feigning sleep he shut his eyes completely and waited for the detectives to leave the house. He heard the front door close, he heard the car doors slam shut, he heard the engine start, but only when he heard the car drive off, did he open his eyes.

Christ that was close. He was going to have to watch his step with Stanford; the man was nobody's fool. He would lay off the whisky until this mess with the car was cleared up. He couldn't afford any more slip ups like tonight. He looked at the bottle longingly, there wasn't much whisky left, might as well finish it off. He poured it all into his tumbler and started to drink. By the time the glass was empty Michael couldn't even be bothered to go to bed. Instead he staggered from the chair towards the sofa and heaved himself on it. Seconds later he was asleep.

**

'Do you think it was him who hit the girl?' Sharon asked Stan once they were both back in the car.

'Killed the girl.' He corrected

Sharon cringed at the rebuke. 'Where to now, Sir?' She asked quietly.

'Let's go to the pub.'

Sharon stared at Stan, it took a few seconds for her to realise he meant them to check out Michael Barton's alibi, she was still smarting from his remark about Jill Mason.

Stan noticed her slight hesitation and winked at her. 'Surely you didn't think I was suggesting dereliction of duty in favour of getting pissed.'

'Not at all, Sir,' she replied, smiling at him and starting the car.

For a Friday night the place was fairly quiet. About half a dozen men leaned against the bar at varying intervals. A group of middle-aged men were at the end of the bar laughing loudly. A handful of couples were dotted about the place sitting at tables, and two men in their twenties were having a loud conversation at another. Freddie Mercury's voice blasted out from the juke box. An attractive young woman smiled at them as they approached the bar. Her smile soon changed to a look of wariness as Stan showed his ID and asked if any of the staff working tonight had been working on Wednesday.

'I was working Wednesday night,' she told them.

'And you are?' Stan asked.

'Debbie, Debbie Murray.'

'Do you remember a tall, thin, fair-haired man in his early thirties in the bar that evening?'

'Was his name Michael?'

'Sounds like him,' replied Stan. 'What time did he arrive?'

'About nine o'clock.'

'Was he alone?'

'Yes,' Debbie replied nodding her head.

'Did you talk to him much?'

'Yes quite a lot, he seemed such a nice guy. He told me his wife had died recently. I think he said Wednesday had been their anniversary. He was so sad and the way he talked about his wife, well he obviously loved her very much. I was almost jealous, when I think of the wasters I've been out with.'

'Did he flirt with you at all?'

Debbie looked slightly embarrassed. 'Look I liked the guy I found him attractive and I flirted a bit with him. At one point I thought he was interested, I caught him eyeing me up a couple of times while I was serving other customers; obviously I was wrong. He had two or three whiskies phoned a taxi and left.'

'What time was this?'

'About twenty to eleven.'

'Did he appear drunk when he came in?'

'Didn't look like it.'

'Was anyone else working that night?'

'Just Steve; he was working in the office from eight thirty onwards. He popped out from time to time to make sure I wasn't too busy on my own, but I never was.'

'No one served him apart from you?'

'That's right.'

'Did he talk to any other customers in the bar?'

Debbie shook her head slowly before replying. 'No, I'm sure he didn't.' Stan thanked Debbie for being helpful before he and Sharon left the pub; they also left Debbie wondering what the police wanted with the attractive stranger from a couple of nights ago.

CHAPTER 32

Forensics had confirmed the traces of blood found on the front of Michael Barton's car belonged to Jill Mason. There had been no match for the fingerprints inside the car. However, a lighter found under one of the seats had come up trumps. A partial print on it belonged to a Danny Brogan, who already had a couple of charges of shoplifting under his belt. They had brought him into the station for questioning. Danny, of course, denied everything, insisted he'd lost the lighter weeks ago and had been at home all Wednesday night. His mother had confirmed this and they'd had to let him go.

Stan had believed him; he was sure Danny hadn't been anywhere near the car but was certain he knew something.

Sharon had been thinking the same thing. 'Did you see the look on his face when you showed him the lighter?' Without waiting for a reply she continued. 'He knows who had it in the car. I'd stake my wages on it. He's covering for somebody and my money's on the brother.'

'Mine too; let's get something to eat and then we'll pay brother Joey a visit.

***

Joey had been shitting bricks ever since they had crashed the car. The night they had taken the car had been fun. They had driven around for hours. Joey had wanted to abandon it, burn it out even; but Tam had had other ideas. He said they should keep it for a while. He had parked it in a street, near his house, which had more than its fair share of bashed up cars already littering it. They had gone back to the car on Friday after school and piled in, only this time everything had gone wrong. Tam had been showing off, driving too fast, he had gone through a red light and the police had spotted and chased them. Tam had crashed into a lamp post and the three of them had been lucky to get away.

The initial euphoria he had felt at outwitting the police and escaping had disappeared when he couldn't find Danny's lighter and he realised he had either dropped it in the car or when he had fled from the police. Danny's prints would be on it as well as his own and Danny's prints were on file. If the lighter was in the car, he was finished. Joey was more afraid about what Danny would do to him than the police. He had stayed at Steph's house since the crash, but had been too afraid to tell either Steph or Tam about the lighter.

He needed clean clothes and had phoned the house and asked if Danny was there. When his mother said no, he hurried home, grabbed some clothes, another pair of trainers, and shoved them in a holdall. He was about to leave the house when his mother dropped the bombshell.

'Don't know what your brother's done this time, but the polis dragged him off again this morning.'

Joey stared at his mother in horror. He had to tell Steph and Tam now; he couldn't keep this to himself any longer. He ran from the house, down the stairs, out the close and onto the pavement. He had only moved a few yards when he saw Danny coming towards him. Joey turned and ran in the opposite direction. He could hear Danny bearing down on him from behind. Rationally he knew he could not out run him, but fear of what his brother would do to him made him try. It was no use; Joey felt Danny's hand grab the hood of his jacket.

'What the fuck have you done?'

A fist connected with his right ear and he yelled in pain. Desperately he tried to field off Danny's punches, without much success.

As suddenly as the punches had started, mercifully, they stopped, and Joey was aware of a woman pulling him away from Danny. He watched in horror as a man snapped a pair of handcuffs on his brother. They were both unceremoniously shoved in the back of a car and driven to the police station; Danny's second visit of the day there.

Joey was trying hard to be brave; he was in the interview room with the detectives who had stopped his brother from half killing him, and his mother.

'Where were you on Wednesday night?'

'No comment'

'Were you with your brother Danny on Wednesday night?'

'No comment!'

Keep saying no comment to all their questions like they do on the telly, he told himself. Only, the people on the telly who sat and said no comment always looked calm and in control, and not in the least bit scared; whereas Joey was terrified. He sensed the man was getting angrier every time he uttered the words. Eventually the man banged his fist down hard on the table.

'Listen sonny, we have a stolen car, which knocked down and killed a girl on Wednesday night. The driver didn't stop and a lighter with your brother's prints was found in the car. There were other prints on the lighter which match those taken from inside the car. What are the chances when we take yours, they'll match up? Now you can sit there and say no comment, till you are old and grey, but a girl is dead because of you, a girl the same age as your brother.'

Shocked at what Stan had just said Joey blurted out. 'We didnae kill nobody. We only took the car for a drive. I swear we didnae knock anybody doon. Please you've got to believe me. All we did was drive aboot.' Joey was almost hysterical now.

'Let's start at the beginning,' Sharon said; a soothing tone to her voice. 'Where did you get the car from?'

'Ardencraig Road.'

'Where on Ardencraig Road?'

'At the old folk's home; the one that's all shut up now, Windlaw.'

'And this was Wednesday night?'

'Yes.'

'What time?'

'Dunno.'

'Think Joey, its important.'

A few seconds elapsed. 'Nine o'clock I think. Hey, hang on a minute.' Now Joey was quite animated. 'I got a text message just before from Jen, this girl that fancies me,' he said almost apologetically, digging the phone from his pocket. 'You can check the time.'

Stan took the phone from him as Sharon continued. 'Who were you with?'

'No one, I wis on my own.'

'Don't mess me about, Joey, you said we.'

Joey stared at her miserably; Steph and Tam would kill him if he shopped them to the polis.

'Listen carefully, Joey, a girl is dead, do you hear; D E A D.' She spelled out the word, emphasizing every letter. 'Now is not the time for keeping your mouth shut through some sense of misguided loyalty. Now, who were you with?'

Joey's shoulders sagged in resignation. 'Steph Peters and Tam Bolan.'

'Addresses?'

Joey replied, wondering if Steph and Tam would ever forgive him.

'The three of you took the car from outside the

old nursing home on Ardencraig Road, on Wednesday night, is that correct?'

Joey nodded and mumbled. 'Yes.'

'What made you take that particular car?'

'It was open.'

'Open; do you mean unlocked?'

'Not just unlocked, the door was open, light on, radio on, even the keys were there.'

'Where were the keys Joey?'

'In the ignition.' An unspoken 'duh 'was tagged onto his reply as if Sharon was an idiot. 'It was because of the radio we found the car. Steph heard it first, and then me and Tam came oot the bushes to see where it was coming from.'

'What were you doing in the bushes?'

'Smokin, havin a laugh.'

'How long had you been there?'

'Aboot half an hour.'

'Do you remember seeing the car there when you arrived?'

Picking absently at a grubby cuff, he shook his head and replied. 'No.'

'When you came out the bushes, did you see anyone else?'

'There was a guy further along the road.'

'On which side?'

'The same side as us.'

'What was he doing?'

Joey shrugged. 'Just walkin.'

'Walking towards you or away from you?'

'Away. I didnae want to get in at first coz I thought

it was his car.'

'Why did you think that Joey?'

'Dunno, s'pose coz he was the only one there, but he just kept walkin away so it couldnae have been his.'

'What was this guy like; tall, short?'

'Tall.'

'Do you remember what he was wearing?'

Joey shook his head. 'No, it was dark.'

'Think Joey, picture him in your mind, was he wearing a coat or a jacket?'

He thought for a few seconds. 'A jacket, I think.' Then he added more confidently. 'Yes a jacket, he had the hood up.'

'And you're sure you saw no one else apart from this man anywhere near the car?'

'No there was no-one else aboot.'

'Who drove the car Joey?'

A cloud passed over his face. 'Tam,' he said, feeling guilty at betraying his friend.

'Where did you take the car to?'

'Just roun aboot.'

'Where round about?'

'Castlemilk, Fernhill, Cambuslang. Me and Steph wanted to take it up the Braes and leave it there, but Tam said we should hang on to it. We left it in the street next to Tam's hoose. He couldn't find the key on Thursday so it was Friday after school before we took it oot again. That's when the polis chased us and Tam crashed intae the lamppost.'

***

Leave the car on the Cathkin Braes indeed, thought Stan. More likely set it on fire there was what Joey and his pal Steph had really suggested they do. Stan shook his head slightly knowing how close they had come to losing the evidence the car had given up. It was lucky for them that Joey's mate Tam had been naïve enough to keep it.

'Puts our Mr Barton in the frame,' said Stan once Joey had left the station. 'He could have knocked down Jill Mason, drove through Carmunnock, turned right at the roundabout onto Ardencraig Road. He spots Joey and his mates, dumps the car, hoping they'll take it. Let's face it he almost put a sign on it for them saying, take me. A taxi would have got him to Battlefield by ten past nine; buses at that time of night say twenty past; fits the time frame. Check taxi companies, see if anybody picked up a fare for Battlefield from Ardencraig Road on Wednesday night anytime between eight and ten. Also check bus timetables for buses between Castle-milk and Battlefield.'

CHAPTER 33

Michael was worried. D.I. Stanford had visited him again; this time to inform him his car had been involved in an accident which had killed a young woman, and whoever had been driving at the time had failed to stop. Michael had done his best to look suitably shocked. He had told Michael three youths had been questioned and although they had admitted to stealing his car, they had denied knocking down and killing Jill Mason. They had been adamant they had stolen the car from Castlemilk and not Battlefield where Michael had claimed he had left it. D.I. Stanford had made it clear to Michael he believed it was unlikely they had been driving the car at the time of the accident. That revelation had filled him with fear. Stanford had not been forthcoming with any other information and he had been too afraid to ask.

Did the police suspect it was him driving? Were they planning to arrest him? Did they have enough evidence to arrest him? Would the youths who took the car be able to identify him? Michael didn't think so, after all he never saw their faces; therefore, how could they have seen his? These questions had bounced about in his head for hours until he'd thought his head would burst.

At least he still had some form of transport; Louise's car. After her demise he had wanted all her belongings out of the house immediately but had thought it might look a bit suspicious. Instead he had bundled everything into black bags and stored them in the spare room. After a few weeks, which he had deemed a decent length of time, he had sent her jewellery registered post to her aunt Moira and taken the black bags to the nearest charity shop. He had left one framed photograph of them both in the living room for appearances and her car had been parked outside the house ever since, making him look every inch the grieving widower who couldn't bear to get rid of his wife's car. Now he was glad he had kept it.

He tried not to think about the night he had knocked down and killed Jill Mason; it wasn't easy. At first he had been full of remorse and guilt, but slowly those feelings had been replaced by ones of anger. Initially, at Jill herself for not looking before she stepped onto the road; however, the person Michael was really angry with was the blonde from the health club. After all he had only run Jill Mason down because he had been thinking about her. This whole mess would never have happened if it hadn't been for her. Not only had she humiliated him, because of her he had killed and nearly been caught. Well she should pay for what she had done. He would make her pay.

CHAPTER 34

Someone in a car, parked behind Michael, turned on their headlights and startled him. He held his breath until whoever it was had driven away. It was a Friday night and he was parked in the car park of the health club waiting for the blonde to come out. He glanced at the clock on the dashboard; any minute now he thought. He was going to follow her, find out all he could about her and then... He hadn't thought that far ahead. Let's just see where she goes first.

The door of the health club opened, and he watched as two men in their early thirties emerged, followed by a young woman in her mid-twenties. Seconds later the door opened again and out strode the blonde. Michael watched as she marched arrogantly towards her car. She was walking so briskly she overtook the two men and woman who had left the club before her. Michael watched as one nudged the other and both men stared at her.

Unaware or unfazed by the men's attention she unlocked her car, climbed in and drove off immediately. Michael followed. The roads were quiet, and it was easy to keep her car in sight. He had only been driving behind her for about two miles when she turned into a quiet cul de sac and pulled into a parking space. Quickly he parked his own car, switched off his headlights and waited. A few yards in front of where the blonde had parked her car, a leather clad figure with short black hair leaned lazily against a lamp post, smoking a cigarette. Michael watched as the blonde got out of her car and walked along the pavement. As she drew level with the bike, the figure tossed the half smoked cigarette onto the road and grabbed her around the waist.

'Oh shit,' he muttered, waiting for all hell to break loose, remembering his own encounter with her. Seconds elapsed and nothing happened, the blonde made no sound. Michael watched in astonishment as the blonde grabbed the bikers head and pulled it firmly towards her own; both sets of lips urgently finding each other. Michael sat transfixed by the intensity and passion of their kiss. Not quite the ice maiden after all. Finally, they broke apart and Michael caught his breath and stared in disbelief. They had both turned towards him and a street light had illuminated the biker's face; it was the face of a young woman.

Both women walked quickly, arms around each other's shoulders, towards the front door of the nearest house. The blonde unlocked the door and they disappeared inside. From his car he watched, expecting to see a downstairs light come on; nothing happened, the house remained in darkness. Finally, after a few minutes a light did come on; in an upstairs room. Michael caught a glimpse of the blonde standing in her bra before she swiftly shut the curtains.

Now he understood why she had been so aggressive to him that night in the car park. With her looks and stature men were drawn to her. After all he had wanted her the first time he had set eyes on her. He recalled the look the two men had given her only a short while ago outside the club. He felt a measure of sympathy for her; all that unwanted attention. It would always be unwanted, no matter who the man was, because it was the attention of women she craved.

It all made sense; how roughly she had shaken him off when he had touched her arm. He had breached a boundary, he now realised. She had dealt with the unwanted attention by ignoring the looks and the comments, shutting them from her life completely. She had built a mental barrier around herself and men were on the opposite side of it. However, by touching her arm Michael had broken through the periphery of that barrier, invaded her space and forced her to acknowledge him. The anger she felt towards men and the way they perceived her was always there, simmering just below the surface; and at his touch it had boiled over.

Michael actually felt a sense of empathy towards the woman; after all he knew only too well what that anger felt like. He no longer wanted to punish her or felt the need for revenge. He gave one last look at the upstairs window before driving slowly out of the cul de sac.

CHAPTER 35

The enquiry was not going well. Finding who had killed Jill Mason was proving difficult. Stan's gut instinct told him it was Michael Barton and Sharon agreed but they needed to find some proof.

They had both visited Michael at home again and this time had 'invited' him down to the station and questioned him about his movements the night Jill Mason had been killed. His story had never wavered no matter how much Stan had pushed to try and catch him out. It had reminded him of a similar case he had worked on as a young DC. The victim, a twenty four year old woman with a two year old son, had been knocked down and killed by a driver who hadn't stopped. Her body had been dragged face down along the road for fifty yards. The sight of the woman's face had haunted him for a long time afterwards. The vehicle had been a pool car belonging to a building company. There had been no witness to the accident and when they had traced the driver he'd insisted it had been stolen from outside his girlfriend's house, where he claimed he had spent the entire evening. The girlfriend had backed him up. Everyone on the team had thought they were lying but they had stuck to the same story rigidly and no one had seen him drive the car from outside his girlfriend's house that night.

Stan had felt sure the girlfriend would crack and give her boyfriend up when she was shown pictures of the dead woman, but he had been wrong. The girlfriend, a hard-nosed cow, hadn't flinched and insisted her boyfriend had been with her the entire evening.

There had been no witnesses to Jill Mason's death either. The woman who had seen what was thought to be Michael's car turning off the road where Jill's body had been found, was unable to identify the driver.

Checking taxi companies had yielded nothing, none of their drivers reported picking up a fare matching Michael's description between Castlemilk and Battlefield within the time frame that evening.

A search into buses operating within the area pointed to the number 34 service being the only bus that would have got Michael Barton from Castlemilk to Battlefield anywhere near nine o'clock and that would have not arrived in Battlefield until nine nineteen. Although another bus would have got him to Battlefield before nine o'clock it would have left Castlemilk before Jill Mason had left her house. The 34 service had no CCTV and the driver, when they had managed to track him down had not been much help. At present off work with stress he told Stan and Sharon the night they were asking about was the night after his fifteen year old daughter had informed him and his wife she was four months pregnant.

'The older daughter's got a two year old and lives with us now because her boyfriend was beating her up, fuck sake you'd think she have learned a lesson by that; but no she gets herself knocked up too. The wife doesn't keep well, gets bad asthma attacks. No wonder I'm on the sick. I'm at the end of my tether.'

He went on to tell them he had been so worked up about it at the time, he wouldn't have noticed if Jesus Christ himself had walked on the bus and asked for a ticket.

The pub CCTV didn't work properly and therefore didn't record what was shown on the screens. Michael Barton had not been captured on any street CCTV in the area. Stan and Sharon were in agreement if he really did not have anything to do with Jill Mason's death, and had been walking around the area aimlessly for as long as he claimed, he would have appeared on camera at some point.

The jacket had bugged Stan. Joey and his mates had said the person they saw walking away from the car had been wearing a hooded jacket, however Debbie Murray had insisted Michael Barton had been wearing a suit when he had entered the pub. This meant he had to have discarded it somewhere before he went in to the pub. Stan surmised he would probably have pulled the hood over his face as much as possible while on the bus and while getting on and off. By Stan's reckoning the most obvious place to have got rid of it would have been between where he had got off the bus, and the pub. He had organised a team of officers to sift through roadside rubbish bins, situated around the pub and bus route but the jacket had not turned up. He'd also checked the lost property of the bus company in case it had been discarded on the bus, to no avail. They weren't to know it was still riding around in the back of Jason Armstrong's van.

They had asked Debbie if she might have got the time wrong; could it have been nearer half past nine when Michael had arrived. She said she didn't think so, she was sure it was nine o'clock.

***

It was mid-morning and Sharon was standing beside Stan's desk, a Styrofoam cup of coffee in each hand. She pushed one towards Stan and sipped some of the scalding liquid from the other.

'I've been doing a little digging on Michael Barton,' she announced.

'Did you come up with anything interesting?'

'Remember he said his wife died a few months back, well she drowned and he was with her at the time.'

'Any witnesses?' Stan asked, recalling Michael Barton's reaction when he'd enquired about the woman in the photograph.

'He was the only witness and...' She stared at him for a few seconds before continuing. 'He works for a company called Insurance, Insurance, Insurance.'

'An insurance company,' said Stan smiling, thinking he knew where Sharon was going with this.'

'Really? With a name like that I thought it might possibly be a Bakery,' a voice rang out from the desk adjacent to where Sharon stood.

Stan watched her throw D I Barry Wilson a look of disgust as he rose from his desk and sailed towards the door, smug smile on his face. Wilson was a cocky bastard and there was no love lost between the two men. Wilson was conceited and arrogant, more interested in putting away the bad guys for the glory rather than getting them off the street. Added to that he was lazy, he got everyone else to do the donkey work and then waltzed in and took the credit.

He had almost reached the door when Stan rolled his eyes towards the ceiling and replied in a voice loud enough for everyone in the vicinity to hear. 'Tonight Matthew, I am going to be the worst comedian in the world.'

A few people in the office sniggered and Wilson's body momentarily froze before he barrelled his way through the double doors and into the corridor.

Stan winked at her. 'You were saying D.S. Thomas before we were so rudely interrupted.'

'His wife drowned a few months ago, he was the only witness and he works for an Insurance company. At first I thought I might be on to something there; turns out I was wrong they both had good insurance cover. When I say good, I mean adequate not mega bucks; so I did a little more digging. His mother committed suicide twelve years ago and he was the last person to see her alive. A few days ago his car is involved in an accident which kills someone. Now maybe the guy is just unlucky but people seem to die around him.'

'Where did the wife drown?'

'Not far from Tighnabruaich. Apparently, they were out walking and the wife, whose name was Louise, fell from some rocks into the water. She couldn't swim; exit Mrs Barton.'

'Where is Tighnabruaich; the highlands?'

'No Sir, it's just over twenty miles from Dunoon.'

'Right, let's check the ferry timetables.'

'Western Ferries back and forward from Gourock every twenty minutes or so.'

'Good, I'll phone ahead and tell the local boys to expect us.'

Unusually heavy traffic and three sets of road works later, Stan and Sharon finally arrived at the ferry terminal, only to find one had already set sail minutes earlier. It was a cold blustery day, with rain not far away and both Sharon and Stan opted to stay in the car once they finally boarded a ferry. Sharon was pleased to note the crossing was shorter than she had expected; she was not a big fan of boats and the water was not exactly calm.

D I Sandy Johnstone was waiting for them at the local station in Dunoon. He was a large rugged looking man and Sharon couldn't help thinking he would have looked at home on a rugby pitch. He was curious to know why they were investigating

Michael Barton; he had attended the scene of Louise Barton's tragic drowning.

'What did you make of him?' Stan asked.

'He was in shock by the time I arrived at the scene and I have to say I thought it was genuine. Two women stumbled upon him before we got to him; both were interviewed. He told them the same as he told us; there were no discrepancies. I contacted Louise Barton's father and he confirmed she couldn't swim. I also spoke to staff in both the hotels they had stayed in; staff all said the same. No arguments or drunken brawls; Louise and Michael Barton seemed like a happy couple enjoying a weekend break.'

'Both hotels.' Stan said, surprised.

'They stayed the Friday night in Dunoon. Didn't arrive in Tighnabruaich until Saturday night. It's all in here.' He handed the report to Stan. 'Because he worked for an insurance company, I checked out what financially he stood to gain by her death; not much more than most. Do you want to go to the spot where she drowned?'

Both Stan and Sharon nodded in agreement.

D.I. Johnstone looked at the car key in Sharon's hand. 'We'll take my car. It will be quicker.'

Thinking he was taking a pop at her driving skills because she was a woman, she pursed her lips and raised her eyebrows in indignation.

'It's not you; it's the road,' he said; laughing heartily at her reaction, and then added. 'Hope you like roller coasters.'

She sighed. This day just gets better and better.

'The views you will see are well worth the ride,' he assured her.

Unfortunately D.I. Johnstone hadn't been exaggerating about the road; equally he hadn't been exaggerating about the views either, they were stunning. On reaching Tighnabruaich he drove along the shore road through the boatyard and along the coastal trail. The terrain was hard going; the rain had softened the ground and the wheels of the vehicle were sending mud everywhere. Sharon sat in the back praying they didn't get stuck in the mud. She was beginning to feel a bit queasy, this journey on top of the ferry crossing the reason. The thought of having to get out the car and push it from the mud filled her with dread. After what seemed like a lifetime to Sharon, D.I. Johnstone finally stopped the car.

'We're here,' he announced. 'And not a minute too soon by the look of things,' he added; turning in his seat and catching a glimpse of Sharon's face.

'I'm fine,' she retorted; opening the car door and taking deep breaths.

D.I. Johnstone rummaged in the glove compartment and pulled out a small unopened bottle of mineral water. 'Try this it's not cold I'm afraid, but it's wet,' he said pushing the bottle towards her.

Mustering up as much of a smile as she could Sharon took it from him. As she sipped the bottle of water; Stan looked around.

'It's pretty remote here,' he remarked. 'How busy

does it get in summer?'

'Weekends; a few people out walking; but a Monday morning not many people about; even in summer.'

D.I. Johnstone climbed over the wall separating the path from the rocks and Stan and Sharon followed.

'What were they doing on the rocks?' Stan asked.

'Barton said they were having a rest and enjoying the view.'

'It strikes me as a bit odd that someone who couldn't swim would choose to sit on rocks here. After all there is not that much room between the wall and the edge of the rocks. Does the tide go out quite far?'

'No, it doesn't go out much at this point at all.'

The tide was quite high on the rocks and Sharon gave an involuntary shudder. She thought of Michael Barton here with his wife; what had gone through poor Louise Barton's mind as she fell from the rocks and the question that was now in all three minds; did she fall or was she pushed?

'Where did the two walkers find Michael Barton?' Stan asked.

'On the path; a few yards from where the car is parked.'

'And the houses back there?'

'Nobody remembers seeing either Barton or his wife.'

Stan gave one last look around him before climbing back over the wall. Sharon and D.I. Johnstone followed and watched as Stan walked a few yards in either direction of the car and looked around him before climbing back into the car.

'Ready?' D.I. Johnstone asked Sharon.

'As ready as I'll ever be.' She gave him a weak smile.

'The return journey won't be so bad. We'll be stopping at Tighnabruaich to visit the hotel the Barton's stayed in. It will break the journey up and if you're lucky I might even buy you a brandy, medicinal purposes of course,' he said, winking at her.

'Every cloud has a silver lining,' she replied, her voice flat, before getting in the car.

Molly, the receptionist who had been on duty when the Bartons had checked into the hotel, had not been able to add anything that she had not told D.I. Johnstone at the time of Louise Barton's drowning. Stanford asked her if she had ever seen Michael Barton before he had come to stay with his wife at the hotel. He also asked if to her knowledge he had ever stayed at the hotel before, either with or without his wife. Molly was sure she had never encountered either Michael or Louise Barton before they had stayed at the hotel on that fateful weekend. However, she had dutifully checked the booking list for the last two years to no avail. Stanford thanked her and left his card should she remember anything further.

True to his word D.I. Johnstone offered to buy Sharon a brandy before the last leg of the drive back to Dunoon. An offer Sharon politely refused. When they arrived back in Dunoon, he drove them directly to the Hotel the Bartons had stayed in on the first night of their weekend break. Once again, the staff who had encountered the Bartons could add nothing to their original statements and were sure they had never encountered either one of them before.

Arriving back at the police station D.I. Johnstone offered to take them for something to eat. However, one look at Sharon's face and Stan declined on both their behalves. Thanking him for all his help, Stan and Sharon said goodbye and headed toward the ferry terminal, this time with Stan driving.

CHAPTER 36

A small piece of cheese covered in mould and two, slightly rancid smelling sausages were the only items in Michael's fridge. Slamming the door shut in disgust, he opened the freezer. The sight that met him was not much better. The freezer boasted a bag containing two roast potatoes, another with a handful of mixed vegetables and a tub of ice cream which had been there before Louise died, and had long since lost its lid. Throwing the contents of both fridge and freezer in the rubbish bin, he put on his jacket and lifted the keys to Louise's car.

He made his way to the local supermarket, entered the car park and drove towards the front of the store. As he glanced along one of the lanes looking for a parking space, he saw a car leaving a bay. Michael drove towards the space; he had almost reached it when a small mini cooper drove in from the empty space located behind it and parked. Michael hit the horn sharply, intending to draw the driver's attention to the fact that he had been about to park there; if the driver reversed into the space behind, both cars could be parked. The young woman with a mass of red curly hair, sitting behind the steering wheel of the mini cooper, was busily rifling in her handbag. At the sound of Michael's horn, she didn't even bother looking up but continued searching her bag with one hand and gave him the finger with the other. Michael was incensed at her audacity. Shaking and with beads of sweat dotting his forehead, he fantasised dragging the woman from the car by the hair, grabbing the finger she had so rudely gestured at him and snapping it at the knuckle, then snapping her other fingers one by one. Let's see how easily you could give the finger then. The sound of someone tentatively hitting their horn from behind brought him from his reverie. Looking in the rear view mirror he saw three cars were lined up behind and none could move until he did. As he slowly inched forward, the driver of the mini cooper exited her car, clicked the remote to lock it and hurried towards the entrance of the supermarket, all without looking once in his direction. Still furious he drove towards the next available space and parked the car. What was wrong with women nowadays? They thought they could do what they liked and get away with it.

Slamming the car door closed; he marched towards the supermarket entrance. Still thinking about his encounter with the woman, he walked absentmindedly up and down the aisles throwing items in his trolley, until the redhead from outside had him stopping in his tracks. He watched as she reached up to the top shelf, removed a jar and proceeded to read the label. The only other person around was an elderly woman carrying a basket at the bottom of the aisle. Seizing his opportunity Michael walked quickly towards her pushing his trolley. He had almost reached her when she again stretched to the top shelf, this time to replace the jar. This could not have gone better if he had planned it.

Pretending to slip he shoved his trolley as hard as he could against the redhead's back pining her against the shelves, while at the same time crying out. 'Oh no.'

The elderly woman gasped in horror as the redhead cried out in pain.

'I'm so sorry,' he gushed, pretending this time to regain his balance. 'Are you all right?' He watched her intently as he spoke. Would she recognise him from outside and realise he had done this deliberately. He was ninety nine percent certain she had not seen him; she hadn't looked his way even when she'd given him the finger. However, by doing so it surely had to mean she knew a car was trying to enter from the other side. There was a small chance she had glimpsed his face as she had driven into the parking space.

'I think so,' she replied, staring at him and sounding a bit shaky.

Michael breathed a sigh of relief. She obviously didn't recognise him. Are you sure? Do you want to sit down?'

'What the hell happened?' she replied, this time sounding a lot less shaky.

'I slipped, I think the floor is a bit greasy back there. Look I really think you should sit down. I'll get someone to get you a chair and a glass of water.'

'It's ok, honestly I'm fine. I don't have time to sit down.' She snapped the words at him as she turned away.

'Well if you're sure. I'll mention the floor to the manager on the way out. After all something really should be done about it, it's downright dangerous.'

The redhead, was no longer listening to him and had already started to walk away while he was still speaking. Michael made his way into the next aisle. He'd certainly got a measure of revenge on the woman. With a bit of luck, her back would be sore for a good many days to come. Whistling, he continued with his shopping; this time paying much more attention to what he placed in his trolley. As he left the supermarket a large smile spread across his face. Speak to the manager about the floor; I think not.

CHAPTER 37

It had been raining almost constantly for two days. Molly watched great rivulets of water running down the kitchen window as she waited for the kettle to boil. She had just returned from work and was making herself a well-earned cup of tea. She loved her job as hotel receptionist in Tighnabruaich. The only downside was the journey back and forth on days like this.

Something was niggling at Molly. Ever since the police had shown up last week at the hotel and asked her questions about Louise and Michael Barton, she'd had the feeling there was something important she needed to tell them, if only she could remember what it was. It was there somewhere, lurking on the outskirts of her memory if only she could reach out and grasp it.

She took her cup of tea into the living room and settled down in her favourite chair, all the while thinking about the Bartons. One day a seemingly happy couple; the next a tragedy, leaving one partner dead and another grieving.

Thinking about the cruel end to their marriage brought back memories of her own.

She had fallen in love and married a man much more ambitious than she'd realised. He'd worked for one of the local banks and never made a secret of wanting promotion, but Molly had assumed he would be content to apply for jobs within daily travelling distance; how wrong she had been. He'd applied for a job in Edinburgh and got it. When she'd plucked up the courage to tell Richard she didn't want to live there he'd been furious, said he had to take the promotion; this was their future. Finally, they'd reached a compromise. Financially now much better off as Richard had almost doubled his salary, he would rent a small flat, stay in Edinburgh during the week, and at weekends he would travel home.

About four months into this arrangement Richard suggested Molly should travel to Edinburgh for the weekend. He'd made new friends through work and wanted her to meet them. Slightly miffed he wanted to spend the precious little time they had together with others, she agreed knowing she should make the effort to meet his friends.

The weekend had not proved to be the one off Molly hoped. Every few weeks Richard asked her to join him in Edinburgh. She dreaded these visits; they always included socialising with his new friends. They were pleasant enough, but she had nothing in common with them and felt slightly uncomfortable in their company. It all came to a head one night when Richard telephoned and told her his boss had invited them to a party at his home. It was a great opportunity for her to meet more of his work colleagues and their partners. It was also important for him career wise; it would give him a chance at networking. Molly's heart sank.

When Richard finally finished speaking there was a long silence.

'Molly are you still there can you hear me ok?'

'Of course I'm still here, where else would I be?'

'Is something wrong?' His voice sounded slightly puzzled.

'I don't want to go to the party, I hate parties and you know it.' Once started she hadn't been able to stop. 'I'm fed up coming to Edinburgh; I don't even like the place. It's not fair asking me to share what little time we have together with strangers; people I don't even particularly like, and it hurts like hell that you hardly ever want to come home at weekends now.'

'That's not true. I come home most weekends.'

'Most weekends aren't good enough.' She heard him sigh before he replied.

'Molly please, this party is really important career wise.'

She came right back at him. 'More important than your wife's feelings.'

'For God's sake it's a party, a few hours that's all.'

'No Richard I'm not going and that's final.'

There was an uncomfortable silence before he replied. 'Ok, if that's how you feel I'll go alone.'

'That's outrageous and completely unfair.'

'No, it's not, I told you this is really important. I

need to go.'

'But...' She got no further. Richard's voice cut across hers.

'It's also important to have a supportive wife.'

Every word of that conversation was firmly etched on her memory; it had signalled the end of their marriage. It was the first weekend they had spent apart since Richard had started working in Edinburgh. It hadn't been the last. Every few weeks there was a social event he couldn't afford to miss and after her refusal to go to the party, he never again suggested she accompany him. Three months later he arrived home one Saturday morning, sat Molly down on the sofa and told her in shaky voice their marriage was over; he'd met someone else, someone who wanted the same things he did.

Deep down she'd had known this day would come. Their relationship had never really gotten back on track after her refusal to go to the party. They'd slowly drifted apart and Molly had refused to acknowledge it; the thought of losing Richard had been too painful. He had packed what little possessions were still in the house and left. She'd never seen him again.

The pain of losing Richard had been almost unbearable at times, but at least the last time she'd seen him he'd been alive, not a lifeless body dragged from the water like poor Louise Barton.

A sudden thump from above made Molly jump slightly in her seat; that damned cat, she sighed and rose from the chair. She knew exactly what the cat had done; he'd been on the window ledge in the spare room and knocked the small wooden box from the ledge onto the floor. In recent months he'd taken a liking to grooming himself there. It wasn't the first time he'd knocked it over. As she reached the top of the stairs a large streak of dark fur ran past her. Slowly she entered the room; the wooden box lay on the floor as she'd known it would. Blackie hadn't been at the front of the cat queue when the agility qualities had been dealt out. She picked it up and placed it back on the window ledge. A movement outside caught her eye; it was Mrs Crawford who ran the guest house across the road. Molly watched as she lifted a couple of shopping bags from her car and walked up the winding path towards the front door.

At last, like a mist lifting slowly and leaving everywhere visible, Molly clearly remembered what had been troubling her ever since she had talked to D.I. Stanford. It was the way Michael Barton had limped into the hotel with his wife on the Sunday evening; the night before she had drowned. It had been more than a limp; he had almost lurched to the one side. He had looked so odd. Molly had seen someone walk like that before from this very window; a man walking up Mrs Crawford's path.

The day had been extremely hot, and she'd had all the windows open all day, the temperature had been so high she had left cleaning the upstairs rooms until quite late in the evening. When she had finished vacuuming this room, she had closed the window and that's when she'd seen him. She hadn't been working that day and was certain it had been a Saturday; it would be easy enough to check. Molly kept a note of her shifts in her diary.

Had it been Michael Barton she'd seen going into Mrs Crawford's house? He'd certainly had the same strange walk and was about the same height, but Molly had only seen him from the back and he had been wearing a skip hat. She was tempted to go and ask Mrs Crawford about him; she was curious to know if he had been one of her guests or someone she knew personally. However, Molly decided to contact D.I. Stanford instead, he'd given her a card with a contact number on it and it was in her handbag. As she made her way back downstairs, she remembered something else, Michael Barton had been walking normally on Monday morning when he and his wife had left the hotel.

CHAPTER 38

'Guess where we're going?' Stan asked Sharon, replacing the telephone receiver.

'Somewhere warm and sunny,' she replied, sounding hopeful.

'Not quite; Dunoon.'

Sharon's heart sank, remembering the ferry journey. 'What; again?'

'That was the receptionist, Molly, the one from the hotel in Tighnabruaich. She lives in Dunoon and apparently the woman across the road from her runs a guest house. She thinks Michael Barton might have stayed there two weeks before his wife drowned.'

Sharon grabbed her jacket from the back of her chair and followed Stan who was already heading towards the door.

They arrived outside Molly's house less than two hours later. Molly was at the window waiting for them and had the front door open before they had got out of the car. Ushering them into the living room she went off to the kitchen to make some tea. Minutes later she appeared with a tray, holding a teapot and three mugs with sunflowers painted on them, and a large plate bearing the same pattern, filled with chocolate biscuits.

'I hope this doesn't turn out to be a wild goose chase,' she said looking genuinely worried. 'I would hate to think I dragged you all the way down here for nothing.'

Sharon took a sip of her tea and replaced the cup on the saucer. 'Molly, the man you saw walking on Mrs Crawford's path, why do you think it could have been Michael Barton?'

'He was walking really strangely, limping; no worse than limping, almost lurching up and down. I know that probably sounds silly, I mean you see people limping from time to time, but not like this. I don't know why I didn't remember this before, but when the Bartons stayed at the hotel, I saw Michael Barton walk like that.'

Stan and Sharon exchanged looks. No one else had ever mentioned seeing Michael Barton limp and neither of them had ever seen him limping.

'Was he limping the whole time he stayed?'

'No. That's what's so strange, I only saw him walk like that the once; on the Sunday. My shift was over but I was still in the hotel talking to Pete, the Barman; I had a book in my car for him. I popped out to the car to get it and one of the other guests cornered me outside. He's an older gentleman and stays frequently at the hotel. Unfortunately, he seems to think of the staff as his own personal servants for the duration of his visits. I was waylaid by him for about five minutes and when I returned inside with the book, the Bartons had entered the hotel and almost reached the reception desk. That's when I noticed Michael Barton walking strangely. I remember thinking at the time; it was odd I hadn't noticed him walking like that the day before when they had checked in. However, the next morning he hadn't been walking like that either and at the time I just surmised he hadn't been limping the night before at all, he had merely stumbled. Now, however, thinking back I know he didn't just stumble because I walked behind them both until they reached the stairs.'

Stan made some notes while Sharon continued. 'When you saw the man on Mrs Crawford's path, was he entering or leaving the house?'

'I never actually saw him go into the house, but he was walking towards the front door.'

'You didn't get a look at his face then?'

'No, he had his back to me and he was wearing one of those skip hats.'

'Did you ever see Michael Barton wearing a hat like that during his stay at the hotel?'

'No.'

'And you are sure it was the Saturday night exactly two weeks before the Bartons stayed at the hotel?' Stan asked.

'Yes I'm sure. I keep a note of my shifts in my diary and it was the Saturday during the summer that the weathermen were all claiming had been the hottest day of the year, with record temperatures. It was the only Saturday I'd had off in five weeks.

Someone at work even joked afterwards it had been worth waiting for.'

'Can you remember if there were any cars parked outside Mrs Crawford's house when you saw this man walking up her path?' he asked.

Molly thought for a few seconds before answering. 'No, I really am sorry but I can't remember.'

Stan and Sharon thanked Molly and left the warmth of her house to brave the wind and rain outside. Optimistic they may be on to something they crossed the road and opened the gate leading to Mrs Crawford's garden. In the summer the garden probably looked a picture but today it was a mass of dripping green vegetation. When she opened the door, Mrs Crawford appeared somewhat taken aback to find the man and woman on her doorstep were detectives seeking information about a former guest. The name Michael Barton meant nothing to her; she was sure no one of that name had stayed in the house recently. Dutifully she invited them in and gave them the guest register to look over.

'I insist all guests' sign in on arrival and sign out on departure,' she informed them.

Only one name appeared against the date on the register when Molly had glimpsed the man with the strange walk on Mrs Crawford's garden path. The name was Martin Brown.

'Same initials,' muttered Sharon, glancing at Stan.

'Do you remember this man; Martin Brown?' Stan

asked.

Mrs Crawford squinted at the register, when she saw the date against his name her eyes lit up. Ah yes I remember him well. It's the date you see; my only niece had given birth to a baby girl the day before.'

'Was he alone?'

'Yes he was.'

'Can you describe him to us?'

'He was tall and thin and he was wearing glasses. Hard to tell what age he was; early thirties maybe, but I'm not sure'

'Hair colour?' Sharon prompted.

'I don't know, he was wearing a hat.'

'What; even at mealtimes?' Stan asked.

'He didn't have any meals. He only stayed the one night and he didn't want an evening meal; only bed and breakfast. On Saturday night he changed his mind about the breakfast; asked if he could have a couple of filled rolls to take with him instead. He said he wanted to make an early start.'

'Did he say where he was going?' Stan continued.

'No, I don't think he did'

'What time did you speak to him on Saturday night?'

'About ten o'clock, maybe even later, I'm really not sure.'

'Did you notice anything odd about the way he was walking?'

'What do you mean?' Mrs Crawford asked, looking puzzled.

'Was he limping at any time?'

'He definitely wasn't limping when he arrived or when he left.'

'What about when you spoke to him on Saturday night?'

'Well I didn't actually see him walking on Saturday night. He was already on the stairs when I came to answer the service bell. He asked for the rolls instead of breakfast and I agreed. When I left him, he was still standing on the stairs.'

'Did you talk to him much?'

'No. To be honest my niece had had a difficult time giving birth and there had been some complications. Thankfully she is fine now, but at the time I was really worried about her. When he appeared at the door and asked for a room, I was in two minds whether to turn him away. He was such a well-mannered man and when he said he only required bed and breakfast for one night I agreed to let him stay.'

'Did he say anything at all about where he had come from or where he was going?' Stan asked, trying to keep a note of exasperation out of his voice.

'No, sorry, I'm not being much help here am I?'

'It's ok,' said Sharon reassuring her. 'Could anyone else have spoken to him, Mr Crawford, perhaps?'

'My husband died many years ago.' Her voice sounded flat. 'I live alone and there were no other guests. The couple who had stayed the week before left after breakfast on the Saturday morning and no one else was booked in until the following Friday.'

'Did you happen to notice what kind of car he was driving?' Sharon asked.

'I don't think he had a car, there didn't seem to be one parked outside while he was here.'

'Are you quite sure you have never seen this man, either before or since he stayed the night here?'

'Quite sure,' said Mrs Crawford confidently.

Stan kicked a stone towards the gutter in disgust once they had left Mrs Crawford's guesthouse and were out of earshot. 'Any B&B's I've ever stayed in the landladies have been nosy little buggers, usually trying to get your life story out of you before you even reach the top of the stairs. Christ, Freddy Kruger could have stayed the night and the most she would have to say about him would be; he wore a hat and a nice stripy jumper.'

'Oh come on sir, that's a bit harsh, after all she was worried about her niece,' replied Sharon, trying not to laugh. 'I wonder if Michael Barton wears glasses.'

'Even if he doesn't wear them, he could have picked up a pair of reading glasses from any chemist for a couple of quid. Combine that with a skip hat pulled down low and she...' Stan jerked his thumb towards Mrs Crawford's guesthouse. '... will never be able to positively identify Michael Barton and Molly whatshername only saw him from the back; again wearing a hat.'

Sharon pulled up the hood of her jacket as the rain started again. 'I'm thinking it's not beyond the bounds of possibility that Michael Barton did a little reconnaissance mission a couple of weeks before he brought Louise Barton here. Disguised himself just enough so no one would recognise him, parked his car well away from the guesthouse. Had a good look around and decided where the best place to throw his wife into the sea would be.'

'I think there is a good chance you're right but proving it is going to be difficult.' Glancing at Sharon he added, mischievously. 'You know strictly speaking it's not actually sea it's...'

'The Firth of Clyde, I know, so you can spare me the geography lesson,' she replied, cutting him off midsentence as she climbed into the car.

For the most part Sharon and Stan hardly spoke on the return journey home, both deep in thought, each mulling over what they had learned so far about Michael Barton.

'Maybe we are approaching this from the wrong angle.' Sharon said when they were back in Glasgow and had been stopped at yet another set of traffic lights.

Stan looked at her, raised an eyebrow but said nothing.

'Michael Barton came on the radar because we think he knocked down and killed Jill Mason,' she continued. 'Then we started to look at the facts surrounding his wife's untimely death and now today we're looking at events slightly before her death.' The lights changed to green and Sharon put the car into gear and drove forward. 'What I'm saying is, we are working backwards all the time and not really getting anywhere. Why don't we go right back to his mother's suicide and start working forward?'

Stan stared at her for a few seconds. 'Ok let's do

it your way,' he replied, nodding his head in agreement.

CHAPTER 39

Simon was on his way to the company where Louise had worked; a visit he was dreading. He had refrained from calling there for as long as he could; preferring to contact the company by phone. However, the orders placed by phone had been nowhere near as good as when he had visited in person, and Simon had been a salesman long enough to know he could easily lose this company as a customer, if he didn't make regular visits. In today's world the marketplace was too competitive to allow personal matters to compromise sales. After all he reminded himself, you're a grown man who had an affair with a married woman and now it's over; not some schoolboy with a teenage crush.

When Louise had ended their affair, Simon had taken it much harder than she could ever have imagined. Louise had made her choice. She had chosen her husband over him and he had known she would not change her mind. He had never tried to contact her; instead he'd decided to look to the future and get on with his life. He'd dated someone, met through a mutual friend a few times, but had found himself constantly comparing her to Louise. Unfortunately, she had never measured up. It hadn't seemed fair to continue to see her, as it was obvious to Simon she'd wanted more from the relationship than he had.

As he walked into the building, Simon felt more nervous than he could remember feeling in his entire life. The receptionist recognised him and told him Mr Boyd was expecting him and he should go straight through. Gerald Boyd's office was located to the rear of the main office; anyone going there had to pass through the main office first. Simon took a deep breath and opened the door. His eyes sought out Louise's desk immediately; it was empty. He didn't know whether he felt relieved or disappointed. The receptionist must have phoned ahead, to announce his imminent arrival, because Gerald Boyd opened the door to his office as Simon approached.

Three quarters of an hour later he emerged from his appointment with Gerald Boyd in a buoyant mood. He'd managed to secure a lucrative order for the next six months.

Walking towards the door at the front of the main office; Simon's eyes once again sought out Louise's desk. His heart missed a beat; there she sat, head bent low, reading from a sheet of paper, her hair falling forward covering most of her face. He'd almost reached her desk when she stood up and walked towards him. He stopped in his tracks and blinked, it wasn't Louise; he was looking at a complete stranger. The woman was much taller than

Louise and her hair was slightly lighter. Aware he was staring at her she asked. 'Can I help you?'

Simon cleared his throat. 'I'm looking for Louise, I thought this was her desk, but I must be mistaken.' Looking around the office and not seeing her he continued. 'Do you know where she is?'

The woman's face clouded over. 'I don't think anyone called Louise works here,' she answered, not meeting his eyes and looking helplessly around her. 'I'm quite new here so you might be best to speak to Julie.' She pointed to the girl sitting at a desk opposite and hurried away.

Hearing her name mentioned Julie looked up from her desk.

Simon approached Julie's desk and tried again. 'Hi I'm looking for Louise.'

A strange look passed over Julie's face. 'LLLouise.' she stammered.

'Yes Louise Barton, do you know where she is?'

'Louise is dead,' replied Julie, her eyes filling up with tears.

Simon had to grip the edge of Julie's desk to steady himself. His voice was almost a whisper. 'What do you mean dead?'

'She drowned.'

'Drowned,' he replied, horrified. 'When, for God's sake when did this happen?'

'In the summer.'

The summer? No that couldn't be right; he had seen Louise many times throughout the summer. This girl Julie must be confusing Louise with someone else, there must be another person called Louise working here. The relief he'd momentarily felt was cruelly snatched away from him with Julie's next statement.

'It happened at the end of August, she had gone on a weekend break with her husband Michael; she fell off some rocks and drowned.'

He watched as Julie lifted a paper hankie from a box on her desk and blew her nose. He had to get out of here, he felt sick, and he needed some air. He almost ran towards the front door and only just made it outside before throwing up. Eventually he stopped retching and took a few deep breaths before stumbling towards his car. He heaved himself inside and let his head lean back against the headrest. Louise had died at the end of August that meant she had died not long after the last time he had seen her. Simon remembered that night only too well; she had told him she was not leaving Michael, he had been so angry he had forced her to leave the flat, virtually thrown her out. In the weeks that followed he had been bitter and angry and had thought her a selfish cow. His beautiful Louise was dead; the pain was almost unbearable. Tears coursed down his cheeks and dripped off the edge of his chin. He didn't have the energy to wipe them away nor care who saw him crying.

CHAPTER 40

A check of the current electoral roll against that of the one at the time of Abigail Barton's suicide, had shown three names appeared on both registers; Timothy and Violet Shepherd and Samuel Bruce.

No one answered the door when they rang Samuel Bruce's doorbell, however, they fared better at the Shepherds, both Timothy and Violet were at home.

Sitting in the Shepherds' living room Sharon looked around her and found it hard to believe how anyone could live among such clutter. There was far too much furniture in the room and every surface was covered with ornaments. The whole place was spotless, and Sharon could not help but wonder how many hours a week Violet Shepherd put in cleaning this room alone. Compared to her minimalist living room, the Shepherds' was like Aladdin's cave.

Violet and Timothy didn't get many visitors and were happy to chat to Stan and Sharon about Michael and Peter, the two boys who had, while growing up, lived next door.

'Good kids, they were,' said Timothy.

'Helpful too, especially Michael,' added Violet. 'Many a time I came back from the shops and realised I had forgotten something. Michael would be only too happy to run down to the corner shop for me. Of course, I'd always give him something for himself. Not at all like the kids round here nowadays; they want to know how much they will get first, make sure it's worth their while.'

'And that's the ones you can trust not just to bugger off with the money,' her husband added.

'I remember the day they moved in.' Violet Shepherd continued. 'Michael was only a baby and Peter was a toddler. Abby, their mother, was a different person in those days. She was so bubbly and happy, always smiling. Peter; that was their father's name too, doted on the boys and Abby doted on him. After the accident she became a shell of her former self.'

Sharon stared hard at Violet. 'What accident?'

'Peter Barton was killed in a car crash going to work. The boys were only young. Michael took it especially hard, didn't talk for days. Abby was never the same it was as if she was passing the time rather than living. She told me once she wasn't afraid of dying, said she was looking forward to it because she could be with Peter again. They say time is a great healer and she was still young, I hoped she would meet someone else and be able to move on, but she never did. Sometimes I felt sorry for the boys, she always seemed so detached from them. I suppose that's what made them so close; they only really had each other for comfort.'

'They got on well together as children then?' Stan asked.

'Oh yes,' Timothy answered. 'Michael was the quieter of the two, a sensitive boy. Peter was different, not a tearaway you understand, but he had a few scraps in his time. Not many kids messed with Peter or Michael for that matter and those that did usually ended up with a bloody nose or thick ear; courtesy of Peter.'

'Oh yes Peter was very protective of his younger brother,' agreed Violet. 'I remember one boy calling Michael a nasty name because of his leg...'

'His leg,' interrupted Stan, immediately. 'What about his leg?'

'As a boy Michael was always climbing something, trees, fences, sheds, you know what some boys are like. Anyway, he fell from a tree and smashed his leg up pretty bad. He took a long time to recover and even longer before he walked properly again. Even then some days he started walking fine but by the end of the day he would be walking funny; sort of bouncing up and down, because his leg was playing up.'

'So Michael Barton walked with a limp, a limp that came and went,' Sharon said looking at Violet Shepherd.

'Yes the fall left a weakness,' she answered and then continued with her story. 'This day some boy was being mean to Michael because of his leg. Peter walked up to him and kicked him really hard on the shin. I saw it all from the window. The boy yelped in pain and started to hop about holding his leg, before he had had time to recover Peter kicked him hard on the other shin and promised to break both his legs if he ever called Michael names again. Michael looked up to his older brother; depended on him really in many ways. I think that's why he took it so hard when Peter left.'

'Why did Peter leave?' Stan asked.

'He went on holiday and never came back.'

'So Michael didn't go with him?'

'No Michael was still at school, Peter had left school had a good job too. He went to Spain with his mates and that was the last we saw of him. His mates came home, and he stayed. Abby told me Michael had sat at the window most of the day waiting for Peter to return but he never did. He didn't even come back for his mother's funeral.'

'Now Violet,' Timothy said reproachfully. 'The boy didn't know his mother was dead. Michael didn't manage to find him in time for the funeral. Oh don't get me wrong the lad tried his best but Peter had moved on from the last address they had for him.'

'Yes Tim, but even when Michael did track him down, he didn't come home did he? No he left Michael to deal with everything. Remember he told us the day he came to clear out Abby's house. He was genuinely upset Peter had not come back to help.' Violet sounded slightly annoyed.

'Yes, I know dear,' Timothy Shepherd answered in

a soothing voice trying to placate his wife.

'Did anyone ever see Peter after he went to Spain?' Sharon asked.

Violet answered. 'No but he phoned a few times at first and then sent the odd postcard. The post-cards usually came when he'd moved on somewhere different. Abby showed me a couple of them.'

Stan looked at Timothy Shepherd. 'When did Michael move out of the house?'

'A few years before Abby died. Once he started working the boy got his own place.' Violet Shepherd looked uncomfortable as she added. 'I know you shouldn't speak ill of the dead, but I think by that time Abby's drinking was getting a bit out of hand.' She looked at her husband hesitantly, then gave a little shrug and continued. 'After her husband died, Abby started to drink, oh don't get me wrong you never saw her drunk, well not when the boys were young. She drank before going to bed, told me her-self it helped her to fall asleep and she took pills for depression. That's why I don't believe she ever meant to kill herself, it was just an accident; she took too many pills and drank too much.'

'What can you remember about the day she died?' Sharon asked gently, she knew Violet and Timothy Shepherd had found her body; she had read the report on Abigail Barton's death.

Violet buried her face in her hands for a few seconds before answering. 'It was awful. Michael phoned on the Tuesday and said he was a bit wor-ried he had been trying since the day before to contact his mother and there was no reply. He was laid up himself with some sort of bug and asked if I would mind popping next door to check on Abby. I thought she had probably just unplugged the phone after a few drinks and forgotten to plug it back in; she had done it before. There was no reply from the doorbell. I started to feel uneasy, I looked through the letter box and shouted on her, but Abby didn't answer.'

'She came back and got the spare key,' interrupted Timothy. 'We've always had one since the boys were little. We both went in and found Abby dead on the settee.'

Changing the subject slightly, Stan asked the Shepherds if they had ever met Louise Barton, Michael's wife.

'Only the once.' Violet answered. 'We bumped into them quite by chance one day while shopping in town. They both looked so happy. I'm really pleased Michael met someone as nice as her.'

Stan waited for Violet Shepherd to continue but she said nothing.

'You do know she is dead,' he ventured.

Stan watched as the colour drained from Violet Shepherd's face. Looking at her husband she replied. 'No, we didn't, when did she die?'

'August, last year.'

'Oh my God, poor Michael, he must be in bits,' said Violet wrapping her arms around herself. 'We were away most of August, staying with my sister in Devon. We had such a lovely time. To think we were enjoying ourselves when poor Michael's wife had died, it's just so unfair. What he must have gone through, it's unthinkable.' Her eyes glistened with tears. 'Oh Tim that's why we never got a card at Christmas.' She looked at Stan and Sharon then sniffed. 'I know some men don't bother with cards, but he'd always sent us one before.' She sniffed again. 'He always put wee notes in too. That's how we knew he'd got married a few years back.'

As they rose to leave; Stan asked Timothy Shepherd when would be the best time to catch their neighbour Samuel Bruce, for a chat.

'Old Sammy's not there anymore, got taken off to the hospital six weeks ago. I'd forget about chatting to him; the poor sod's got senile dementia. He should have been taken into hospital a long time ago if you ask me. It wasn't safe him living there himself in that state for so long.'

'Well D.S. Thomas, you must be feeling pretty pleased with yourself.' Stan winked at her as they walked towards the car. 'Good call going back to Michael Barton's old house, good call indeed.'

CHAPTER 41

'Do you think Michael Barton's mother really meant to hill herself?' Sharon asked Stan the day after they had visited the Shepherds.

'What; you mean as opposed to taking too many pills and booze at the one time?' Stan shrugged. 'Who knows, probably more likely to have been an accident, there was no note. However, no point in losing any sleep over that question, it's one that's not likely to be answered. Right now, I am more interested in how his wife died.'

'I have a meeting at two o'clock with Susan Gibson, one of the two women who found Michael Barton after his wife drowned. Unfortunately, I still haven't managed to contact the other one, Marie Clark.'

'I've got a dentist appointment at two thirty.' Stan replied, pulling a sour looking a face. He hated going to the dentist. He'd had toothache on and off for weeks, the tooth was almost completely black, and he knew it had to come out. 'Once I'm back I'll try to get a hold of Marie Clark.'

Sharon decided to leave immediately and grab a bite to eat on the way. It would make a welcome change to eat something which really appealed. Stan was all burgers or rolls and sausage. The one time she had hinted at having something different he had shoved a bag of chips smothered with gravy in front of her. After wolfing down a ham and cream cheese bagel and a diet coke she made her way to the address she had for Susan Gibson. She found it easily, a quiet street with a row of terraced houses on both sides all with perfectly manicured lawns. As she walked towards number thirty eight, she caught a glimpse of someone looking out from behind a curtain of the house across the street.

Sharon rang the bell and the door was opened almost immediately by a tall attractive looking woman in her fifties.

'How can I help?' Susan Gibson asked, once they were both settled in large comfortable leather chairs in her sparsely, but expensively decorated lounge.

'I understand you found Michael Barton the day his wife drowned.'

'Oh yes and quite a fright he gave me and Marie that day. At first, I thought he might be drunk, he was weaving about on the path up ahead. When he saw us he started staggering towards us. I have to admit I was a bit frightened, there was no one else about and well you read about such terrible things happening to people these days. He was muttering something. We couldn't make out what it was, but as he got closer we heard him say something about his wife, and he kept saying please help me. By this time, I realised he wasn't drunk or crazy, just really upset. I thought his wife must have fallen or taken a bad turn. When he led us onto the rocks and there was no woman there, I did start to feel uneasy again. Then I noticed a woman's bag lying on the rocks, that that's when I started to think she might have fallen in. Mr Barton was soaking wet and I remember thinking that's why he is wet; he has been in the water.'

'Did he at any time say to you she had fallen from the rocks into the water?'

Susan Gibson thought for a moment before answering. 'No he didn't; he just kept saying he couldn't find her. I told Marie to call the police. She couldn't get a signal and had to climb back over the wall onto the path. Between you and me I didn't feel comfortable being left alone with him on the rocks. Something about the man unnerved me. I feel quite guilty saying that after all the poor man's wife had just drowned but that's how I felt,' she said, giving a slight shrug of her shoulders.

'Did he say anything to you whilst you were on your own with him?'

'No, I asked him if his wife had fallen in and he nodded his head. I asked him where and he just sat down on the rocks and stared at the water. Marie came back and asked him the same questions, but he never answered. I suppose the poor man was in shock. The emergency services arrived more quickly than I had expected, I found out later he had already called them.'

'Were you and your friend Marie on holiday or just enjoying a day trip?'

'No it wasn't a day trip; the weather had been so good we decided to take off for a few days. We're both widows with no commitments, she explained. We left early on Saturday morning and went to Arrochar first. We stayed the night there, and then drove to Kames on the Sunday afternoon; it's beautiful around that area and so peaceful. We intended to stay until Wednesday but when that poor woman drowned neither of us were in the mood for a holiday anymore and we left for home the next day.'

'Had you ever seen Michael Barton either alone or with his wife before that day?'

Susan Gibson moved her head slightly from side to side. 'No; definitely not.'

'What about your friend, did she mention if she had seen him before?'

'No, I don't think so. Of course you would have to ask her to be certain, and that won't be possible for a while; she's in Australia for six weeks visiting relatives. She left only last week.'

Sharon tried not to show her disappointment. As she rose to leave, she asked Susan Gibson if she had seen Michael Barton limping at any time. Susan said she hadn't seen him limping; he had been weaving about when she had first spotted him, by weaving she had meant not walking in a straight line, but no, definitely not limping.

By the time Sharon got back to the station Stan had returned from the dentist; one side of his face looking slightly larger than the other.

'How did you get on with Susan Gibson?' he mumbled with some difficulty.

Sharon made a face. 'Nothing we didn't already know from the witness statements, and I'd forget about trying to contact Marie Clark; she's in Australia.

'When is she due back?'

'Away for six weeks; left last week, you do the maths.' She scowled and sat down with such force the chair rolled a few feet backwards. 'Instinct tells me he killed Jill Mason and he had something to do with his wife's death. As money does not seem to have been an issue, I'm going to dissect both his wife's personal life and his before I leave this alone.'

Stan had to admire her enthusiasm and wished he could muster up the same, but right now all Stan wanted to do was load up with painkillers and crawl into bed. The tooth hadn't given up its place in his mouth easily. He shuddered at the memory of the crunching noises he had heard, as bits of tooth broke away while the dentist tugged at it.

True to her word, the next day Sharon dragged Stan off to visit Louise Barton's father. Stan was in a grumpy mood, he hadn't got much sleep the night before; his mouth had been too sore. The pain had eased off slightly by morning, but eating hadn't been easy, and he had given up on his breakfast; with the result he was not only tired but hungry too.

Louise Barton's father was frail and painfully thin, and Sharon couldn't help but feel glad they had come to speak with him today; he didn't look as if he would be around for much longer. His sister fussed over him, putting an extra cardigan round his shoulders and telling him to pull his chair nearer the fire. If Stan and Sharon had hoped George Rutherford would dish the dirt on his son in law, they were sorely disappointed. In fact, he told them he couldn't have wished for a better husband for his daughter. They had loved each other very much and Michael had really looked after Louise. He had been glad his daughter had found someone like Michael. Even when he had moved here to live with Moira, they had both visited often. His sister agreed with everything he said. When Stan asked about Louise's friends her father said to his knowledge the only friends she had kept in touch with since marrying Michael were Liz Walker and Grace Black.

The heat inside the house had been oppressive and Sharon was glad to leave and be outside in the fresh air 'I don't believe for one minute Michael Barton was the goody goody husband the old boy thought he was,' she said, her voice sour as she unlocked the car.

CHAPTER 42

'Thank goodness you're here.' Anne said when Michael arrived in the office ten minutes late and feeling rough; too much whisky the night before again the reason. Thinking, fuck off what's it got to do with you anyway, he completely ignored her and walked towards his desk. Sarah stepped in front of him and blocked his path.

'Ken Paterson has called a staff meeting in his office.'

'When?' Michael replied, wondering what the meeting was about.

'Now.' Sarah almost shouted the word at him, the irritation obvious in her tone. 'We have been waiting for you to get here.'

One by one they slowly filed into Ken Paterson's office all thinking the same. What was the meeting about? It wasn't unusual for him to call staff meetings, he held them regularly, but the staff always knew about them a week in advance; an impromptu one like this had never happened before. The reason soon became clear, Ken Paterson wasted no time in telling them he was resigning. His wife had been offered a job abroad; initially, on a three year contract. It was too good an opportunity for her to turn down and Ken had decided to take the plunge and go with her. If all went well they did not intend to return.

Listening to him, Michael could not make his mind up whether he admired the man or thought he was being extremely stupid. On the one hand it took a lot of guts for a man to put his wife's career ahead of his own. On the other hand, should a man really be trailing in the wake of his wife? Michael concluded Ken was making the biggest mistake of his life. After all he had treated Louise like an equal and she had betrayed him. His boss was going one step further and allowing his wife to become the dominant partner by putting more importance on her career than his own. It was a recipe for disaster as far as Michael was concerned and he was quite sure his superior would live to regret his decision. Of course there was no way he was going to voice these opinions, to do so would have been quite inappropriate; he did not know the man well enough. However, more importantly this meant his job would be up for grabs and Michael had his eye on it. As the others moved towards their superior shaking his hand and wishing him well Michael looked around. He could easily imagine himself sitting in this office, he would rearrange the furniture a bit, move the desk and chair nearer the window, which looked directly onto the street below. He would have plenty of time to look out of the window, once the job was his; unlike his superior he would delegate most of his work to the other staff members. A slight shiver of excitement rippled through his body at the thought of the power he would have over the staff and the respect he would command from them. His thoughts were interrupted by the sound of his name being called. The others had all left the room and Ken Paterson was looking at him enquiringly. Knowing he had been caught grinning like a Cheshire cat and feeling slightly foolish; he quickly rose from his chair and walked towards his soon to be ex superior, hand outstretched in a congratulatory fashion.

He hardly did any work during the rest of the day, he could not concentrate. All he could think about was Ken Paterson's job and the competition he would be up against. Apart from Bill and two women who worked in the claims department, Michael had been there the longest, hopefully Bill would not apply; he hadn't when Ken had got the promotion, however, his wife had been extremely ill in hospital at the time and that obviously had been part of the reason. He needn't have worried; Bill made it quite clear later in the day that he had no intention of applying for the position. He told Michael his wife's health was and always would be poor and he didn't want any added responsibilities at work. Michael felt like dancing round the staffroom when Bill told him this, however, he managed to looked suitably sympathetic and told Bill he was quite right his wife had to come first; whilst thinking silly old fool. That narrowed it down somewhat; he would be up against Margaret Jenkins and Sandra Fairweather, both of whom worked in the Claims Department upstairs. He was sure both would apply; they had done the last time when Ken had gotten the job Michael had only just joined the company at that time. Margaret was the only real competition, Sandra's absence record was appalling and he was quite convinced that fact alone would rule her out completely.

Eventually five o'clock came and Michael could leave. He couldn't get home fast enough. Fumbling with the key to open the door he almost ran to the kitchen, once inside the house. Yanking open a cupboard; he grabbed a glass and poured himself a large measure of whisky. His celebration was premature, he knew, but he would get the job; he was going to make sure he did. He held the tumbler up to the light, the whisky would have to go until after the job was his; but tonight the whisky bottle was his best friend. Michael raised the glass to his lips and started to drink. Hours later he dragged himself off to bed and set his alarm clock to go off forty five minutes earlier than usual. He knew he would be feeling rough from the whisky in the morning and he wanted to have something to eat and be wearing a freshly ironed shirt before setting out for work.

The interviews were to take place a week on Friday. Ken Paterson had given four weeks' notice and the company wanted the post filled and his replacement in the job as soon as possible. Michael was ecstatic to learn, the following day, that Margaret Jenkins would not be applying for the post. Apparently, she was pregnant; this had come as a shock to everyone, not least Margaret herself who was forty one. She hadn't intended to announce her pregnancy quite so soon, but everyone asking her why she was not applying for the job had forced her hand. Not only was she not applying for the promotion, once the baby came along she intended to resign. Never in his life had Michael been so thrilled to learn someone he knew was pregnant. This was great news; however, there was bad to follow. The company had another branch in the north of England and Michael learned, later that week, someone from there had also applied. No one seemed to know anything about him, and it was driving Michael nuts not knowing what kind of competition he was up against.

He spent every night on the internet researching the company. He read and re-read everything he could find. He trawled through books on interview techniques and questions; imagining the questions he would be asked and how he would answer. He stopped drinking completely and started arriving at work half an hour earlier than usual every day.

Six people, including Michael were to be interviewed. The employee from England, John Forbes who worked in the same office as Michael; pleasant enough, but young and inexperienced as far as Michael was concerned. The same could be said of Alan Brown who worked in claims and was also applying. Sandra Fairweather, whom he'd ruled out as any sort of competition. The biggest shock had been to learn that Sarah Greene had applied. The cheek of the woman, she had hardly been here five minutes and was applying for promotion. The sheer arrogance to think she could do the job better than him, when he had years of experience filled him with rage.

Eventually the day of the interviews dawned. When his turn came Michael took a deep breath and strode confidently into the room.

When he emerged from the room thirty minutes later he was still smiling. The interview had gone well. He felt relaxed, all the preparation had paid off. Unless the unknown applicant had a good few years of experience more than himself under his belt, the job would be his. All six candidates were to be informed at four o'clock which one of them had been successful. Michael had gone directly to lunch after his interview; lunch being two double whiskies and a packet of crisps in the nearest public house. Waiting for four o'clock to arrive was agonising; he lost count of the number of times he looked at the clock on the wall. The hands tormenting him as they slowly crawled their way round and round.

At three fifty five, the first of the candidates to be interviewed that morning was summoned back to the interview room, signalling the panel had come to a decision. One after another they entered the room, all went in hoping for good news; but only one person received it and that person was not

Michael.

The shock of being told he had been an unsuccessful candidate had made him feel sick. The panel's decision had been like a punch in the stomach and the bright smile he had gone into the room with had slid down his face, like tiles with too little adhesive slide down a wall, eventually shattering as they hit the floor. Shattered was exactly how Michael felt sitting in that room.

The stinging disappointment at not getting the job was soon replaced by almost uncontrollable anger when he discovered the successful candidate was none other than Sarah Greene.

He had gone directly to the nearest pub at five o'clock to drown his sorrows. How could they have given the job to her of all people? She was nothing but a two-faced bitch, pretending to be nice to him after Louise had died and then stabbing him in the back applying for a job that should have been his. He hated her more than he had ever hated anyone in his life. Well she would pay, like everyone else who crossed him she would pay, and he would enjoy collecting the debt and wiping the smug smile from her face. A couple of people standing at the bar eyed him suspiciously as he staggered slightly, spilling some of the whisky from his glass. Michael didn't notice; he was caught up in a drunken fantasy of slapping Sarah across the face time and time again until not only was the smile gone but so were most of her features.

CHAPTER 43

The sound of the doorbell wakened Sarah: disorientated and thinking it was her alarm clock she reached out and pressed the button to switch it off. Thirty seconds later she heard the sound again, and this time realised someone was at her door. She could hardly move her head from the pillow. Anne and Linda had taken her out, directly from work, the night before to celebrate her promotion; and celebrate they had. After two bottles of wine Linda had ordered cocktails, and Sarah and Anne had been only too happy to drink them. The doorbell rang again, and Sarah swung her legs slowly out of bed. Holding her forehead with one hand; she gingerly made her way to the front door. Opening it slowly, she was confronted by a smiling Penny who had bypassed the street level door by pressing the service button. She held a bottle of champagne in one hand and a card in the other. One look at Sarah and Penny burst out laughing.

'Has someone been at Sam and Ella's place again?'

Sarah made a face; visiting Sam and Ella's place was a standing joke between herself and Penny when one of them had overindulged the night before.

'I suppose a glass of champagne's out of the question.' Penny continued, raising the bottle slightly.'

At this suggestion Sarah clamped her hand firmly over her mouth and ran for the bathroom.

'I'll take that as a yes.' Penny laughed as she made her way into the kitchen and switched on the kettle.

By the time Sarah emerged from the bathroom Penny had two cups of steaming hot coffee on the kitchen counter. One look at Sarah and instead of offering her one of the coffees she guided her from the kitchen.

'Back to bed for you, my girl,' she said firmly, pushing Sarah into the bedroom.

Sarah, who was only too happy to go back to her bed, climbed in obediently. Penny returned to the kitchen poured the coffee down the sink, filled a glass with cold water, removed two paracetamol tablets from her handbag and made her way back to the bedroom. Placing them on the bedside table beside Sarah, who had already gone back to sleep, she quietly made her way towards the front door and left the flat.

Sarah slept uninterrupted for the next two hours, when she awoke, she saw the water and pills immediately and smiled at Penny's thoughtfulness. She sipped some of the water and swallowed the pills washing them down with some more water, then snuggled back down under the covers and slept for a further hour. This time when she awoke, she felt a whole lot better. Getting out of bed, she made her way towards the kitchen to make herself a cup of coffee and a slice of toast.

The bottle of champagne and the card that Penny had left caught her eye; she opened the card. Penny was a good friend, one of the best. Rummaging in her handbag she found her mobile phone and sent a text message to Penny. The message consisted of just one word. "Thanks." Sarah knew her friend would realise she was not just thanking her for the card and champagne but also for her compassion earlier.

After a shower and ensconced in a well-worn, but comfy tracksuit she felt almost human again. As she wandered from the bedroom into the lounge she spied three envelopes lying on the mat behind the front door. She picked them up; all three looked like bills. At least she would have a bit more money now that she had been promoted. The first two were addressed to her but the third was addressed to Mr and Mrs G Morven, her next door neighbours. Intending to put it through their letterbox, she opened her front door.

The sight that met Sarah stopped her from completing that task. Guy and Valerie Morven were trying, unsuccessfully, to negotiate a piece of, from this angle, unidentifiable furniture into their home. Three words sprang to mind; Car Boot Sale. The Morvens were always going to them and returning with armfuls of objects they had purchased at bargain prices. God knows where they put it all.

As Sarah watched, Guy Morven bellowed at his wife in exasperation. 'To me, to me.'

Sarah had an almost uncontrollable urge to giggle. It was like watching the Chuckle Brothers.

'It won't budge,' Valerie Morven snapped back at her husband.

Taking a few steps closer she saw it was a small sideboard and it was now quite firmly wedged in her neighbours' doorway. 'Do you need some help with that?' she asked.

'Is the pope a catholic? Of course we need some help'

Not sure if she was more taken aback by what Guy Morven had said or the tone of his voice, Sarah went to their aid. She had barely touched the sideboard when Valerie Morven gave an almighty push which sent it hurtling to the side and jammed one of her fingers between the door post and the edge of the sideboard.

'Damn it Val, you're going to scratch it.' Her husband yelled as Sarah hollered in pain.

Incensed, Sarah glared at him while she gingerly rubbed her finger. Guy Moron, which at this point Sarah thought was more of an apt name than his own, was obviously more concerned that his wife might have damaged a piece of second-hand furniture than the fact that she had almost amputated her neighbour's finger. Thankfully he had at least tilted the sideboard slightly, releasing her finger, the second she had yelled out.

'On the count of three push hard to the left. One,

two, three.'

Sarah and Valerie both did what sergeant major Guy demanded and thankfully the sideboard careered into the Morven's hallway.

After a quick inspection of the sideboard Guy finally asked Sarah if her finger was all right.

'Well I suppose it must be, after all it's still attached to my hand,' she replied, looking pointedly at it.'

Valerie looked positively mortified and Sarah was glad to note her husband Guy now looked rather sheepish.

Retrieving the letter that she had left on her own doorstep when she had gone to their assistance she shoved it into Guy's hand. 'I think this belongs to you.' He was now looking more uncomfortable with every passing second.

'I really am sorry about your finger. Come on in and I'll put the kettle on.'

'No thanks I've just had one,' she quickly replied. Her headache was beginning to return and the last thing she wanted to do was sit in her neighbours' house and make polite conversation. Then, not wanting to appear rude she added, smiling. 'Another time, perhaps.' Before beating a hasty retreat back to her flat and firmly closing the door.

CHAPTER 44

A visit to Liz Walker convinced Sharon if not Stan they were on to something. Liz had been only too happy to talk about her late friend.

'Louise was a lovely person, bright and bubbly; nothing was ever too much trouble. Too soft for her own good, sometimes; Grace used to say. But I suppose that was what made Louise, Louise if you know what I mean.'

'How well do you know Michael Barton?' Sharon asked her; desperate to know if Liz's opinion of him would be the same as his father in law's.

'I don't really know him at all. I only met him a couple of times. Weddings, funerals etc. With four kids Dave and I don't get out much together. Dave catches up with his mates every few weeks and I catch up with Grace and Louise whenever I can.' Her expression crumpled and she sniffed. 'At least I did until...' She didn't finish the sentence.

Sharon waited while Liz fished about in her pocket for a hankie and blew her nose before asking. 'Do you think they were happy together?'

'Yes I think so. Louise always seemed happy enough and never hinted that anything was wrong in their marriage.'

Treading carefully Sharon asked Liz, her voice quiet. 'Do you think Louise might have been having an affair?'

Liz gave her a half smile before replying. 'Funny you should ask me that; the last time the three of us were out Louise seemed different somehow, as if she knew something we didn't. For a laugh I asked her if she had a lover; she scoffed at the idea, but there was definitely something. I'm sure she was on the verge of telling us what it was then Grace got called away to the phone and the moment passed. Grace came back to the table moaning and complaining and we started talking about something else.'

Stan and Sharon left Liz Walker's house and went directly to speak with Grace Black.

'Someone's done well for themselves,' whistled Stan, looking up at the block of flats on the harbour development site where Grace Black lived.

If the outside had impressed Stan he must surely be bowled over by the inside, thought Sharon, as Grace Black showed them into a large room expensively decorated and overlooking the river; she certainly was.

Grace told the same story as Liz; she didn't know Michael particularly well she had only met him a handful of times. Grace said he had always appeared pleasant enough, maybe a bit too clingy for her liking but it hadn't seemed to bother Louise. As far as she was concerned Louise had been happy with Michael and there had been no marital problems.

When Grace mentioned she never socialised with them as a couple. Sharon asked her why not.

Grace sighed. 'I had already divorced my husband by the time Louise met Michael, and Liz was single; she hadn't met her husband Dave until the following year. It had always been a girls' night out and had just stayed that way even when Louise and Liz married.'

'Liz told us she thought Louise was hiding something, do you think she could have been having an affair?'

'I know that night Liz thought she might be, she even joked about it but I thought it more likely she was pregnant. She seemed too loyal to have an affair; still how well does one person ever know another?' Grace gazed towards the window, leaving Stan and Sharon with the distinct impression she was thinking about her ex-husband.

'How did Louise seem the last time you were all together?' Sharon asked her.

'Happy, animated even, that's why I thought she might be pregnant. However, later that evening Liz had been talking about her kids and Louise had said she intended to wait a while yet before having a baby. I did think it was a bit odd at the time; in the past she had often talked about having children and I'd got the idea she and Michael had been trying to have a baby, but I must have been wrong.'

Or maybe things had changed between Louise and her husband and she no longer wanted a baby with him, Sharon reasoned.

'Liz thought she might have been about to tell you both something important when you got called away to the phone, did you think that too?'

'Liz already asked me the same question and truthfully, I don't know. If only I hadn't got called away to take that bloody stupid phone call that never was.'

'Both Stan and Sharon looked at her puzzled and Stan asked. 'Who was on the phone?'

'That's the sixty four million dollar question, whoever it was hung up when I answered. I dialled one four seven one, but the number had been withheld; the strange thing was I don't remember telling anyone where I was going that evening and I had my mobile with me and there had been no missed calls.'

'So, Louise Barton had a secret and one she didn't share with her closest friends.' Stan mused once they had left Grace Black's apartment block. 'Liz thought she had a lover and Grace thought she might be pregnant. We know from the post-mortem report Louise Barton had never been pregnant. Maybe Liz Walker was not the only person to suspect Louise had been having an affair, maybe Michael Barton had also suspected as much; it might explain the phone call.'

'Of course; if Grace Black didn't tell anyone where she was going that night, whoever had phoned her at the restaurant had to have been informed by either Liz or Louise she was going to the restaurant, Liz would tell her husband Dave who she was going out with and Louise would tell Michael.'

'Exactly.'

'Ok say Louise was having an affair and Michael Barton was on to her, why phone the restaurant and ask for Grace. Just because Grace and Liz were there wouldn't be proof that Louise was, she could be using them as a cover, called off at the last minute and sneaked off to meet her lover.'

'Yes, but what if Michael Barton already knew his wife was in the restaurant, he could easily have followed her and if the other two had already arrived before Louise he wouldn't have known for sure Louise was meeting her friends and not her lover. He can't risk going into the restaurant to see who she's with. So what's the next best thing?'

'A phone call,' said Sharon nodding in agreement. 'Someone wanted to know if Grace Black was in that restaurant.'

Stan looked at his watch. 'Tomorrow we'll go talk to Louise's former workmates but for now it's time to call it a day because somewhere in some pub there's a pint with my name on it.'

The thought of a nice cold beer appealed to Sharon. 'Mind if I join you?'

'Don't you have someone to rush off home to?' Stan replied sounding surprised.

'Only a moggie, who, when I don't turn up will trot round his trusty band of neighbours, most of which will be at home and only too willing to feed and water him, or in one case feed and double cream him.'

'What are we waiting for?' Stan rubbed his hands

together. 'First round is on you.'

'I knew there'd be a catch.' Sharon replied, shaking her head and laughing.

Forty minutes later they were seated in Stan's local, both sipping a pint of Tennents.

'What happened to what's his face?'

'Doug. I gave him his marching orders a couple of weeks ago. I had to really; he gave me an ultimatum; him or the job. It was a case of, get your coat Doug.'

'Sorry.' Stan said, knowing she was trying to make light of it by joking. Although the job had not been the cause of his own marriage breakdown, he knew the strain it put on relationships. Over the years he had seen quite a few of his colleagues' marriages crack under the pressure.

'It's for the best.' Sharon continued. 'The writing had been on the wall for a while and in some respects it's a bit of a relief. At least I won't have to see the wounded look in his eyes; the one he gave me every time I turned up late or called off at the last minute. He had the knack of making me feel guilty most of the time. His constant complaining about me putting my job first and neglecting him was getting me down. When he suggested I get another job; told me our relationship would never work otherwise, that was the final straw. I think he wanted a partner who would be in the kitchen at five o clock making dinner with a fresh ribbon in her hair, and quite frankly I'm not a fresh ribbon in her hair type of girl.'

Stan stared across the table at the young woman

sitting opposite, her thin wiry frame encased in faded jeans and a long sleeved t-shirt. He had never seen her wear anything other than jeans. She was very attractive, but wore no make-up, her skin had a scrubbed clean look to it and her hair was scraped back from her face in a ponytail. Stan's eyes glistened with amusement.

'No Sharon, definitely not a fresh ribbon type of girl.'

'I'll take that as a compliment shall I?' she replied, raising her glass towards him.

The next morning when Stan and Sharon arrived at the small logistics company where Louise Barton had worked a rather snooty looking receptionist announced they were twenty minutes late. In clipped tones she explained they would have to wait as Mr Boyd was now in a meeting with someone else. Ten minutes later the receptionist demanded they follow her as she led the way to Gerald Boyd's office. Thinking the receptionist would have been better suited to the army as a career; Sharon made a face at Stan behind her back before following her.

Gerald Boyd had nothing but praise for his former employee. She had been competent, hardworking, loyal, got on well with the other staff; a good all-rounder as he had eloquently put it. He knew nothing about her personal life but suggested they talked to Julie. Julie worked at the desk opposite the one which had been occupied by Louise and he said he had often seen them chatting and laughing together.

With tears not far away Julie said the same as the others. Louise had never given her any cause to think her marriage was anything other than happy. She had never met Michael, but Louise had talked about him often. She had got the impression from Louise anything she wanted Michael went along with it.

Then they struck gold. As they were about to leave Julie turned to Sharon and said. 'You're the second person to have asked me about Louise recently.'

'Oh really, who was the other?' Sharon asked keeping her voice even.

'Simon, he's a salesman, he comes in from time to time. He didn't know Louise was dead and asked where she was. When I told him what had happened, he looked really upset and practically ran from the office.'

'What is Simon's second name?'

'I don't know but Mr Boyd will be able to tell you.'

'Do you know if Louise ever saw Simon outside of work?' Sharon asked feeling sure they were now onto something.

Julie looked uncomfortable as she stared at both of them. 'They used to flirt with one another, and I think she went to lunch with him once.'

CHAPTER 45

Simon Preston was surprised to find two detectives on his doorstep and appeared visibly shaken when they informed him they wanted to talk to him about Louise Barton.

It was a blessed relief to be able to talk to someone about Louise, until now he had never told a soul about his relationship with her. He'd kept their affair a secret because he had promised Louise he would. When she'd ended their affair, amongst the feelings of anger and bitterness, there had been a niggling feeling of foolishness. He'd been stupid to think she would leave her husband for him; people who had extra marital affairs rarely did leave their spouses, and that had been enough to stop him confiding in any of his friends. Feeling foolish was one thing, but looking foolish to his contemporaries was another and he didn't want their pity.

Once started talking about Louise, like water pouring through a dam, he couldn't stop. He told them everything.

'I met Louise at her office. She was beautiful; there was real chemistry between us, and I asked her out the first day I saw her. She said no at first. I knew she was married and it was wrong but I wouldn't let it go. The next time I visited her office I managed to persuade her to go for lunch and that was it; there was no going back for either of us.'

'What exactly did Louise tell you about her husband?' Stan asked him.

'Not much. I know in the beginning, she felt guilty about our affair. She told me he was a good husband and loved her dearly.'

'What do you mean in the beginning, did something happen to change that?'

'He started drinking heavily and it was taking its toll on her. I know she dreaded going home because he was usually drunk. I told her to leave him; move in with me. I really did think she was going to, but...' Simon stopped mid-sentence and shrugged. He could still remember, clearly, the feeling of shock when Louise told him she was staying with Michael, how he'd virtually thrown her out of the flat and the almost unbearable emptiness he'd felt after she'd gone.

'Was he ever violent towards her?' Stan persisted.

'No I don't think so, she never said he had been and I never saw any bruises or marks on her.'

'Do you think her husband knew she was having an affair?' Sharon asked him.

'I know Louise thought he suspected she was seeing someone. She was convinced that was the reason he was drinking so much.' He shrugged again. 'I'm not so sure, I mean he never said anything; accused her, or asked her outright. Surely if he had suspected his wife of having an affair, he would have brought it out into the open?' Simon said looking from Stan to Sharon then back to Stan.

'Sometimes people ignore situations they don't want to deal with.' Stan replied. 'Did you ever meet Michael Barton?'

'No and I never want to.' He shuddered at the thought. 'If it wasn't for him Louise would still be alive.'

'What makes you say that?' Sharon asked him.

He sniffed derisively. 'One minute he's drinking himself into oblivion and she's all set to leave him, the next he stops drinking and turns into the perfect husband and Louise decides to stay.' Sharon and Stan exchanged looks as he ranted on. 'That girl at the office said she fell off rocks and drowned. I bet he had her clambering all over the bloody place; more interested in finding somewhere to fish than his wife's safety.'

'Did Michael Barton often go away on fishing tips?' Sharon asked him.

'That was all part of the new-look Michael.' His voice was loaded with bitterness as he continued. 'He had gone fishing for the first time the weekend we split up. It was to be our first weekend together. Instead we argued because she wouldn't leave him and that was the last time I saw her.' He stared at the floor for a few seconds before glancing back at the two detectives. When he met Sharon's eye his memory slowly began back pedalling to thirty seconds earlier. How quickly she had asked him why he blamed Michael for Louise's death and the looks between both detectives while he'd been speaking. The realisation stunned him.

'My God; you think he killed her.'

Keeping his voice even, Stan replied. 'We are investigating another matter entirely and at this point are merely talking to people who know Michael Barton and who knew his wife Louise.'

'But you must think her death is suspicious otherwise you wouldn't be here.'

'As I said Mr Preston, we are investigating another matter entirely, thanks for your time,' Stan said, rising from his seat.

For a long time after the two detectives left, Simon sat motionless, going over every inch of the conversation he had just had with them. The same two questions going round and round in his head. Had Louise been murdered by her husband? Did the police suspect that was what had happened? The pain Simon had felt when he'd discovered Louise was dead had been bad enough, but the guilt he now felt was much worse. If Louise had indeed been murdered by her husband, then he was partly responsible because in all probability the reason Michael Barton had killed his wife was because she had been having an affair with him.

CHAPTER 46

That bloody dog was barking again. Michael heard it the minute he turned into the street. He hated dogs, probably because he had been bitten by one as a small child and had spent most of his childhood being afraid of them. He could never understand why people who owned dogs doted on them and treated them like one of the family. As far as he was concerned dogs were a nuisance, they fouled the streets, they smelled, and the sound of their barking grated on his nerves. One of his neighbours, an elderly lady who lived alone, called Mrs Campbell had got a dog about a year ago and called it Muffy; so Louise had informed him at the time. His lack of interest meant he could not have told anyone what breed it was. Some sort of terrier he thought, it looked the same as the ones he remembered seeing on the front of old postcards. Usually there were two a black one and a white one. Scottie dogs his mother had called them.

Mrs Campbell had recently had her old wooden gate replaced with a new wrought iron one; leaving a larger space between the gatepost and the hedge than had previously been there. The dog had taken to squeezing itself between the two. Once out on the street it spent most of the time running up and down the pavement barking to get back in to Mrs Campbell's garden. Another reason not to like dogs; they were stupid. It couldn't even work out it could get back into the garden the same way it got out. He suspected the old dear was a bit deaf and if she was at the back of the house, she didn't always hear it barking. Sometimes other neighbours, tiring of hearing it, would go out and open Mrs Campbell's gate for it to get back in; Michael had done it himself a couple of times.

Seeing Michael getting out of the car Muffy ran towards him, hopefully. Clutching four bags of shopping and shutting the boot of the car at the same time, he did not see the dog, at his feet, as he stepped onto the pavement and inadvertently stood on its paw. The little bastard snarled at him before limping off. Incensed Michael carried his shopping into the house. As he put the bags down a packet of digestive biscuits fell out hitting the floor. Great; now I've got a packet of broken biscuits. He peeled open the packet and was pleasantly surprised to find only the first few were in bits. Smiling to himself he shook them from the packet onto the palm of his hand and made his way back outside onto the pavement where a rather subdued Muffy was sniffing about. The dog eyed him warily but when Michael held out a morsel of biscuit the dog walked slowly towards him. Michael gave the dog the piece of biscuit and backed his way along the path holding out another, the dog followed him along the path and into the house. Once in the kitchen Michael opened the back door and placed the rest of the broken biscuits on the patio. Muffy was delighted and munched into the unexpected treat while Michael opened his garden shed.

One minute the dog was happily eating; the next it was lying dead, head caved in on the patio, thanks to Michael and a garden spade.

Wrinkling his nose in distaste he stuffed the dead dog into a bin bag, tied the top ends together and dropped it unceremoniously in the rubbish bin. 'Bye bye Muffy,' he muttered replacing the lid. Taking a brush and shovel from the garden shed he quickly brushed up the remaining biscuits and crumbs from the patio, turned on the garden hose and quickly washed the spade on both sides. Replacing all three items back in the shed he returned to the house, put his shopping away in record time, made himself a coffee and sat down to enjoy the fresh cream donut he had bought himself. Peace, perfect peace.

The next day Mrs Campbell approached him as he left the house. 'Mr Barton have you seen my dog, Muffy?' she asked him, close to tears.

Yes, it's in my dustbin with its head smashed in; want to see? Instead, looking the picture of innocence and a note of concern in his voice he asked. 'Is Muffy missing?'

'I can't find her, poor Muffy I haven't seen her since yesterday.'

'Try not to worry; I'm sure she'll turn up when she's hungry.' She'll turn up alright; at the dump.

'Oh I do hope you're right.' Mrs Campbell sniffed. 'I don't know what I would do if something happened to her.'

'I'll keep a lookout for her.' Michael said, walking away and smiling as she mumbled her thanks.

He was almost tempted to retrieve Muffy from his dustbin and leave her on Mrs Campbell's doorstep just to find out exactly what the old dear would do when she found out something had happened to her precious Muffy. What was correct behaviour when one's neighbour murdered one's dog, he wondered. He had a sudden image of Mrs Campbell throwing herself on a funeral pyre in her front garden and had to clamp a hand firmly over his mouth to stop hysterical laughter escaping.

CHAPTER 47

Ignoring the usual smarmy grin on Lewis's face, Stan switched on the kettle and placed two heaped teaspoons of Nescafe into a chipped mug. He had just emerged from a meeting with Jill Mason's parents; a meeting which had not gone well. They were both desperate for their daughter's killer to be brought to justice and from their point of view it wasn't happening quickly enough. He couldn't tell them anything more than he had the last time they had spoken, and he sensed they were losing faith in both Stan and his team. He couldn't blame them; he'd made them a promise to catch whoever was responsible and so far he had not been able to deliver that promise. The barely controlled anger in Jack Mason's voice, and the haunted look in his wife's eyes was something that Stan would not be able to forget until whoever killed Jill Mason was safely behind bars.

Although totally convinced it was Michael Barton who had robbed the Masons of their daughter, the problem was Stan had no evidence to support this theory. Jill Mason had been killed by his car, but Michael Barton claimed he had left it parked in

Battlefield much earlier. He'd reported it stolen the next morning when he claimed he'd returned to get it. The car had indeed been stolen and the three culprits caught. All three had insisted they had taken the car from Castlemilk and all three had claimed to have seen someone walking away from it, someone with a hooded jacket. They were adamant they had never driven anywhere near where Jill Mason had been knocked down and Stan had believed them; their recalling of events had been completely consistent. In addition, residents of the houses further down the road had been questioned and a couple of people, who had been out walking their dogs that night, had placed the boys where they said they had been slightly before and at the time Jill Mason was knocked down. Trouble was the boys could not identify the person they had seen walking away from where the car had been left. He had been too far away, it had been dark and he'd had his back to them. Michael Barton had walked into a bar in Battlefield at nine o'clock, according to Debbie, the barmaid, and not wearing a hooded jacket. Even if he had dumped the jacket, which Stan was sure he had done, the time was still out; there was no way he could have knocked down Jill Mason, dumped his car in Castlemilk and then got himself to Battlefield in time to walk into a bar at nine o'clock. Debbie must have got the time wrong, but she was sure she hadn't, and Stan had no evidence to charge Michael Barton with.

Had Michael Barton been extremely clever or extremely lucky, Stan wondered. Sharon was certain he was responsible for his wife's death and was determined to prove it. While Stan agreed she was right, he did not want to end up with a situation where Michael Barton was arrested for his wife's murder and Jill Mason's death was left an unsolved crime. He had to get closure for the Masons and also for himself he realised. Still maybe going after him for his wife's murder was the way they would crack him, only time would tell and at this moment it was their only hope.

CHAPTER 48

The small attractive blonde at the end of the bar was giving him the eye. She had barely taken her eyes off him since he arrived. It was Saturday night and Michael had decided to go out on the town. Catching the blonde's eye, he smiled, she smiled back. A few minutes later the two friends she was with left their drinks on the edge of the bar and walked towards the ladies room; Michael seized his chance and made his way towards her.

Her name was Becky, she was single, worked in the personnel office of a department chain and best of all had her own flat. She also liked the sound of her own voice and prattled on about her friends, family and job. All Michael had to do was smile, make the right noises, buy the drinks and Becky was content. When her friends had returned and saw her talking to Michael, they'd discreetly lifted their drinks from the bar and moved away. Eventually Becky asked him about himself and Michael answered all her questions honestly. He decided making up a fictional life would not be wise; he might trip up and get caught out. No he thought; tell the truth as much as possible and omit the things he didn't want her to know. When he said he was a widower he saw the look of slight surprise that crossed her face. He'd got the same reaction from Tina at the Health Club, he supposed it was because of his age. The word widower always seemed to conjure up an image of an older man to most people. The surprised look slowly faded, and Becky looked almost pleased. He watched her body language with interest. She moved nearer to him, put her hand on his arm, squeezed it gently, and stared into his eyes. In that moment Michael knew she was his for the taking. He also realised something else; the fact that he was a widower was of great appeal to women. It made him look slightly vulnerable and women warmed to him immediately, trusted him, wanted to look after him. Michael smirked at this notion.

'What is it?' Becky asked when she noticed him smiling.

The words tripped off his tongue so easily. 'I was just thinking how lucky I am to have met you.'

Becky was captivated and when Michael asked her if she wanted another drink, she suggested they went back to his house and had one there. No way was he taking her anywhere near his house, so he told a little lie; one he had lined up for just such an eventuality. He told Becky he had recently moved to an old rundown property and was in the process of restoring it. It was like a building site, he told her and there was no heating. That did it, Becky suggested they went to her flat instead.

They left the pub and he put his arm round Becky's shoulders as they made their way towards the taxi rank outside Central Station. Fifteen minutes later they were cosily installed on the back seat of a taxi and on their way to Partick. Becky snuggled up to Michael and he tightened his arm around her. She turned to kiss him, and her short skirt rode even further up her legs, when Michael tentatively placed one of his hands on her legs just under the hem of her skirt he felt her legs part slightly as she moved closer to him. This was turning out to be a very good night; he moved his hand further up Becky's leg.

The next morning Michael awoke to a strange sound, slightly disorientated it took him a few seconds to work out where he was. The petite slim blonde from last night was now a mound of snoring quilt, with blonde hair sticking out, haphazardly. He eased himself quietly out of the bed and dressed quickly; noting that not only were his clothes and the ones Becky had been wearing last night lying on the floor, but what appeared to be most of the contents of her wardrobe were also there. The door straight ahead was open and he could see it was the kitchen. Feeling thirsty he walked towards the sink. The bedroom was untidy, but the kitchen was worse, much worse. There were unwashed mugs and plates lying on every worktop.

'Make a pot of tea and bring it back to bed,' a voice, thick with sleep, said from behind him. 'I think I deserve it after last night.' Becky yawned first then winked at him, as he turned around.

Michael stared at her, did she expect him to be grateful. 'I would if I could be sure to find a clean cup,' he replied sourly. 'Christ, do you ever clean up in here?'

'Sometimes,' she replied sounding completely unperturbed.

He watched as a naked Becky, turned on her heel and strode back into the bedroom. He glanced around the kitchen once more, shaking his head at the mess before following her into the bedroom, to retrieve his jacket.

'Will I see you again?' Becky asked, sounding as if she couldn't care less one way or another.

As he slipped out of her flat, he looked at his phone. He had not intended to see her again but when she had brought the subject up, he had thought why not? She would do if he was ever stuck for female company. He didn't want a girlfriend, after Louise his attitude had changed towards women, completely. All he wanted from a woman was sex and he had no intention of being with the same one too often. Bringing Becky's name up from his phonebook he added S1 beside her name, S for slut and 1 for number one; he would number all the women he had sex with and wanted to see again this way. He would see them when it suited him and if and when they got too clingy, he would delete them from his list. Whistling he walked down the stairs, he was already looking forward to next weekend wondering if he would be able to pick up a different woman as easily as he had picked up Becky.

CHAPTER 49

Sarah pulled her scarf closer round her throat and tucked her arm around Robert's elbow. They had just left La Vita and already she was regretting wolfing down sticky toffee pudding on top of Lasagne. They were making their way towards their favourite wine bar when a couple, further along the road, in front of them had her stopping in her tracks. The sudden tug on Robert's arm had him stopping too; much to the annoyance of the overweight man, walking behind who subsequently slammed into them. Still staring ahead, she muttered an apology, which went unnoticed as the man shook his head, swore under his breath and marched on his way.

'What's wrong?' Robert asked.

'It's Michael,' she replied, still staring ahead. 'Look, he's with a woman.' Robert stared at her, looking puzzled. 'Michael Barton, the guy from work whose wife drowned a few months back.' She turned towards him. 'I can't believe he's out with someone else already.'

'It could be anybody, a...'

She cut him dead. 'Well it's hardly a sister or casual acquaintance, for God's sake look at him he's all over her. C'mon,' she said pulling on his arm. 'I want to see what they're up to.'

'You're not seriously suggesting we follow them?'

'Yes I am, now hurry up before we lose sight of them,' she replied, grabbing his hand and dragging him behind her.

They followed Michael and the woman onto Renfield Street. By the time they had managed to cross the road, dodging traffic and getting tooted at twice by irate drivers, Michael and the woman had taken a right turn into Gordon Street. When they reached Gordon Street themselves, they were just in time to witness Michael and the woman joining the end of a small queue.

'Damn, they're waiting for a taxi.'

'As opposed to what?' Robert asked, sounding slightly irritated.

'I was hoping they would go into a bar; where we could have watched them.'

'Well that's not going to happen,' he said, firmly taking her hand and leading her back in the direction they had come.

The wine bar was dark and warm, candles fluttering on every table. Robert and Sarah were sitting comfortably at a table in the window. They were both sipping glasses of Chardonnay, poured from a bottle nestling in a bucket of ice on the table.

Robert stared at Sarah and asked. 'Were you serious when you said you wanted to follow Michael into a bar and spy on him?'

She nodded at him. 'Yes I was.'

'Why would you want to do that?'

Placing her glass on the table she stared at Robert for a few seconds before answering. 'There's something about that guy that's just not right. His wife's only dead a few months and he's out on the town with someone else. They were much to cosy for it to have been a friend.'

'People deal with grief in different ways. Just because he's not sitting at home every night with a box of tissues doesn't mean he's not suffering.'

'But that's the whole point. He arrives at work looking every inch the grieving widower. He comes in late most days, looking hung-over, he hardly does any work. Everyone covers for him and I turn a blind eye because we all feel sorry for him. He's led us all to believe he goes home every night after work to an empty house and hits the bottle.'

'Well maybe he has decided to try and get his life back on track. You must admit sitting in the house alone and getting blind drunk night after night is not exactly a healthy option. Being out with another woman does not necessarily mean he has got over his wife's death or misses her any less.'

She glanced around the bar. 'I know what you're saying makes sense, but I never really liked the guy, there was always something about him I didn't trust, and he could be quite nasty sometimes with his comments. Even when the promotion came up it crossed my mind it was a bit odd that he'd gone for the post. It was so soon after her death, I thought going for promotion would have been the last thing on his mind. I told myself I was being mean for thinking that way and it was probably the best thing he could do to help him cope, but I didn't really believe it.' She took a sip of wine. 'If I'm being honest deep down I thought it was slightly inappropriate and I've always had the impression he resented me for getting the job. He's never said anything, again it's just a feeling I can't shake off. I suppose what I'm saying is while everything you've just said makes perfect sense there's always the possibility, he has got everyone fooled and Michael Barton is playing us all for mugs.'

Robert sipped his own drink before answering. 'Why would he do that?'

She shrugged her shoulders. 'Who knows, maybe he's a Jekyll and Hyde character.'

'Or maybe you're being a bit paranoid.' He said and laughed.

Sarah thumped him, playfully on the arm before continuing. 'Even from a distance there was something different about him tonight; a spring in his step.' She gave a deep sigh. 'Perhaps I'm reading too much into this and being a bit mean, grudging him a bit of happiness so soon after his wife's death.' She reached over the table took Robert's hand and squeezed it. 'Maybe you just have a mean, paranoid girlfriend.' They both laughed.

When Sarah awoke the next morning the first thing she heard was the steady, rhythmic sound of Robert's breathing as he lay beside her. She thought back to the night before; it had been perfect. Then she remembered seeing Michael Barton with a woman. It had certainly hit a raw nerve. Had she been justified thinking he was taking them all for mugs at work? She hadn't come to a decision before Robert stirred awake and reached out for her.

CHAPTER 50

His watch showed twenty past nine; Michael was late for work again and had a hangover. He lumbered towards his desk ignoring the others in the office. As he sat down, he glanced towards the door of Sarah Greene's office. The office that should have been his. It was closed as usual; she was always in before him, even when he was on time and that wasn't very often. The only positive thing to come out of her getting the job over him was she no longer worked in the main office. He couldn't care less whether she knew he was late or not, just let her dare to say something to him; he would soon put her in her place. When Sarah had been promoted Michael had decided there was no way he was going to let her boss him around. However, so far she had left them all pretty much to get on with their own work and had not tried to throw her weight around; he couldn't quite make up his mind if he was relieved or disappointed. As he glanced at the door again it opened and out she walked. He watched as she made her way purposely towards him.

'Michael can I have a word please, in my office?'

Slightly taken aback at her abrupt tone he looked

at his watch and replied. 'Give me half an hour to finish these.' He shuffled some papers for effect. 'Shall we say ten o'clock?' His tone matching her own.

'No, Michael not ten o'clock, now please.'

Feeling mortified he looked around him, apart from Linda who was openly staring at him and obviously listening to every word, everyone else either had not noticed the exchange between himself and Sarah, or were pretending not to. Sarah had reached the door of her office and was standing arms folded across her chest waiting for him. He bristled with anger, how dare she humiliate him like this, she was making him look like some naughty schoolboy being dragged out of class by the headmistress. Well this would be the first and last time she did that he decided, standing up and striding towards her.

***

Sarah was beginning to think addressing Michael's timekeeping might not be such a bad idea. After all, if he was over his wife's death enough to start dating, surely he could manage to get himself to work on time. Yesterday the decision of whether to say something to him or not had been made, when she had received a call from a client who gave them a lot of business, and was one the company could not afford to lose. Michael was the person the client had been dealing with, but no one had known where he was so the call had been put through to her. The client was not happy and after investigating the complaints neither was Sarah. She had eventually found the file on Michael's desk buried under a mountain of papers, some of which she knew should not be there.

Shutting the door, Sarah gestured for him to sit down and made her way to her own chair. Before Michael had a chance to say anything Sarah asked him where he had been yesterday afternoon.

'At the dentist.' He snapped the words at her defensively.

'I wasn't aware you had a dentist appointment yesterday.'

'Well I did,' he replied, sounding almost childish.

'In future all requests for time off are to be notified to me in the first instance. That includes all doctor, dentist, optician, hospital appointments, etc.'

Michael opened his mouth to retort and was silenced by Sarah putting her hand up firmly in front of her face, palm facing outwards, as she continued. 'After all that was the rule when Ken Paterson worked here, and as far as I'm aware the rules have not changed, therefore, I expect the same courtesy from the staff as was afforded to him.' Looking him directly in the eye she continued. 'Yesterday I received a call from Harpers; it appears they have some concerns regarding the way business is being handled.'

'I'm dealing with Harpers and everything is progressing smoothly.' He almost snarled the words at her.

'Not according to them and after going through their file I have to agree.'

'Well that's funny because the file is on my desk,' he replied, sounding slightly supercilious and leaning back in his chair.

'Not anymore.' Sarah gestured to the folder in front of her.

'How dare you rummage through my desk.'

'Look Michael I'm sure I don't have to tell you how important the Harpers business is to this company. I shouldn't need to go rummaging,' she said holding up the folder and waving it in front of him. 'This should have been dealt with weeks ago.'

There was a short silence before he replied. 'Ok I'm on it.'

'No Michael, you're not, from now on I am going to deal with Harpers myself.' Before Michael could protest, she continued. 'In fact, I think it would be a good idea if you went back to your desk and made a note of everything you are working on at the moment and at what stage you are at. I suggest we meet back here at three o'clock and go through everything together.' Sarah could see he was furious and to take the heat out of the situation she added. 'If you feel your workload is too much, we can always divide it up amongst the rest of the staff. After all it wouldn't be fair if one person was snowed under with work and another was sitting there hardly doing a thing.'

***

Michael said nothing, he could hardly believe the way she had just spoken to him. He wanted to lunge across the desk and grab her by the throat and it took every inch of willpower he had not to. Instead he clenched his fists tightly and simply nodded as he stood up and walked from the room. He went directly to the men's toilet and shut himself in a cubicle. Only then did he unclench his fists and notice the blood where his nails had been digging into the palms of his hands. Shaking with rage he looked at the tiled wall and imagining Sarah Greene's face, slammed his right fist hard against it. Such was his fury, he didn't feel a thing as his knuckles glanced off the tiles. Still smarting from the dressing down Sarah had given him, he returned to his desk. Common sense told him no one would have been able to hear what had been said in her office, but paranoia made him look around at his co-workers one by one.

He was incensed at her, who the hell did she think she was? Michael made up his mind there and then that Sarah Greene would pay and pay dearly for today. He would make her regret she had spoken to him the way she had. In fact, he would make her regret ever applying for promotion in the first place. Anticipation of the revenge he would mete out made him shiver slightly. He could hardly wait; but wait he must. Just like with Louise every detail had to be planned meticulously. Planning was everything, it meant the difference between getting away with something and getting caught; he would start by appearing to acquiesce to Sarah's demands. Quickly he jotted down everything he was working on and at what stage he was at with each. He then tidied his desk and filed everything away that should not be there, a job he had been meaning to do for a long time.

At exactly one minute to three Michael got up from his desk, lifted his notepad and walked towards Sarah Greene's office.

CHAPTER 51

The first thing Michael did on entering the house was turn on the central heating. He peeled off his rain sodden jacket, dropped it on the floor and with shaking hands poured himself a generous measure of whisky. The damp shirt clung to the back of his neck as he slumped into an armchair and thought over the events of the last few hours.

He had left the house around 8pm and made his way to the city centre. His encounter with Becky last week had made him eager for Saturday night to come around.

He visited three bars before someone caught his eye. Her name was Paula and she was with her friend Maggie. He'd hoped Maggie would get the message and disappear, he even made a few subtle hints but Maggie stuck to Paula like glue. In fact, he got the distinct impression she did not particularly like him. When the bar closed the three of them made their way to the taxi rank. Once in the queue Michael snuggled up to Paula and whispered. 'Let's put Maggie in a taxi of her own and we can get one together.'

Paula stared at him looking slightly puzzled. 'I

thought you said you lived on the south side of the city.'

'Well I do but...' He got no further before she replied. 'We're going in the opposite direction.' Michael tried again this time nuzzling into her neck. 'I know but I thought maybe I could come home with you.'

She giggled before replying. 'I don't think so.'

He pulled her closer and began caressing her back while staring into her eyes. 'I want to spend some time alone with you.'

She kissed him lightly on the lips. 'Sounds good. I'll give you my number and we can go out together one night, just the two of us.'

'He moved one hand nearer her breast and pressed himself against her. 'What's wrong with now?' He felt her pull away.

'When Maggie and I go out together we share a taxi home together.' Her voice had a slight edge to it.

'But I thought...'

'Well you thought wrong. I'm not in the habit of taking men home I've only just met.' Although her voice was sharp, she looked crestfallen.

Too late he realised Paula had wanted a boyfriend from their encounter not just sex. Putting up with her sour faced friend and buying them both drinks all night had been a waste of time. His mood turned dark and he left the queue without saying a word to either of them. Aimlessly he walked around the city centre streets, too wired to go home.

'Lookin for business darlin?'

He glanced at the source of the slow monotone voice; a young girl, eyes, sunken so far into the sockets they looked black, stared back at him. He ignored her. Another woman wobbling in high heeled scuffed boots came towards him but when a car slowed down, she changed direction and went towards it instead. He kept walking until a scrawny female with mousy brown hair tied in a ponytail blocked his path.

'See anything you like?'

She had a slight lilt to her voice and didn't appear to be under the influence of either drink or drugs. Seconds ticked past before Michael did something he never imagined he ever would. He asked the question. 'How much?' subsequently paid the money she asked and allowed her to lead him up a dark lane. Once there as the woman unzipped his trousers, he grabbed her right breast hard and felt her wince. Knowing she was in pain excited him, so he squeezed harder and the more he hurt her the more aroused he became. Her head moved slightly to the side and his hand left her breast and grabbed her ponytail yanking it so hard she cried out. The woman raised her skirt and he caught a quick glance of her crotch before his erection slammed inside her. With every thrust he pulled on her hair harder until he climaxed.

As he'd left the prostitute in the lane re arranging her clothing it started to rain and he'd had to walk more than half way home before he'd managed to get a taxi.

Feeling sorry for himself; he poured another generous measure of whisky. The gratification he'd felt while having sex with the prostitute filled him with disgust and self-loathing He wasn't stupid, he knew it had to do with the pain he had inflicted on the woman, it had been the same with Tina when he had slapped her, however tonight had been better, much better. He'd never felt ecstasy like that with anyone before not even with Louise and it filled him with shame. Thinking about Louise made him angry. This is what she had reduced him to; having sex in a filthy lane with a woman who had the smell of countless men already on her. Rage bubbled inside him, and in that moment he wished his wife was still alive so he could kill her over again. He had killed her too easily, he should have made her suffer, really suffer that's what she'd deserved.

'Fucking bitch,' he screamed, hurling the whisky bottle at the wall as hard as he could. It smashed, sending glass flying in all directions, the amber liquid running in rivulets on the soft beige paint. Seconds elapsed then Michael stood up and kicked the coffee table as hard as he could sending it hurtling to the same fate as the whisky bottle.

When he finally fell asleep in the early hours, he dreamed of Louise again. This time he was walking along a busy street and caught a glimpse of her face in the crowd. His heart missed a beat, he knew it couldn't be her, she was dead. He scanned the crowd and saw her face again; she was getting closer; it was definitely her. His legs stopped moving, he was rooted to the spot, people were banging into him, muttering their annoyance and still he couldn't move. As she drew level he watched in disbelief as she smirked and winked at him before sailing past. The dream changed. He was in a room with the two detectives who had questioned him about his car. The woman had her back to him, but the man was asking where Louise was. He tried to tell him Louise was dead, she had drowned, but the detective would not believe him. He leaned in close to Michael's ear and said he knew Louise was still alive and he was going to find her. Then the female detective turned around, and Michael backed away, his legs buckling beneath him as he stared at the face of the prostitute from a few hours earlier.

He awoke bathed in sweat, fear creeping over him, could Louise really be alive? Was it possible that she had duped everyone? He had pushed Louise off the rocks and then she'd disappeared. Had she swum away leaving him to think she'd drowned? No that was stupid, he told himself, Louise couldn't swim. Irrationally he wondered if she had secretly learned and faked her own death. When he'd caught his wife meeting her lover, he'd convinced himself she was a self-serving, conniving, whore who had duped him for years into believing she was a sweet respectable woman. What if he had been wrong and Louise had thought her life with him so awful, she'd taken a lover and faked her own death to escape him. He had deliberately pushed her off rocks. If she really was still alive, she could easily have him put in jail for attempted murder. My god was she out there somewhere biding her time, lulling him into a false sense of security. Of course she wasn't, he'd seen her body. He'd had to identify it in the morgue. No, Louise was very definitely dead. It was a stupid dream nothing more. However, not wishing to risk returning to it by trying to get back to sleep, he swung his legs over the side of the bed and stood up.

The events of the night before played over and over in his head as he started to make his way downstairs. His biggest mistake had been going after Paula in the first place. On reflection, he decided bold brassy women, like Tina, were the best type to chat up. They let you know exactly where you stood. Either they told you to get lost from the outset, or they made it obvious they were interested and had the confidence to let you know where they expected the night to end.

CHAPTER 52

Sixty five pounds - Sarah whirled around the room clutching the one five and three twenty pound notes, a broad grin spreading across her face. She had sold one of her paintings. She glanced down at the notes almost disbelievingly; someone had paid her for painting a picture; something she loved to do.

It had all come about quite by chance when she'd gone to the hairdressers to have her hair cut. The salon had recently been revamped and Sarah had complimented Marla, the owner on her choice of colours. Jerking her thumb at the half dividing wall that now split the salon into two sections, Marla had confided the wall needed something, but she was not sure what. Sarah had laughed and said she would bring in a couple of her paintings to hang there, she hadn't been serious, painting was just a hobby to Sarah; a way to relax but Marla had seemed really interested and had made Sarah promise to bring in some of her work on Wednesday evening.

Feeling slightly awkward she'd arrived at the salon at the agreed time, clutching as much of her work as she could carry. Marla had been really taken with the paintings, so taken, she had asked Sarah to do an enormous one for the wall, featuring a pair of scissors, a comb and hairdryer. Never having attempted anything like that before she'd been a bit dubious but Marla had been convinced she could do it. She told Sarah she was going on holiday at the end of the week and until she completed the painting, she should hang a couple of the ones she had brought with her on the wall.

'You never know, someone might want to buy them.'

Who would buy a painting in a hairdressing salon? Sarah laughed at the thought. It, therefore, came as a surprise when a week later Brenda, Marla's sister who was keeping an eye on the salon while Marla was on holiday, phoned to say someone wanted to buy one of the paintings she had hung on the salon wall. Unknown to her Marla had put small 'For Sale' signs beside her paintings when she had left the salon. Brenda asked how much she wanted for the paintings. Sarah had no idea, she'd never thought for a minute someone would want to buy them.

'Probably about twenty pounds,' she ventured, tentatively.

'They're worth more than that. Ask for sixty five to start with, you can always drop the price.'

Sarah was doubtful but let Brenda negotiate the price and the woman paid the sixty five pounds readily, knowing she was getting a bargain.

Penny had been on at her for ages to sell her

paintings, but she'd never thought they were good enough. Robert agreed with Penny, which had been in stark contrast to Gordon who had never been enthusiastic about her art. Reluctantly he had let her hang one in the flat and that had only come about because both Penny and a couple of his friends had banged on about how good it was and how perfectly it fitted in with the decor. Robert, however, was extremely supportive and had suggested she sold her paintings on the internet. A friend of his designed websites and Robert assured her he would be more than willing to help her set up her own website. Sarah had refused his offer but now selling a painting had given her confidence in her work and she vowed to ask Robert to contact his friend. She realised there was money to be made from her art and there was no better way of making money than by doing something she loved.

She could hardly wait to start on her painting for the salon; but wait she must because she wanted to discuss colours with Marla. When it was finished, she wanted this painting to be exactly as Marla had envisaged it. For now, she would have to content herself with making a few preliminary sketches. Glancing down at the money one more time she laughed out loud before stuffing the notes into the pocket of her jeans. She almost ran towards the table where her phone lay, she had to tell both Robert and Penny the good news.

CHAPTER 53

There was something vaguely familiar about the blond stranger standing on Timothy Shepherd's doorstep. When he smiled and said hello, Timothy quickly realised it was Peter Barton. Sure, he was older, thinner and blonder; however, there was no mistaking Peter's toothy grin. Even if he hadn't been completely certain, one quick glance down at his hands would have confirmed Timothy's suspicion; for Peter had a round, red birthmark, the size of a ten pence piece on the back of his left hand.

He grabbed hold of Peter's arm and welcomed him into the house. He was really pleased to see him and wanted to know all about his travels, but Peter wanted Michael's address and once given it left almost immediately. Timothy tried his best to make Peter sit down and have a cup of tea. He wanted to hear all about his life and what he'd been up to and was disappointed when Peter made it clear he wanted to get to Michael's house as soon as possible. He wished his wife was in the house, she would have made Peter stay longer. Violet was at the local shops and although she'd only gone for bread and milk, she would be at least thirty minutes, probably longer. Violet knew just about everyone in the neighbourhood and always stopped to chat to most of them. He also knew she would be furious with him when she arrived home to find Peter Barton had been here and Timothy had let him leave before she had come home.

As he wrote down Michael's address, he thought it only fair to warn Peter that his brother Michael had lost his wife in a tragic accident not that long ago. A strange look passed over Peter's face and Timothy Shepherd was left wondering if Peter had even known Michael had been married. Should he also mention the visit Violet and himself had received from the police? Again he wished Violet was at home, she would know what to do for the best. Truth is, Timothy had thought about that visit often and wondered what the hell it had all been about. They had definitely been interested in Michael Barton's life more so than Peter's, of that Timothy was certain, the big question was why. Was Michael in trouble, or was he just an old man jumping to the wrong conclusions. The latter he hoped, deciding to say nothing to Peter about the visit from the police.

Timothy Shepherd was correct; Violet was furious with him when she returned from the shops to find Peter Barton had been and gone.

CHAPTER 54

The sound of the doorbell startled Michael. Hauling himself from his chair, he walked to the front door, opened it, and stared at the man standing on his doorstep. He was tall and painfully thin, with long straggly, blonde hair. His skin, almost the colour of mahogany, had a leathery appearance to it, attributed to years of over exposure to the sun. Both men stared at each other; the thin blonde man was the first to speak.

'Hi Mikey,' he screeched.

Michael could not have been more shocked if he had opened the door to find a little green man with horns on his doorstep. He stood completely dumbstruck and watched as his brother bounded into the house. Even after all this time, Michael had recognised him instantly. He watched as Peter walked towards the lounge, guided presumably by the sound of the television. Quietly he closed the door; he could hardly believe what had just happened. Peter had breezed into his house as if he had only just popped out to the shops twenty minutes ago when in fact, he had buggered off abroad more years ago than Michael could remember.

'Are you not pleased to see your big brother?' Peter asked as Michael followed him into the lounge.

'Yes of course, but how did you know where to find me?' Michael replied; looking puzzled.

'I went back to our old house. Mr Shepherd gave me your address. Nice house Michael, you've done well for yourself.' Peter said, his gaze travelling around the room. He lifted the framed photograph of Michael and Louise and stared at it. 'Is this her; Louise?'

'Yes.'

'Mr Shepherd said she drowned. Jesus, Mikey; what happened?'

The Shepherds must have read about her death Michael decided, but did think it strange they hadn't sent a condolence card. 'I don't want to talk about it. And for God's sake stop calling me Mikey, my name is Michael.'

'Oh bruv I'm sorry.'

'Peter why exactly are you here?'

'Do I need a reason to visit my wee brother?'

'No, but you've never bothered before, not even when our mother died.'

Peter had the good grace to look a little sheepish at this remark. 'I am sorry about that really I am, but by the time you got in contact with me the funeral was over, there didn't seem any point. If I'd known before the funeral I would have been there, truly.'

'If you had bothered to stay in touch, let us know

where you were, I could have contacted you in time for the funeral. After all you knew she would die one day, she wasn't going to live for ever; didn't it ever occur to you when she did I would have enough to do without turning amateur detective to track you down.'

'I know I should have stayed in touch, I wish I had, but I didn't; please Michael don't hold it against me. After all I'm here now and...' Peter stopped talking mid-sentence and started smiling.

'And what?' Michael asked.

'I am starving; what have you got to eat?'

Michael could scarcely believe his cheek. 'What would you like: Lobster Thermidor, or Chateaubriand perhaps?'

Undaunted by Michael's sarcasm Peter continued to smile. 'Got any eggs?'

Michael crossed his arms in front of his chest. 'Yes.'

'Good I'll have poached eggs on toast, thanks,' replied Peter before throwing himself onto the chair Michael had been sitting on minutes earlier. He propped his feet on top of the coffee table which was now a bit lopsided after its recent encounter with the wall.

Michael looked at his brother and shook his head before slowly making his way toward the kitchen.

What the hell was Peter doing here? Why now after all this time? Just visiting my arse; he was up to something. By the time the snack Peter had requested was ready Michael had decided either his brother was here to ask for money, or someone was after him; maybe even both: either way he was in trouble, of that he was sure. Carrying a plate in one hand and a mug of steaming hot tea in the other; Michael walked back into the lounge. Peter was dozing in the chair. Michael stood in silence and watched him. He looked peaceful and relaxed not like a man in trouble or one with money worries. Had he misjudged his brother or was he just good at masking what was really going on? Probably the latter he decided, after all he was good at covering up things himself; his mother's death, Louise, Jill Mason. Good acting skills must run in the family he concluded nudging Peter's leg with his own to wake him. Peter looked up groggily at Michael's face and noticed the look of amusement that had crossed it.

'What's so funny?'

'Nothing,' he said handing over the plate and mug.

Michael watched as his brother wolfed down the food from the plate. He had mixed feelings about Peter being here. He had missed his brother over the years. As children they had always been close, and he had missed that closeness as he had turned from child into adult. He had spent years wishing Peter would come home. He had lost count of the number of times, in the early days after Peter had left, he had answered a knock at the door hoping for the very thing that had happened tonight; his brother to be standing there. It had never happened, and Michael had stopped hoping it ever would a long time ago. The fact that Peter had turned up now out of the blue made him feel both joy and resentment in equal measures. He was curious to know what Peter had been up to all these years, where he had been. However, at the same time he didn't want Peter to realise how badly he had once missed him and how inquisitive he was about his life. After all Peter had never shown any interest in Michael's life, even now he seemed more interested in filling his stomach than anything else. It also threw a spanner in the works as far as his plan for Sarah was concerned.

Finishing the last of the toast; Peter looked up and caught Michael watching him. 'Got any vodka?' he asked.

'Afraid not; only whisky.'

'Whisky it is then,' replied Peter, rubbing his hands together, leaving Michael in little doubt he expected him to get up and pour him one immediately. Shaking his head again Michael complied.

CHAPTER 55

A few days after Peter had arrived on Michael's doorstep, he told him the real reason he had turned up out of the blue. As Michael suspected, Peter had got himself into a spot of trouble.

He had been having an affair with the wife of the owner of the bar where he had been working and things had started to get out of hand. The affair had only ever been a bit of fun to Peter; not so, however, to Tracey the lady in question. Although according to Peter, Tracey was no lady. She had taken the affair too seriously and wanted to leave her husband. Unfortunately for Peter, she was putting pressure on him to leave with her. Tracey's husband was a pretty heavy guy, with some pretty heavy mates and Tracey was an unhappy, bitter woman. She had threatened to let her husband in on their little secret if Peter didn't comply. Peter had been smart enough to work out Tracey's husband would come after him either way. Getting out of Spain as quickly as possible and alone had seemed the intelligent option.

When Michael returned home from work the day after Peter had told him about Tracey, the house was empty. His first thought was his brother had disappeared abroad again. A quick check of his bedroom proved Michael wrong. What little belongings Peter had brought with him were still scattered around the room.

Since arriving Peter had slipped into a routine of watching television into the early hours of the morning. He stayed in bed until around one o'clock; once up he made himself something to eat and then wandered off to the local shops to buy a paper and cigarettes. Usually he came straight back and read the paper from cover to cover before switching on the television and settling down on the sofa to start the whole process all over again. Michael was glad Peter was off the sofa and out. It had begun to irritate him watching his brother lounging about doing nothing. However as the hours ticked by, he started to feel slightly uneasy, where exactly was his brother and what was he doing? At five past eleven Michael had to wonder no more, a drunken Peter stumbled back into the house, threw himself onto the sofa and buried his head deep in his hands.

Puzzled Michael asked. 'What's wrong?' His brother ignored him, and he tried again. 'Peter what's happened.'

Finally Peter looked up and answered him. 'I went to visit Brian and Gavin.'

Michael was confused. He would have expected his brother to be in a better frame of mind than he was after catching up with friends he hadn't seen for years. 'Did you have some sort of argument with them?' Then added. 'Surely you weren't fighting with them,' his gaze automatically resting on Peter's hands checking out his knuckles.'

'No I haven't been bloody well fighting. Chance would be a fine thing.'

'What do you mean?'

'Brian is in London, been there for years apparently, and Gavin...' He swallowed before continuing. 'Gavin is dead.'

'Jesus.' Michael said, completely taken aback. 'How?'

'Cancer. At twenty two, bloody cancer.' His head drooped down. 'His father dropped dead of a heart attack the day after the funeral. You should see the state of his mother; she's skin and bones.'

Michael had a hard time imagining a thin Mrs Stafford, she had always been extremely overweight. His brother looked guilt ridden. He could understand why. While Peter had been bumming around Spain, living life like it was one big holiday, back home one of his best friends had been dying.

Suddenly he looked up at Michael, his voice sharp. 'Did you not know about this?'

Irritated at his accusing tone he shot back. 'Why would I? They were your friends. I hardly saw them after they came back from Spain and I moved out our old house years ago.'

'I know.' His brother's voice now sounded defeated. 'I just thought maybe mum would have heard and mentioned it to you.'

'Huh. You know what she was like. Too wrapped

up in herself to care about anyone else.'

'I'm sorry Michael,' he whispered. 'Sorry about mum, I mean. Tell me...,' he faltered. 'Tell me what happened.'

Michael stared at him for a good ten seconds before answering. 'Not tonight. I think you need to rest now.' His voice was brusque.

Peter offered no resistance as Michael pulled him to his feet and steered him towards the stairs.

CHAPTER 56

The sound of the alarm clock wakened Sarah from a deep sleep. She stretched out and turned it off knocking over an empty mug at the same time. She could hardly believe it was time to get up and that she had been sleeping for six hours; it felt like only a few minutes earlier she'd closed her eyes.

Robert had taken her to London for the weekend. They had travelled down on Friday morning and travelled home on Sunday evening. He'd suggested she spend the night at his flat and return home early this morning to change before going to work. Sarah, however, had opted to come home last night, even though it had been quarter to twelve when they'd arrived back in Glasgow and Robert's flat had been nearer. Now she was glad she'd made that decision.

As she quickly showered, she thought back over the weekend, it had been perfect. She'd really enjoyed herself and realised she had far more in common with Robert than she'd ever had with Gordon. She knew she should stop comparing the two of them, but she couldn't help it. Another plus for Sarah was the fact that Penny genuinely liked Robert. Whereas with Gordon; she had merely put up with him for her sake. Penny had recently started dating a guy named Tom, the four of them had gone out one night and Robert and Tom had hit it off immediately. All in all, life was good and Sarah was feeling happier now than she had felt in a long time.

The only fly in the ointment was Gordon, she acknowledged. He was still calling her from time to time much to Robert's surprise. Last Saturday night she'd been in the kitchen preparing dinner when her phone had started to ring. She had shouted to Robert to answer it. It had been Gordon and she wasn't sure which one of them had got the biggest surprise when he had.

When Robert had brought the phone to her Gordon had started quizzing her immediately.

'Who was that?'

Her voice was short when she answered. 'Robert.'

'Is that the same man I saw you getting into a taxi with a few weeks ago?'

'Yes.'

His next question came back at her quickly. 'Has he moved in?'

'No. Look I really need to go I am in the middle of cooking dinner.' She was resentful at his questions and it showed in the tone of her voice. When she hung up Robert looked at her enquiringly.

'That was Gordon, my ex.'

'Oh I didn't realise you kept in touch with him.'

'I don't. He just phones from time to time. I'm usually pretty offhand with him but he doesn't seem to take the hint. I suppose he will eventually. I actually feel quite sorry for him now.'

'You're too soft.' Robert said. 'It's time to tell him to stop phoning. After all he didn't spare your feelings when he went off with Prue. You're not doing him any favours allowing him to keep in touch if he still harbours thoughts of the two of you getting back together.' A look of panic crossed his face. 'Is that what you want?'

'No I don't. There is no way that is ever going to happen.'

She really had to do something about Gordon, she had hoped he would get the message that she had moved on with her life and simply stop phoning; but he hadn't. Truth be told, she was beginning to get a little worried that Gordon was turning into a bit of a stalker. A couple of times recently she had got the feeling she was being followed, she had never actually seen him on either of these occasions and both times had told herself she was just being silly. If he was following her about, she had to put a stop to it now before it got out of hand. The phone calls had to stop too, especially if they were making Robert feel insecure, there was no way she was going to let Gordon influence any part of her relationship with Robert. She decided the next time Gordon phoned she would tell him firmly not to contact her again.

CHAPTER 57

Know your victim well, he thought, feeling smug. He certainly knew his victim well. Michael had been following Sarah Greene around for just over three weeks now. It had been incredibly easy because in the main, the woman was a creature of habit. A boyfriend that stayed over at weekends. Two out of three Fridays she had met him after work and they had gone for a bite to eat. Once they had gone away for the weekend. Monday nights she met a friend after work for a couple of drinks. The pictures on Tuesdays or Wednesdays with the same friend she met on Mondays. Thursday nights she had been consistently on her own in her flat for the last three weeks. A conversation he had overheard in the office, a few months ago, came back to him. Sarah and Anne had been banging on about having me time and Sarah had said Thursday nights were her me time nights. Even if the flat was a mess she did no housework but spent the evening doing exactly as she pleased, whether that be reading, watching television or sometimes relaxing in a hot bath with a glass of wine, she mentioned something else too but Michael had stopped listening by that time.

He had eavesdropped enough on their conversations in the past to know she had been in a relationship which had gone tits up not that long ago. Little wonder, from what he had seen of Sarah Greene's life so far it appeared to be one big routine. She probably only had sex on certain nights at certain times. Poor sod probably got fed up waiting around for it and buggered off. He laughed hysterically as he imagined her saying to her partner. 'Oh no no no, this is Thursday night this is my me time night, you'll have to wait till next Tuesday at ten for sex.'

Well dear Sarah, me time alright, only one of these Thursday nights it's going to be my me time, not yours.

He had followed her home and watched her enter the communal door. From across the road he had waited until a light had come on in one of the darkened windows to identify which flat was hers. He had done this four times in all; reassuring himself he had got the correct flat, each time the same light had come on about a minute after she had disappeared inside the door.

He wanted to get into her flat, but he did not want to risk getting caught breaking in, what he needed was a set of keys. As luck would have it, he got his chance a few days later. Thinking she was in her office he knocked on the door; he had some documents for her to sign. There was no reply, but he had gone in anyway. Sarah hadn't been there, but her handbag was on her desk wide open, a set of what looked like house keys lying at the top. He quickly snatched them out of the bag and shoved them in his pocket. Walking back into the main office he glanced at the clock, it was half past twelve and Sarah usually went for lunch at one. Michael grabbed his jacket and left the office. He went directly to an express key cutting service and had copies made. When he returned, he sat at his desk pretending to work until Sarah left her office to go for her lunch. The only other person around at this moment was Bill. Michael waited a few minutes then casually lifted some papers and walked towards Sarah's office. He knocked on the door and when there was no reply, he opened the door and walked in. He quickly took her keys from his pocket and slipped them under some papers roughly where her bag had been, leaving one of the keys sticking out just enough for her to notice they were on her desk. The last thing he wanted was for her to go home without them and cause a big fuss because she thought her keys were missing. That would ruin his plans completely. No, she must think they had merely fallen out of her bag while it was on her desk earlier and had lain there ever since. Leaving Sarah's office he glanced at Bill who was clearly engrossed in whatever he was doing. Good he thought, chances are he won't even have noticed I was in her office.

He would wait until she had gone for her afternoon tea break then he would slip back in and make sure she had found the keys. If they were still where he had put them, he would move them, make them easier to spot. It didn't come to that, when he next got his chance to look in to her office they were gone. She had obviously found them and returned them to her handbag. He breathed a huge sigh of relief. So far so good, everything was going according to plan.

Peter turning up out the blue had been an interruption he had not envisaged when he had first started following Sarah, however, his brother was so wrapped up in himself half the time that he didn't appear to notice whether Michael was around or not. He wanted to talk to Peter, tell him the truth about what had happened to their mother, but he had no idea how his brother would react to the truth. Would he even care? On the one hand Peter couldn't wait to get away from their mother and had left him to cope with her alone, at an age when he should not have been burdened with that responsibility. He hadn't even bothered to stay in touch, a handful of phone calls in the first couple of years then a postcard once a year if they were lucky. Peter had definitely not thought much of their mother, or of you, a little voice inside his head told him. Not for the first time Michael forced himself to question whether Peter had not only wanted to get away from their mother; had he also wanted away from him too? After their mother died, and he had eventually tracked his brother down, Peter had appeared neither upset by her death or interested in how Michael was feeling. He could understand how Peter had resented their mother and wanted out of the house, he had felt the same and had left the minute he started work. What he could not understand or forgive was Peter leaving him on his own with her while he had still been virtually a child. If the roles had been reversed, he would never have done that. It hurt to face the fact perhaps Peter had not loved him quite as much as he had loved Peter. Indeed, since his brother had arrived on his doorstep a few weeks ago Michael had come to the conclusion that the only person Peter really cared about was Peter. Not being upset that his mother had died was one thing, especially since they had never been close. But how would he feel when he found out the truth, that Michael had found her alive and instead of calling an ambulance had deliberately left her alone in her house to die. The time was drawing nearer to telling Peter, but first things first. He had to deal with Sarah Greene.

CHAPTER 58

'Sarah can I take you out for dinner? I really want to talk to you face to face. Please, it's important.' Gordon's voice pleaded with her over the phone.

It was Sunday evening, exactly a week since she had returned from London with Robert. She took a deep breath, glad her ex was on the other end of a phone and not standing in front of her, and answered. 'Look Gordon I think it would be best if you didn't contact me again. I've moved on with my life; met someone else and I think it's time you did the same.'

'But Sarah...'

Her own voice cut across his. 'No buts Gordon. We're over; I'm sorry I don't love you anymore.' There was a long silence and she knew she'd hurt him, but he had to face facts. 'Please don't contact me again,' she said and hung up.

It had been hard to speak to Gordon like that; she felt cruel. Not wanting to stay in the flat alone, she went to visit Penny.

'You did the right thing,' her friend reassured her, when Sarah told her what had happened.

'There's no reason to feel bad. After all Gordon

brought about this whole situation when he went off with someone else. He didn't care about your feelings at the time either.'

'I know you're right, he didn't.'

'Personally if I were in your shoes the last thing I would be feeling is guilt. Now let's crack open a bottle of wine and celebrate you kicking that jerk into touch.'

She nodded and forced a smile as Penny went off to fetch a bottle from the kitchen.

Valerie and Guy Morven were just ahead of her on the stairs when she returned home a couple of hours later. Mellow from the wine, this time when Guy Morven offered her a cuppa she accepted. It was just what she needed, someone making her a nice hot drink, a bit of inane chitchat, before walking the last few paces to her own flat and tumbling into bed.

CHAPTER 59

The mission had started; Michael had been impatient for Thursday to arrive since the weekend. He slipped away from work directly after everyone returned from their afternoon tea break. He left his suit jacket over the back of his chair to create the illusion he was still around somewhere and slipped on an outdoor jacket which he had left in the staffroom earlier. He retrieved Louise's car from the King Street car park where he'd left it that morning. Before driving off, he removed his jacket and pulled on an old track suit on top of his shirt and trousers, then slipped his feet into tatty trainers which were waiting there for him.

Parking the car a good half mile from where Sarah lived, he placed the keys he'd had cut to her house together with a pair of woollen gloves in one pocket, a length of plastic clothes line in another and retrieved the screwdriver he'd placed in the glove compartment that morning. Shoving the screwdriver inside the cuff of his sleeve to conceal it; he got out of the car, locked it and quickly walked towards the tenement building where he knew Sarah Greene lived.

As luck would have it the rain, which had been on and off all day, started again and grew increasingly heavier the nearer he got to her building. Not many people were about and those who were, paid no attention to the man in a tracksuit with the hood pulled up and head bowed against the rain. Almost everyone he passed had hoods up, some struggling with umbrellas and all were walking as fast as they could. He pulled out the gloves from his pocket, put them on and grasped the set of keys. Striding confidently towards the door he tried one of the two keys that looked alike into the lock. It didn't turn; quickly he tried the other and breathed a sigh of relief when it did. Slipping quietly up the stairs he arrived at Sarah's door and immediately removed the screwdriver from his sleeve and snuck it under the doormat. Swiftly unlocking the two locks on her door he let himself into the flat and locked the door behind him.

The bathroom was the first door on the right as he entered the flat. Michael had a quick look in there and immediately moved on to the next room, which was the kitchen. A couple of mugs and a plate were standing on the draining board. Michael shook his head; lazy bitch. He started opening cupboards, eyeing the contents before passing on to the next, leaving the doors open. The first was stocked with pasta, rice, pickles, salt, pepper, sauce bottles and a few spices. The second held an assortment of tins; soup, vegetables etc. As he was about to move onto the next cupboard something caught his eye; a tin larger than the rest; a picture painted on the outside, the kind people called tea caddies years ago. His mother had had one, only she had not kept tea in it, but money for emergencies. Michael lifted out the tin carefully with gloved hands and opened the lid; inside he found two twenty pound and two five pound notes. He surmised Sarah Greene's mother had done the same as his own and Sarah had carried on the tradition. Folding the money, he unzipped his tracksuit jacket pocket and slipped it inside then redid the zip. He left the tin lying on the work top and opened the remaining cupboards; one held an array of pots and pans, the other some dishes. He moved on to a drawer unit and opened the drawers one by one. The first drawer contained cutlery, a mismatch of bottle openers', vegetable and meat knives in the second, table mats in the third, dish towels in the fourth, the fifth drawer was almost empty apart from a roll of sellotape, a notepad and some envelopes. He left them all lying open Apart from the money; there was nothing worth taking from the kitchen.

The next room held the biggest surprise for Michael, he was dumbfounded to find it decked out like a small art studio. There were several canvases of various sizes stacked against two of the walls. Michael bent down and quickly looked through them. The paintings against the wall nearest to him were all of either vases of flowers or plants. The ones against the farthest away wall were all paintings of fruit; a bowl of mixed fruit, a bowl of oranges, a bowl of apples and several smaller canvases featuring two items of fruit such as, kiwis, plums, peaches and one with a bunch of grapes. Beside these some sketches of a hairdryer were neatly stacked. Michael shook his head; he preferred landscapes and could not understand why anyone would want to hang a painting of a bowl of fruit on their walls, much less a hairdryer. There was no doubt Sarah had painted these herself; her name was scrawled across the bottom right hand corner of them all. Nothing would have given him greater pleasure than to deface them. His hand itched to drag a knife or scissors through each canvas time and time again. He resisted the temptation knowing it would be a big mistake. The break-in had to appear random. A quick in and out for money and jewellery. There was always the chance damaging the paintings could be construed as personal and it was a chance, he was not willing to take. Straightening up he walked towards the centre of the room, where an easel stood holding a large canvas. The painting; the head of a white lily against a dark grey background was unfinished but the detail so far was magnificent, the artwork, much better than in the canvases Louise had shelled out a small fortune for. Michael grudgingly admitted to himself that Sarah Greene had real talent. How fitting, thought Michael as he left the room that she should be in the process of painting a white lily, the flower of death.

Next he entered the living room; a small cabinet was situated at one end of an alcove, a large rubber plant at the other. Two sofas identical in style one pale blue and one cream and both with a collection of blue and cream cushions sat at angles facing the mantelpiece, a coffee table in front of them. Large church candles stood at either side of the mantelpiece, in the middle was a small carriage clock which was either broken or needed a new battery, as the time showed ten fifteen. A flat screen television was fixed to the wall above the mantelpiece and a large canvas depicting an orchid graced the opposite wall. Michael did not need to look at the signature at the bottom to know Sarah had painted it herself. With the exception of the type of flower, it was almost identical to the unfinished painting on the easel, next door. Michael left the living room and entered the last room; Sarah Greene's bedroom. It was painted in creams and beige with matching curtains and duvet. The bed had a couple of cream furry cushions propped against the pillows and nestling against them sat a rather old and tatty looking teddy bear. Michael raised his eyes towards the ceiling. What made grown women want toys from their childhood sitting around their bedrooms. Louise had been the same; only with her it had been a small furry cat missing a tail. She had insisted on keeping it on her dressing table. It had been the first thing he had thrown into one of the black bin bags, he'd used to get rid of her belongings.

The furniture was all pine and not very good quality. He opened all the drawers and rummaged among the contents, deliberately spilling some of them onto the ground. A small jewellery box sat on the dressing table, he looked inside. Most of it was costume jewellery except for a couple of rings, a bracelet and three pairs of earrings. He grabbed the lot and put them in the same pocket as the money he had taken from the kitchen. Next he made his way to the wardrobe and opened both doors. A shelf at the top held several handbags which Michael quickly searched, they were all empty. He felt along every bit of the shelf at the back, but there was nothing else. He stepped back and looked at the bottom of the wardrobe, every inch was covered with shoe boxes, most had at least another three stacked on top of each other and some had a lot more. Bending down Michael lifted the lid off one and looked in; a pair of black court shoes greeted him. Quickly he pulled the lids off all the boxes. He had to pull several out to get to the ones at the back. All held shoes with the exception of one, which had some old photographs in it. Thinking the woman could have given Schuh a run for their money, he checked the time on his watch and surveyed the room, which by now was a complete mess. Only two drawers remained unopened, the ones in the bedside tables, and Michael made his way towards them. The first was empty and he walked round the bed to the other side. This one held a couple of paperbacks, a pen, a passport, and an assortment of documents and receipts. Leaving the bedroom, Michael pulled the door almost closed and walked towards the kitchen door and did the same. These were the only rooms where he had disturbed anything, and he did not want that fact to be noticed by Sarah from the hallway.

Michael made his way towards the only door he had not so far opened in the hall; it was a cupboard; a small walk in cupboard like he had hoped it would be. A few shelves at the back housed some tools, shoe polish, cloths, brushes, several pots of paint and three box files. An ironing board was propped against one wall, an iron sat beside it on the floor, together with a vacuum cleaner and a laundry basket. Michael entered the cupboard pulled the door towards him leaving it open just a crack which was enough to afford him a good view of the hallway, took the length of nylon clothes line from his pocket and waited for Sarah to arrive home.

Eventually he heard her key in the lock, seconds later he heard the door close and she walked into his line of vision. Immediately she stuck an umbrella in the bottom of the coat stand in the corner, then peeled off her coat and hung it on one of the hooks at the top. As she turned away from the stand Michael pushed the door of the cupboard open and walked out. Sarah immediately jumped back, and Michael watched as the look of fright on her face changed to one of almost relief when she realised it was someone she knew, to that of one of confusion and then suspicion. Michael knew she was scared, he could see it in her eyes as her gaze darted towards the front door. She backed up a few paces making the distance between them further, pulling her shoulders up, she asked in a cold voice. 'What the hell are you doing in my flat Michael?'

Top marks, even though she was obviously shit scared she was trying to gain the upper hand with arrogance. He had expected no less from her; he would have been disappointed if she had crumpled immediately and made a run for the door. Feeling like an actor stepping onto the stage; Michael took a tentative step towards her keeping one hand firmly hidden behind his back, he outstretched the other towards her palm up hoping to make himself look totally unthreatening.

'I'm so sorry Sarah but something terrible has happened and I didn't know where else to go.' His voice wobbled as if he was about to burst into tears.

'What is it, what's happened?' She asked, sounding confused.

Michael raised his hand slowly to his forehead and started to sway slightly. 'Can I have a... can I have a glass of water, please.'

Thrown completely off guard, she answered. 'Of course,' and without thinking turned towards the kitchen.

With one quick movement Michael pounced throwing the clothes line over her head from behind and pulled it tight against her throat. She started to struggle immediately, her hands grasping at the twine round her neck. 'Stop struggling or I'll pull tighter,' he whispered in her ear, deliberately pulling tighter to make his point.

'I said stop struggling or I'll pull tighter,' he said

again, this time louder as she blindly tried to grab at his head with one hand.

The command appeared to filter through to Sarah's brain because she stopped thrashing about trying to grab at him.

'That's better, now put your hands out in front of you where I can see them and spread your legs wide apart.'

Sarah didn't move.

'Now.' He yelled in her ear. 'And don't even think about kicking me or I'll pull so hard on this wire you'll be dead in seconds.'

CHAPTER 60

This can't be happening; it's some kind of nightmare, any moment I'm going to wake up. She wanted to believe it too, but deep down, as she stood there, arms outstretched, legs wide apart Sarah knew this was no nightmare. The pain around her neck as the thick twine bit into her flesh was too real. My God was this how her life was going to end; strangled in her own hallway by one of her co-workers.

She had arrived home to find Michael Barton hiding in her hall cupboard; why was he there and why was he trying to strangle her? He had fooled her completely. How could she have been so stupid? The second she had turned her back on him she knew it was a mistake, she'd actually tried to turn back to face him, but he had been too quick for her and now he had something tied round her neck choking her, and all the time she could hear his voice ranting in her ear, his hot breath on her neck.

'It really is your own fault. You brought this all on yourself. Stealing a job that should have been mine. Humiliating me in the office; telling me how to do my job. Nobody does that to me and gets away with it.' He pulled tighter on the twine.

She squeezed her eyes shut; tears coursed down her cheeks as he continued.

'You're going to pay the price for crossing me; everyone always does in the end. You're a selfish bitch, just like my mother and she paid the ultimate price for her selfishness. She paid with her life. I could have saved her. She was still alive when I found her, but I didn't. I left her to die alone. It was what she deserved. Then there was my ever loving wife; only Louise had not been what she seemed. Louise was a whore, fucking another man behind my back and laughing at me. Well I had the last laugh when I pushed her off the rocks. And that stupid girl, who had been too dim-witted to look out for traffic before stepping onto the road. That was a mistake I thought she was someone else. If only she'd turned round, I would have seen her face and braked.'

Terror clutched at Sarah's heart, as she listened to the awful things he was saying, and the venomous tone of his voice. Only two thoughts raced through her mind. He's completely mad, and he's going to kill me. Blind panic made her grab at the twine around her neck again and instantly she felt him pull it tighter. I'm going to die. He was pulling harder on the twine now and she knew with every fibre of her being he would not stop pulling on it until she was dead. Somewhere from amongst the horror came a moment of clarity. If he thinks I'm dead, he'll stop. I have to make him think I'm dead; it's my only chance. Knowing she would have to buckle her legs under her which would put more pressure on her neck filled her with terror. I can't, I'll choke. You're going to die if you don't a voice from within argued with her. I've got to do this, I've got to; it's my only hope. Blackness was creeping around her, everything was fuzzy and slightly out of focus. She could still hear Michael's voice, but she could no longer hear what he was saying, he sounded so far away. Finally summoning up the courage she let her body go limp, she felt the twine slice into her throat; the pain was excruciating. She was falling downwards, blackness was closing in. It's too late, I should have done this earlier, was the last thought Sarah had before the blackness engulfed her completely.

***

Michael looked down at the now still body of Sarah Greene at his feet.

'Not quite so superior now, are you?' he whispered.

Bending down; he loosened the twine from around her neck and slipped it in his pocket. He still felt incredibly angry. He should have made her suffer before he'd strangled her, terrorised her and savoured her fear. Lifting his right foot off the ground he slammed it as hard as he could into her face; there was a dull thud as the back of her head hit the skirting board. He wanted to kick her again and again, but common sense prevailed, he had to get away from the flat as quickly as possible. He stood behind the front door and listened, he heard nothing; pulling up his hood and slowly easing the door open he stepped out and retrieved the screwdriver from under the door mat. He rammed it in both locks moving it from side to side doing as much damage to them as he could. Next he placed the screwdriver against the facing and pulled the door tight against it then he worked the screwdriver from side to side damaging the facing. When he was satisfied the door looked as if it had been forced open from the outside he placed the screwdriver inside his sleeve, pulled the door almost shut, wiped his feet thoroughly on the doormat, slipped quietly down the stairs, and made his way back to his car. Once inside the car he quickly slipped off the tracksuit and trainers. He put the shoes and jacket he'd left in the car back on. He lifted the money and jewellery he'd taken from Sarah's house from his tracksuit pocket and placed it in a small plastic carrier bag along with her house keys, which he carefully wiped with the tracksuit jacket. Next he wiped the screwdriver and placed it along with the tracksuit bottoms and trainers in a black bin bag and tied both bags securely.

Slipping the gloves off first, he started the car and headed for home. Roughly half way through the journey between Sarah's house and his own Michael stopped the car, put on the gloves and disposed of the small plastic bag, the black bin bag and then the gloves themselves. He had intended placing them into a roadside dustbin, however, he'd spotted a large half-empty skip parked outside a shop that appeared to be in the process of being renovated. No one was about and he had thrown them in there instead.

When he finally reached home, Michael parked the car and looked towards the house, no lights were on but he knew Peter was home. He could see the flickering images of the television reflecting on the lounge window. He knew he would find Peter sprawled on the sofa, too lazy to get up and switch the lights on when it had got dark. Michael stared at the house for a few seconds and thought about Peter. It was time to tell his brother the truth about their mother's death. With a heavy sigh, he got out the car and walked with trepidation towards the house.

CHAPTER 61

Gordon shrugged on an old jacket he had hadn't worn in over a year and went outside. It was cold, wet and windy and he shoved his hands deep into his pockets. The lining was burst in one and his finger slipped through the small hole and hit something metal. He grabbed hold of it and tugged it back through the hole. It was a set of keys to the flat he had once shared with Sarah. So that's what had happened to them. Both he and Sarah had pulled the flat apart looking for the keys and not finding them. Sarah had been annoyed with him for being so careless.

Gordon stared down at the keys in his hand. He really wanted Sarah back and to make amends for what he'd done. He had been a fool to get mixed up with Prue; she had been the total opposite to Sarah in every way. Sarah was thoughtful and generous while Prue was self-serving and far from the original dumb blonde Gordon had thought her to be when he had first been introduced to her. His relationship with Sarah had been on an even footing, both enjoying equal status within the relationship. Then Prue had come along, all simpering and helpless and Gordon had fallen for it.

He had been out with some workmates and she had started chatting to one of them, called Guy, apparently, she was friendly with his sister. Guy had introduced them, and Prue had made it obvious she was interested. She was attractive, with a great body. The first night he'd met her she'd made him feel strong and in control. Insisting he escort her home, telling him all her friends had left while she had been chatting to him and she did not feel safe out alone at night. She had left him that night standing on her doorstep wanting so much more than the warm passionate goodnight kiss he had received. She had said the words, same place same time next week, softly in his ear as she had closed the door and Gordon had been hooked. He couldn't wait for the following Friday and this time Prue had not left him on the doorstep.

From the beginning she had taken a submissive role in their relationship, making him feel like lord and master and the feeling of power had been the best aphrodisiac. However, Prue was not the dumb blonde Gordon had thought her to be. Now he knew the real Prue; calculating and manipulative and much smarter than him. Feeling foolish he realised she had controlled him like a puppet master, a puppet. Putting just enough pressure on the strings, ensuring the marionette performs exactly as required. He had been the willing victim and performed exactly as Prue had required. In the few months he had been with her, he had spent a fortune on clothes for her, paid a deposit on a car for her and worst of all had almost bought a house because she wanted him to. Shaking his head at his own stupidity, he remembered the weekly shopping trips she had insisted he accompany her on. At the time it had all been a novelty to him as Sarah had always preferred to go shopping either with Penny or alone. Only now he realised it had not been his company Prue was after on these trips; it had been his wallet. She had never asked him for money; she had been much more subtle.

On that first Saturday shopping spree Prue had bought herself a reasonably priced dress, then she had tried on a pair of expensive shoes and squealed with delight, dancing about the shop murmuring how they were perfect; exactly what the dress needed to set it off. Then she had asked the price and looked crestfallen when the assistant had told her they were ninety five pounds. Slowly she'd started to take them off moaning she would never find a better match for the dress and how much she really wanted them, but there was no way she could afford them. She'd looked so miserable Gordon had launched in without thinking and bought them for her. The next week it had been a seventy pound handbag and two weeks after that a jacket at two hundred pounds. Then there had been the car that had been such a good deal, but the deal was ending that week and she did not have enough for the deposit. Gordon had thought the car overpriced but Prue had worked on him for three days reminding him constantly that was exactly the car she had set her heart on. She frequently mentioned how worried she was that she would never be able to afford one if she could not scrape together the deposit until he had given her the shortfall. Not only did she make him feel like the great provider Prue was always very grateful in the bedroom department, which always helped to soften the blow to his wallet.

When he had left Sarah, he had stayed with a friend for the first week then moved in with Prue. From the outset Prue had made it clear that this was only a temporary measure he had hoped she would come round but Prue had been adamant the flat was not big enough for two. When he had pointed out that the flat was exactly the same size as the one he had shared with Sarah; Prue had flipped. He could see her now standing in the middle of the room hands on hips, nostrils flaring, yelling at him not to bloody well compare her with his ex and not every woman was content to live like a bloody sardine. Then in clipped tones she'd told him there was no room in the wardrobe for his clothes and her own clothes were being ruined because they were all crushed together. When he mentioned the other room, she had given him a withering look and told him the other room was her dining room and there was no way in the world she was prepared to put a wardrobe in there. She would be a laughing stock if she did. It was the one and only time he'd seen her angry.

Later that evening, after make-up sex, Prue had said if he didn't like the thought of living alone in a flat perhaps he should look at the possibility of buying a house big enough for both of them to live in. Buying a house with Prue was not something he had even contemplated but he could not get enough of her and he had to admit it was preferable to them living apart in separate flats. Over the next couple of weeks, he had pored over property guides. However, anything that he thought he could reasonably afford Prue did not like and it soon became clear the type of properties that she was interested in were either out with his price range entirely, or would stretch him financially to the absolute limit. In the end Prue had forced him to move into a cramped bed-sit while she looked about for the perfect house he could afford. Mercifully, she had not found one before she had found another boyfriend with more money and a Mercedes. Although his feelings towards her had started to wane slightly since she had forced him to move out her flat, it had still come as a crushing blow to his ego when she had dumped him for someone else. Knowing what that felt like made him feel even guiltier about what he had put Sarah through.

He wanted Sarah back, he had loved her; still did, however, his lust for Prue had destroyed their relationship and now Sarah had found someone else. He wanted to talk to Sarah face to face, make her understand how much she meant to him. Show her he was serious, that he would never, ever betray her again if she gave him a second chance, but Sarah had refused to meet with him the last time he had contacted her. He turned the keys over and over in his hand and then he came to a decision; he would go to the flat. He didn't know if her new boyfriend lived there or not; he had answered her phone once when he had called her. He wanted to talk to Sarah alone: tonight was Thursday, a night she had always liked to herself when they had been together and he was pinning his hopes on that still being the case.

He stared down at the keys in his hand, finding them was an omen. It was after six o'clock; she should be home from work by now. One last attempt to talk to her; he had to try one more time and if, after hearing what he had to say, she still told him to get lost then he would respect her decision and walk away, because the last thing he wanted to do was upset or harass her. Decision made he transferred the keys to his left hand and slipped them into his other pocket, then turned around and strode purposefully towards the underground.

A sick feeling of nervousness gathered momentum as he walked towards the flat he had once shared with Sarah. The last time he had gone there she had thrown him out. His intention was never to enter the flat using the keys. It was Sarah's now and he respected her privacy, however he knew there was a slight chance she might not let him in if he used the buzzer downstairs. The best course of action would be to open the communal door with the keys, climb the stairs and knock on the door to the flat. It was unlikely she would refuse to open the door to him once he was actually standing on the doorstep. Feeling more and more anxious with each step he climbed, Gordon finally arrived outside the door which he had once known as his own. Taking a deep breath, he reached forward to ring the doorbell. His hand stopped in mid-air; something was wrong, very wrong. The wood on the frame of the door was damaged and as he moved closer to examine it, he saw that the door was not properly closed. He could see one of the locks was also damaged and the wood was badly marked around the other. Gordon's immediate thought was that Sarah had been burgled while at work and had not returned home yet. With a sense of foreboding he gingerly pushed the door open wider. His stomach roiled at the sight that met him. Sarah was lying on the floor, her head at a strange angle, her face bloodied and swollen.

'Sarah!' he screamed; bending down beside her and grabbing her wrist. He couldn't find a pulse. No, no, no, there must be one. He grabbed her other wrist with one hand and wrenched his phone out of his pocket with his other. He felt something, he was sure of it. Letting go of her wrist he punched 999 on the key pad. Panic rising, when the emergency operator answered he shouted. 'Ambulance,' then almost hysterically added. 'And police, get the police.' By this time he had stopped listening to what the woman on the other end of the phone was saying to him, choosing instead to shout the address twice at her before dropping the phone and grab-bing Sarah's wrist again. Alarm coursed through his body; he couldn't find a pulse, but there had been one seconds ago, he was sure of it. He reached out to check for a pulse in her neck and saw the marks. Eyes wide with horror; Gordon realised someone had tried to strangle Sarah. The paramedics arrived to find Gordon sitting on the floor cradling Sarah's head, tears streaming down his face.

CHAPTER 62

Robert stole a glance at Gordon as he paced the hospital corridor. He knew he should feel grateful towards him for finding Sarah and getting her to hospital. If he hadn't turned up at Sarah's flat unannounced, she could have lain there until the next day. She could have died before anyone found her. Something cold clutched his heart at the thought of losing Sarah and he realised just how much he had grown to love her in the short time he'd known her.

However, it was not gratitude he felt towards Gordon it was anger and suspicion. He had been furious to learn that Gordon still had a key to Sarah's flat. Did Sarah know he had a key and could let himself in and out of the flat at any time? Did she secretly hope he would come back for good one day? He knew Sarah had been madly in love with Gordon and had thought they would always be together; she had been completely honest about that. She had even told Robert when Gordon had left her at first, she had secretly hoped he would come back someday. It was not until she'd realised he had been cheating on her and left her for someone else, her feelings towards him had changed. She had assured

Robert there was no way she wanted to get back together with Gordon, she'd moved on with her life and Gordon was firmly in the past. Robert had believed her; he'd been convinced Gordon no longer mattered to her, but what if he'd been wrong. He remembered only too clearly the one and only time he had answered Sarah's phone. Surprised; no probably shocked was a better word to describe how he had felt to find Gordon on the other end. Until that night he had not realised they were still in touch. Sarah had assured him they didn't really keep in touch. Gordon phoned her from time to time and quite frankly she didn't have the heart to tell him to get lost. He had believed her at the time. Now he wondered if he'd been a fool. Did she look forward to his phone calls? Furthermore, did she phone him sometimes? The phone calls, however, were not the major issue; the fact that Gordon still had a key to the flat was.

Sarah had always refused to see him on Thursday nights, telling him it was the one night she set aside for herself. Robert now began to wonder why she had always refused to see him on Thursday nights. Could the reason be because Gordon visited her then? He didn't believe Sarah would be that deceitful, then again she had told him herself she had never thought for one moment that Gordon would deceive her and he had. Was she now cheating on him with her ex-boyfriend?

He stopped pacing the corridor and staring the man opposite directly in the eye asked. 'So, Gordon why exactly did you go to Sarah's flat tonight?'

'There was something I wanted to discuss with her.'

'Like what?' He knew he sounded rude but didn't care.'

'It was a personal matter.'

'Did she know you were coming to see her?'

'What difference does it make?' Gordon sounded irritated.

'It makes a difference to me. Now did she know you were coming to see her tonight?'

Gordon sighed before answering. 'No, she didn't.'

Robert had a moment of relief before another thought started to take shape in his head. What if it hadn't been coincidence Gordon turning up and finding Sarah when he had. If Sarah had been telling Robert the truth about not wanting anything more to do with Gordon; how would she react to him suddenly appearing in her flat having gained entry with a key. They may have quarrelled, and it could quite easily have gotten out of hand. Had Gordon been violent towards her? Dear God had he been the one who had done this to her and ransacked the flat to make it look like a robbery gone wrong?

He knew the police had questioned Gordon at great length, they had questioned him too. Surely there was no way they would allow Gordon anywhere near Sarah unless they had ruled him out as a suspect. Robert stole another glance at him. Maybe they did suspect him and were still gathering the evidence. He certainly looked worried but was it worry over Sarah's condition or of what she might say when she came round. Robert resolutely made up his mind. Until another credible suspect emerged, his money was firmly on Gordon, and there was no way for one second he would leave him alone with Sarah until she came round and could say for definite whether or not it was Gordon who had attacked her.

He looked through the glass at Sarah's bruised and bandaged body hooked up to several machines. She had to pull through this, she had to; the thought that she might not was just too painful to even contemplate.

CHAPTER 63

Jenny Brother and Sharon Thomas had started their police training at the same time and had clicked immediately. On completion of their training they had been assigned to different divisions but had kept in touch and become firm friends. They tried, shifts permitting, to meet up every four weeks. Tonight, they had planned a trip to the cinema and then a bite to eat. However, as Sharon had been about to slip her feet into her shoes Jenny had phoned to say she had got held up, par for the course being a Detective Sergeant. She told Sharon she would not make the cinema but was still up for something to eat later.

Sharon had decided rather than sit about the house waiting for her friend to finish work she would go to the cinema alone and arranged to meet Jenny at a pizza joint near to the cinema, around ten o'clock. The film, a run of the mill chick flick, had kept Sharon's attention for barely twenty minutes, after which time her eyelids had started to droop and she had promptly fallen asleep. Awakening with a start she rubbed her eyes and watched the film for a few minutes before squinting at her watch. Eventually she managed to make out the time and realising there was only ten minutes to go before the film ended, she decided to cut her losses and leave immediately. Much to the annoyance of the four people she had to clamber over before reaching the aisle.

When she arrived at the restaurant Jenny was already seated at a table and halfway through a bottle of wine. Jenny waved to her the minute Sharon walked in.

'Good film?' Jenny asked once Sharon was settled in her seat. Sharon made a face in reply. 'That good,' Jenny said and laughed.

'Put it this way whatever held you up I guarantee it was more exciting. What was it anyway?'

'An attempted murder on a young woman in Ibrox; someone tried to strangle her in her home. It looks like she may have disturbed a burglar, but I'm not ruling out anything until we get the forensic reports back.' Jenny took a sip from her wine glass as Sharon poured some from the bottle into her own glass and continued. 'He left her for dead and made some mess of her face. And for what; a couple of rings and a few quid she kept in the kitchen cupboard, according to her ex who found her. At least the insurance claim should go through without any quibbling as she works for the company.' Raising her eyes towards the ceiling she added wryly. 'Every cloud has a silver lining.'

The mention that the assaulted woman worked for an insurance company immediately made Sharon think of Michael Barton.

'Not a company called Insurance, Insurance, Insurance, by any chance?' she asked half-heartedly.

'Yes, it is as a matter of fact,' replied Jenny, sounding interested. 'Why do you ask?'

'We are looking at a one of their employees in connection with a hit and run.'

'The one in Carmunnock?' Jenny leaned further across the table towards her friend as she asked the question.

'Yes and I think he is beginning to look good for getting rid of his wife too.'

'No kidding.'

'You know Jenny; I wouldn't mind talking to this woman when she comes round.'

'If she comes round, it's not looking too good at the moment.' Jenny replied, finally making eye contact with the waiter who had been hovering about hoping to take their order ever since Sharon had sat down.

It was late when Sharon arrived home, she had insisted Jenny go over every detail of the assault on Sarah Greene. She toyed with the idea of phoning Stan, but decided against it. She had nothing to tell him really, other than the fact that someone who worked beside Michael Barton had been attacked in her home. She would tell him in the morning. Undressing quickly, she slipped into bed and fell asleep almost immediately.

The next morning Stan walked into the office and chucked the unread newspaper he had been carrying under his arm onto his desk. The attack on Sarah Greene had made the front page. Sharon stared first at the newspaper then at Stan as he sat down.

'Guess where she worked?' Sharon pointed at the newspaper. Stan shrugged, indicating he hadn't got a clue. 'Insurance, Insurance, Insurance.' The excitement she felt was obvious in her voice.

'Well, well, well.' Stan laced his fingers together, his two forefingers resting on his chin and leaned back in his chair.

'A friend of mine is working the case and has promised to let me know the minute she comes round.' She didn't mention to Stan that Jenny had said it was touch and go for the victim. Sharon would not allow herself to think the woman would not pull through. It may be just coincidence that she worked beside Michael Barton, but Sharon had a gut feeling there was something to be learned by talking to this woman.

She spent the next hour catching up with paperwork, trying to block out the sound of Wilson's voice. He had bought himself a BMW and was bragging about it to anyone who would listen and unfortunately for Sharon, even those who didn't want to. His voice droned on...brake horse power... cruise control...trapeze alloys... What the bloody hell were trapeze alloys and what was it with men and cars? As long as a car had four wheels and could get from A to B without breaking down that was good enough for her. Doug, her ex-boyfriend had once said only plonkers drive BMW's; well Wilson certainly fitted that bill. The ringing telephone on her desk was a welcome distraction from the sound of Wilson's voice and his incessant talk of cars.

Seconds after answering the telephone Sarah grabbed her jacket from the back of her chair and managed to shrug it on before cutting the connection.

Triumphantly she looked at Stan. 'Sarah Greene has just regained consciousness. She claims Michael Barton tried to kill her.'

CHAPTER 64

Munching his way through a piece of toast Michael surveyed his garden from his living room window. He was on his third cup of coffee; he'd really wanted a whisky but had managed to resist the temptation so far.

Glad he had requested today and Monday as annual holidays, he sat back in his chair and sipped his coffee. Peter was upstairs, still in the same position as Michael had left him last night, after helping him to bed. Positive that Sarah had been dead when he had left her flat, he was completely unaware she was lying in hospital. Unlike when he had mown down Jill Mason with his car and had listened to radio news report after news report to discover if she was alive or dead, he was savouring the moment when he heard Sarah's death confirmed. The build up to that moment had his whole body tingling with excitement, and Michael wanted that feeling to last as long as possible. It was a much better feeling than the one of sheer panic when he had killed Jill Mason. Jill's death had been a mistake, a bad mistake, but with quick thinking and good judgement he had been smart enough to get away with it. If he could kill someone on the spur of the moment and not get caught, then after all the planning he had put into Sarah's death, just like with Louise, he was certain he wouldn't even be a suspect. Another feeling was beginning to creep over Michael; one of invincibility.

It was Sarah who had put the idea of taking the days after he had killed her as annual leave into his head; he sniggered at the irony. She had pointed out a couple of weeks ago that he had more holidays to take before the end of the company's leave year than anyone else and had suggested he started to take some shortly. Taking holidays meant he would hopefully not be in the office when the other employees were informed Sarah had been murdered. Not that he was afraid he would not be able to carry off acting the shocked workmate; oh no, he could do that little performance standing on his head. As far as Michael was concerned Sarah was now out of his life for good and he did not want to waste any more of his time on her or her death than was absolutely necessary. The thought of listening to the other girls wailing and snivelling in the office bored him. He was certain Sarah would be found quickly, his money being on the boyfriend as the person most likely to discover her, if not today then surely at some point over the weekend. With a bit of luck when he returned to work on Tuesday at least the initial snivelling would have stopped.

Michael yawned; he'd not had much sleep. His confrontation with Sarah last night and the conversation he'd had with Peter when he'd returned home, compounded with the amount of whiskey he had consumed after Peter was in bed was beginning to take its toll.

He had poured Peter three more than generous measures of vodka before telling him the truth about their mother's death. 'I could have saved her you know.'

Peter sat up slightly. 'Who Louise?'

'No mum.'

His brother looked puzzled. 'I thought you said she was dead when you found her.'

'I lied.' His voice was almost a whisper.'

Now Peter was sitting bolt upright on the sofa. 'What do you mean?' When Michael didn't answer he raised his voice and asked again. 'What do you mean Michael?'

'Do I really need to spell it out?'

'My God are you seriously telling me you found her alive and deliberately walked off and left her to die.' When he nodded in response Peter continued. 'Why would you do such a thing?'

He was beginning to get annoyed at Peter's reaction after all his brother hadn't given a damn about either him or his mother for years. 'Why do you think? You know what she was like; the booze and the pills. Things got worse after she got sick all she did was moan; nothing I did was ever good enough.' He stared at Peter. 'Let's face it you couldn't wait to get away and you never once came back to see her. Did you Peter?'

His brother reached over and poured himself a generous measure of vodka from the bottle, swallowed it in one gulp and poured himself another. 'Okay I wasn't the world's best son but you; you're a bloody psycho.' His voice grew louder with every word he uttered. 'You left our mother to die alone like some dog in the street. What kind of freak does that?' He hurled his tumbler at Michael, who managed to avoid stopping it with his head by ducking. It slammed into an oak cabinet with glass doors in the corner, smashing not only a door but one of the glass shelves inside. Michael began to feel uneasy. If Peter turned on him, he would be no match for his brother. Although Michael could kill people he couldn't fight. Peter was the fighter in the family, he had always sorted out problems with other kids with his fists, or feet, or both. Michael had never had to fight in his life; for Peter had not only fought his own battles he had fought Michael's too. Luckily, just as quickly as Peter had started shouting at him, he stopped and burst into tears.

He cried for a long time. 'Poor mum,' he uttered over and over again.

Quietly, Michael fetched Peter another tumbler and poured more vodka into it. The two of them sat in silence for a long time Michael refilling Peter's glass time and time again and all the while wondering why Peter was so upset about their mother's death. After all, she had been a crap mother, completely steeped in self-pity and had given both him and Peter an upbringing starved of love and affection. He grew angry thinking about how things had been so bad Peter had buggered off and left him to deal with her alone. Peter had no idea how hard it had been for him. Over the years her drinking had gotten worse and the bouts of depression more frequent. Even when he'd left home and got his own place, he'd still had to visit her, do things about the house for her; there had been no one else to share the burden with. Peter had left without even a goodbye and hadn't bothered to stay in touch; after all a handful of phone calls and postcards over the years didn't quite cut it at staying in touch as far as he was concerned. He hadn't even bothered to come home when he'd found out she was dead. In fact, the only reason he was here now was because by this time some woman's husband was probably after him.

As Michael got steadily angrier, Peter got drunker. Every so often he looked at Michael and shook his head from side to side. When Peter did speak again his words were slurred and Michael was unable to make them out. He leaned in closer towards Peter the next time he spoke and managed to make out the words. '...I should never have left.'

No you shouldn't. It was wrong to leave me on my own with her: I was only a child. He wanted to shout but was too afraid of Peter's reaction. Although Peter was pretty drunk Michael wasn't sure he was drunk enough to be rendered harmless. Moreover, he had a nagging doubt that Peter did not mean he should never have left Michael alone with his mother, but that he might mean he should never have left his mother alone with him. So, he said nothing just kept pouring vodka after vodka into his brother's tumbler until Peter's head started to droop and his eyes began to close. By this time incapable of moving himself; he allowed Michael to propel him into the hall towards the stairs. Getting up the stairs was awkward. Michael had to half carry him and lost his balance twice. Luckily each time he managed to grab the banister and slam Peter into the wall to avoid them both tumbling down the stairs. Eventually they reached the top and panting from exertion, Michael steered his brother the last few feet into the bedroom he had begun to think of as Peter's. When they reached the middle of the room Michael let go of Peter and watched as his brother flopped forward; the top half of his body landing on the bed. Breathing heavily, he stared down at him for a few seconds before bending slowly and swinging both Peter's legs upwards onto the bed. Walking towards the door he turned and looked at his brother once more before switching off the light and closing the door. Feeling utterly exhausted, both physically and mentally he retuned downstairs and poured himself a very large whiskey. He lost count of the number of times he refilled the glass before curling up on the sofa and falling into a deep sleep.

Something at the bottom of the garden to the right

caught his eye, there was no wind; everything else in the garden was still, yet he was sure the leaves of the rhododendron bush had moved. He stared hard, his gaze roving over the bush from top to bottom, not seeing anything out of the ordinary. Maybe he had been mistaken, just when he had almost convinced himself this was the case, the leaves moved again and this time he caught a glimpse of a face. Someone was hiding in his garden. Initially he felt outraged and banged his mug down on the windowsill, fully intending to go outside and confront whoever it was. Slowly the feeling of outrage turned to one of unease as he surveyed the rest of the garden. Although the front hedge was pretty high it was also slightly bald in patches and Michael could see movement on the pavement beyond, yet no one had walked past his gate in either direction. Slowly Michael lifted his right foot to take a step backwards and as he did so his stomach roiled at the sight of Detective Inspector James Stanford opening his gate. Just like before Stanford had seen him; only this time he never took his eyes off Michael as he strode confidently along the path towards the front door.

The next few minutes were a blur, he found himself standing in the kitchen and could not remember getting there. Stanford was grabbing at his wrists although he couldn't remember letting him in. The detective's mouth was moving but Michael could only make out certain words above the sound of blood pounding in his ears. 'Michael Barton...attempted murder.....say anything...' He knew more people had entered the house at least one had come in through the back door. Then he heard a woman's voice.

'Sir, you'd better come and see this.'

Michael cast his glance towards the ceiling; they'd found Peter.

Realising he had been handcuffed; snippets of what Stanford had said before he went upstairs finally started to make sense. He had been arrested for murder, no; attempted murder was what he had said. My God Sarah was still alive; but how? Fear gripped Michael like a vice at the dawning realisation not only was the bitch still alive to point the finger at him for trying to kill her, he had confessed to her about his mother, Louise, Jill Mason and with no time to set the scene to look like suicide, they now had Peter to add to their list. He didn't care about the others, however, he was genuinely ashamed that he had killed his brother.

Feeding his brother the deadly mixture of vodka and crushed sleeping tablets, the ones the doctor had prescribed for him after Louise's death had proved harder than he had realised it would. It had drained him emotionally; he had felt real guilt afterwards, a feeling that was somewhat alien to him. He had crushed the sleeping tablets a few nights earlier, once Peter had gone to bed and added them to an already opened bottle of vodka which he had hidden at the back of a cupboard in the kitchen. He had waited until he had told Peter the truth about their mother's death before he had started to pour him drinks from that bottle. Peter had actually made it easier for him when he had thrown the glass. He had casually lifted the vodka bottle and taken it into the kitchen and swopped bottles when he had replaced the glass that Peter had smashed. He had helped Peter upstairs while he was still alive; he hadn't wanted to watch his brother die in his lounge.

As Michael was led out to the waiting police car in handcuffs, he felt no remorse for the others only regret at being caught. He should have been smart enough to check Sarah Greene for a pulse before he had left her flat. He had been so sure she was dead he hadn't bothered and that had been his downfall. He berated himself for having been so careless. All the planning and attention to detail had been in vain; at the last hurdle he had slipped up and slipped up badly. Not only had he tried and failed to murder Sarah Greene, he had also confessed, almost bragged about his other crimes. Michael felt his face flush with embarrassment at his own arrogance and stupidity.

CHAPTER 65

Sarah had to stay in hospital for over a week after she regained consciousness. She'd suffered a broken jaw and swelling to the side of her head where it had slammed into the wall, when Michael had kicked her, and which the doctors were keeping their eye on. Gordon visited her every day, until the day she told him she intended to move in with Robert when she was discharged from the hospital.

Gordon looked devastated by this news. 'Sarah I really don't think that's a good idea.'

'Well I do. Robert has arranged for time off work and quite honestly after everything that's happened, I'm not ready to go back to living in the flat at the moment. In fact, I'm not sure I ever will be.'

'Sarah, think about this, moving in with Robert is a big step. You hardly know the guy.'

She fell back against the pillows. 'Look Gordon it's not up for debate. I'll always be grateful to you. You saved my life. But we both need to move on.' She took a deep breath and added. 'In different directions.'

He hadn't come to visit her the next day or the day after. He finally returned the day before she was due to be discharged and wished her well, adding if she ever needed him for anything not to hesitate to call. Sarah watched him leave, shoulders hunched in resignation. He had never really given her a proper explanation as to why he had turned up at her front door that night. Only that he had wanted to talk to her about something. He had never said what it was, and Sarah had not asked. She had a fair idea he had wanted to ask her to give him another chance and as she had no intention of doing that, she had not pursued the conversation. What she needed to do now was put all her energy into making a full recovery, not fretting over Gordon's feelings.

She could hardly wait for the trial and the chance to face that bastard Michael Barton across the courtroom. She had never liked the man and had often thought there was something off about him, but even she hadn't pegged him as a killer.

Although the hospital was warm, she shivered slightly as memories of the night he had tried to kill her returned. The biting pain as he pulled tighter and tighter on the twine around her neck made her instinctively put her hand to her throat, touching the marks she knew were still there. His hot breath in her ear as his toneless voice hissed on and on recanting the other deaths he had been responsible for. She squeezed her eyes shut and made herself take deep breaths. She would not allow the fear she felt to overwhelm her. She would stay strong and Robert would help her, of that she was certain.

CHAPTER 66

So the bitch had outwitted him. It had all come out in court; how she had pretended to be dead so he would loosen his grip and he, like an idiot, had fallen for her act. She had recounted his confession to finding his mother alive and deliberately leaving her to die, killing Louise and running over Jill Mason, because he thought she was someone else; her voice loud and confident. Smug cow; he had wanted to lunge at her across the court and strangle her, this time with his bare hands. He hated her more now than ever; she had made a fool of him yet again and this time it had been for the whole world to see. The trial had been all over the media.

As for Stanford and his sidekick, who did they think they were, digging around in his past, asking old neighbours about his childhood. Quizzing people who'd known Louise. They had even dragged Simon Preston into court. The humiliation he'd endured listening to him telling everyone how he had loved Louise and she had loved him but had been too loyal to leave her husband. The bile rose in his throat. Loyal indeed, he could think of many words to describe Louise; deceitful, adulterous, liar, whore. Loyal was certainly not one of them. By the time Simon Preston had finished giving his evidence he had managed to make Louise look like she had been an angel.

Strangely until now, he had never felt any animosity towards the man Louise had had an affair with. Whether Louise had pursued Preston, or he had pursued her Michael had always held Louise to blame for the affair. His wife had been an attractive woman and he wasn't stupid, he knew other men had given her admiring glances; he had caught a few at it. After all it was in men's nature to eye up women, he did it himself. He had trusted her implicitly and had always imagined she would have rejected any advances from other men with some dignity, but she hadn't. Instead she had rolled over and opened her legs and that he could never forgive. Now he wished he'd gone after Preston too.

Standing ram rod straight, his left foot beating a steady rhythm on the worn grimy floor of his cell, he stared at the wall opposite. His voice was barely a whisper. 'I'll show them all; make them pay for humiliating me. Preston, Stanford and his bitch sidekick. Nobody does that to me and gets away with it. As for Sarah Greene I'm going to finish her off completely and this time there will be no slip ups.' The now familiar arousing sensation of anticipation coursed through his body, and he grinned. Meticulous planning was the key and he had plenty of time for that.

ACKNOWLEDGEMENTS

This book has been a long time in the making and my thanks go to family and friends, for all their support and encouragement, especially my husband Jim, and children, Jamie and Rachael. To mum and dad, Kathleen and Ian Walker, who always encouraged my love of reading and to dad, who encouraged my love of writing, a huge thanks, it has helped enormously.

My sincere appreciation to all members of Kelvingrove Writers Group, past and present, for their inspiration and suggestions, especially Pat Feehan, Linda Bell and Mike Gill who gave copious help during editing.

To Jamie Maclaine, Rachael Maclaine, Alison Cassells, Margaret Sherwood and Elaine Sherwood, for accompanying me on location jaunts and to Elaine Sherwood and Ian Pickering for answering my questions on police procedure, I am forever grateful.

Gratitude to Nikki Cameron and David Pettigrew, tutors of creative writing classes I attended, for their invaluable advice and motivation.

Printed in Great Britain
by Amazon